ELMH

P9-DGM-236

3 1135 01896 2180

Scott had been walking with his hands in his pockets, but as Lauren unlocked her car and pulled the door open, he quickly propped his hands on the roof, caging her in.

She stood stock-still. She didn't turn around to face him. It was as if she was waiting to see what he'd do next before she moved.

"I meant what I said, Lo."

"About what?" Her voice was low, husky.

"I don't do relationships. At least not in the traditional sense. I'm not going to lie: I want you. So if you decide to walk down this road with me, you need to know that there's no happily ever after at the end of it. No love or prolonged commitments. It'll be raw and consuming, but eventually it'll be over. Can you handle that?"

Lauren started to turn around but Scott pressed himself against her, putting a stop to her movement. "Don't answer me right now. Think about it. I need you to be sure. The last thing I want is to hurt you, Lo." He pressed a soft kiss to the nape of her neck that was somehow both innocent and filthy. "I'll see you tomorrow." And with that, he pushed off the car and left, hoping like hell her answer would be yes.

THE BEST MEDICINE

ALSO BY ELIZABETH HAYLEY

*Pieces of Perfect**
Sex Snob
*Picking Up the Pieces**
*Perfectly Ever After**

**A Pieces Novel*

THE BEST MEDICINE

A Strictly Business Novel

ELIZABETH HAYLEY

ELMHURST PUBLIC LIBRARY
125 S. Prospect Avenue
Elmhurst, IL 60126-3298

A SIGNET ECLIPSE BOOK

SIGNET ECLIPSE
Published by the Penguin Group
Penguin Group (USA) LLC, 375 Hudson Street,
New York, New York 10014

USA | Canada | UK | Ireland | Australia | New Zealand | India | South Africa | China
penguin.com
A Penguin Random House Company

First published by Signet Eclipse, an imprint of New American Library,
a division of Penguin Group (USA) LLC

First Printing, June 2015

Copyright © Shauna Johnson and Sarah Glasgow, 2015
Penguin supports copyright. Copyright fuels creativity, encourages diverse voices,
promotes free speech, and creates a vibrant culture. Thank you for buying an
authorized edition of this book and for complying with copyright laws by not
reproducing, scanning, or distributing any part of it in any form without permission. You are supporting writers and allowing Penguin to continue to publish
books for every reader.

SIGNET ECLIPSE and logo are trademarks of Penguin Group (USA) LLC.

ISBN 978-0-451-47552-7

Printed in the United States of America
10 9 8 7 6 5 4 3 2 1

PUBLISHER'S NOTE
This is a work of fiction. Names, characters, places, and incidents either are the
product of the author's imagination or are used fictitiously, and any resemblance
to actual persons, living or dead, business establishments, events, or locales is
entirely coincidental.

If you purchased this book without a cover you should be aware that this book
is stolen property. It was reported as "unsold and destroyed" to the publisher and
neither the author nor the publisher has received any payment for this "stripped
book."

For our kids. To show them that wishing on a star isn't just a cliché. Those wishes can actually come true.

Chapter 1

Temporary Insanity

"If one more douche bag gets handsy with me tonight, I'm going to go 'Kung Fu Fighting' on his ass," Lauren yelled over the blaring techno and raucous crowd.

"Tell me about it," Simone agreed. "I haven't been groped this unappealingly since I was in the back of Todd Grady's car in eleventh grade."

"Doesn't he go by 'Tina' now?" Cassidy asked.

Simone widened her eyes and slowly nodded her head. The girls instantly broke out in hysterics.

Lauren relished these nights with her girlfriends—casually drinking in Mickey's Bar and Grill and flouncing around the dance floor like deranged *Riverdance* rejects. The four of them—Lauren, Simone, Cassidy, and Quinn—had been the Fantastic Foursome since middle school, though Lauren had known Quinn since kindergarten, when she'd dragged Quinn out of the lunch line so they could go outside for recess early. They'd been friends ever since.

Lauren took a sip from her glass and tasted diluted

Malibu. "I'm getting another drink. Maybe the alcohol will kill the STDs that are seeping out of these cretins. Anyone else need anything?" Her friends all shook their heads, causing Lauren to say "lightweights" over her shoulder as she pushed her way toward the bar. With school starting in two weeks, Lauren intended to take full advantage of the last few days of summer before she'd have to buckle down and get into student mode.

Eight years ago, Lauren had thrown her small crew for a loop when she'd announced that she was going out of state for college. But that sojourn had only lasted two years before she'd returned to Virginia, taken some time off from school, and ultimately gotten her life back on track. Now, at twenty-six, she was about to finish her last year of graduate school at George Mason University and couldn't wait to join "adulthood"—a place her friends had entered years ago.

Once she arrived at the bar, she smoothed down her canary yellow halter top, which had ridden up as she pressed her way through the multitude of men. Lauren flagged down Sam, one of the bartenders she knew, and held up her glass to him. He gave her a swift nod and set about mixing her drink. Lauren and her friends had been coming to Mickey's since they were twenty-one. Her parents had known Mickey since they were kids, so she'd always felt comfortable there despite the influx of drunk, horny guys.

"Can I buy you a drink?"

Lauren cringed as soon as she recognized the voice. She took a deep breath before turning around to face the man who had shamelessly been trying to get into her pants since tenth grade. "Hi, Josh," she said, feigning a small smile. Lauren had always been good at reading people. It was part of the reason she had changed her major from marketing to psychology when she enrolled at George Mason. And she knew *exactly* what kind of man Josh was, which is why she had no interest in being around him.

"Hey, beautiful. So how about it? Can I get you a drink?" Josh winked at her, which reminded her of her great-uncle Thomas, who had an odd tic that caused his eyelid to spasm constantly.

The image made her laugh abruptly, which earned her a curious look from Josh. *Great, now* I've *suddenly become the weird one*, she thought. It wasn't that Josh was unattractive: he was tall, well-built, and had a handsome face. No, the real problem was that his dick had been buried in more holes than a homeless dog's bone. And since he was an arrogant prick, those holes didn't always belong to Virginia's classiest bachelorettes. Lauren regarded him with the same wariness a child would a party clown: he was fun to laugh at, but the last thing you wanted was to find yourself alone in a room with him.

"Sorry. You just reminded me of something really funny."

Josh smiled, thinking her words were a compliment. "Oh yeah? What would that be?"

"Uuuh." Lauren dragged the word out, trying to think of the right way to phrase her response. "My uncle used to wink at me a lot. Well, not just me. It wasn't like some creepy thing where he'd wink at his young relatives. He had this spasm problem. Not that you looked like you were spasming. I just don't see a lot of people wink, so when you did it, that's what I thought of." Lauren was rambling and from the bemused smirk on Josh's face, she could tell he thought he was flustering her. Which he was, but not for the reason he thought. "Anyway, we have a tab running, so I'm all good on the drink. Thanks though." Lauren turned back toward the bar just as Sam set the Malibu and 7-Up in front of her.

"Anything else?" Sam asked, glancing quickly at Josh and then back to Lauren.

"You got an exit strategy back there anywhere?" Lauren asked quietly so Josh wouldn't overhear.

"I can pull the fire alarm," Sam joked.

Lauren smiled widely. "I'll keep it in mind."

Sam wiped the bar between them with a wet dish towel. "Well, I'm here if you need me," he said before walking away to help another customer. Lauren smiled again. Sam had been best friends with her older brother, Cooper, and always looked out for Lauren when she was at Mickey's. He had become a sort of surrogate older brother over the years, even if it was only between the hours of ten p.m. and two a.m.

Lauren turned back around to face Josh, hoping to quickly give him the brush-off so she could return to her friends. But, not expecting him to be standing so close to her, she nearly collided with him. Her drink sloshed over the side of her glass and splashed onto Josh's gray T-shirt.

"Shit, sorry," Lauren apologized as she reached toward the bar to grab some napkins, putting her drink down so she could help dry Josh's shirt.

"No worries. It'll dry. Though if you were feelin' like you needed to make it up to me, I'd accept a dance as payment."

The thought of dancing with Josh made Lauren's stomach flip. She felt her lips turn down in disgust before she had time to stop them. She noticed his eyes narrow at her reaction and desperately tried to recover. "I, uh, think I've done enough damage to you for one night. God only knows what would happen to you if you tried to dance with me." She let out a small laugh that sounded as half-hearted as it was.

Josh leaned even closer, causing his torso to connect with Lauren's chest. She silently cursed her size B breasts. If they'd been larger, they would've kept Josh farther from her face. "I think I can handle myself," he replied.

Lauren hoped that was true since she had *no* intention of handling any part of Josh. The very thought made her shiver in repulsion. Of course, Josh took the slight movement of her body as an invitation. He began leaning down toward her, eyes closed. Lauren suddenly understood why women in horror movies never ran until it was too late. It took her brain a while to accept that this nightmare was actually a reality. Just as his lips were about to connect with hers, she threw her hand up, causing him to kiss her palm.

His eyes jerked open. "What the hell was that?"

"Uh, my hand?" Lauren wasn't sure why it came out as a question, but it had.

"Yeah, I figured that much out." Josh backed up a bit, heat radiating off of him. He was pissed. "You're a real fucking tease—you know that?"

Lauren's back straightened. If this douche bag wanted to start name-calling, then he'd found a willing adversary. "And you're a fucking misogynist. Since you're clearly an idiot, let me take the time to spell something out for you: I'm. Not. Interested. Now get the hell out of my way so that I can go back to people whose company I actually enjoy." She sidestepped Josh quickly and began walking toward her friends, not even bothering to pick up her drink.

Josh stood stock-still for a moment, clearly stunned by Lauren's words. But that didn't last long. Lauren hadn't made it more than five steps before she felt a firm grip on her biceps and was pulled toward a small alcove off to the side of the bar. Once the destination had been reached, Josh spun her around and thrust her roughly against the wall. The impact caused her breath to leave her momentarily, but she recovered quickly.

"Don't you ever put your hands on me again!" Lauren yelled in Josh's face. If he thought she was going to back down, he was sorely mistaken. When it came to fight-or-flight situations, Lauren always fought. Her brother had taught her how to handle herself when she'd grown boobs, and she'd been ever thankful for it.

Josh pushed against her, putting his arms on the wall on either side of her head in an effort to use his size and proximity to intimidate her. And while the situation did cause fear to bubble within her, she'd never let it show.

"You're so sexy when you're mad," Josh rasped into her ear.

"Josh, I'm giving you one last chance to back up before I seriously lose my shit." Lauren's voice was strong and laced with a warning that she had every intention of following through with.

"Stop playing hard to get, baby. I know you want it. I can see how hard your nipples are through your shirt. And I bet if I touch that sweet pussy, I'll feel how wet it is for me. Maybe I should prove it to you." Josh's hand quickly skated down the wall and landed on the button on Lauren's jeans. He fumbled for a couple seconds before all hell broke loose.

Lauren may have been more than a little tipsy, but that didn't make her more tolerant of Josh's inappropriate behavior. It made her rail against it with a fervor she'd only felt a few times in her life. Reflexively, she brought her fist up in a lightning-fast move and connected with Josh's windpipe. He staggered back, gripping his throat, but Lauren wasn't done. She brought her heel down hard on the top of his flip-flop-clad foot, then brought her knee up to connect with his balls, causing Josh to double over with a pain that she was sure radiated through his body.

Lauren stepped closer to him, needing to make sure he knew that she wasn't scared of him. She'd just kicked his ass, and she'd do it again. *Anytime.* "Fuck with me again, and a broken dick and a sore throat will be the least of your problems."

Josh straightened slightly, his hands still covering his groin, and looked at her with venom in his eyes.

Lauren turned sharply and walked quickly out of the alcove and back toward the bar. When she heard heavy footsteps behind her, she spun her head to see Josh following. She quickened her pace, realizing that she was dealing with a special kind of moron. Reaching the bar, she yelled to Sam to get his attention. His furrowing brow let her know he noticed the worry on her face. "Time for the fire alarm," she mouthed, hoping he had suddenly learned to read lips. He looked at her, confused. "Fire alarm!" she yelled. Recognition seemed to dawn on his face, but Lauren couldn't be sure because a shrill alarm began to blare, diverting her attention.

It took Lauren a moment to realize what happened

after that. She registered people running for the exit, pushing one another to get out of the packed building. Fights broke out around the bar and outside due to the throng of bodies trying to escape through the same door. Tables broke, glasses shattered, and screaming filled the air. Lauren caught sight of Cassidy, Simone, and Quinn and ran toward them.

"What the hell is going on?" Lauren yelled over the noise.

"Guess there's a fire," Quinn explained, fear etched on her face.

"A fire? There's no smoke or anything. Who said there was a—" *Fuck my life.* Lauren hadn't really thought about the consequences of someone *other* than Sam hearing her yell. But clearly, someone else *had* heard her, and they'd pulled the fucking fire alarm. "Shit, girls, come on. We gotta get out of here." It took them quite a while to push through the crowd and make it out the front doors. Had there really been a fire, they would've been goners. Finally they made it outside just as the fire trucks were pulling up. Lauren watched in horror as police tried to calm the raging crowd.

"It was her. She said it."

Lauren turned toward the voice and saw a thick blond girl pointing her out to police. Lauren had never really been the type to wish ill will on strangers—until that moment. "Ladies, we need to skedaddle. Now." Lauren tried to corral her friends by urging them toward the street.

As they reached the edge of the sidewalk, Lauren heard the voice that caused her blood to boil nearly out of her skin. "Way to go, you crazy bitch."

Lauren's eyes finally came to rest on the prick. Reacting on pure adrenaline and hatred, Lauren grabbed the drink Cassidy was still holding and hurled it toward Josh. Unfortunately, Lauren was quite a few years removed from her days on the high school softball team. Her velocity had remained, but her aim had evidently disappeared. The glass she'd thrown sailed wide, completely missing Josh. Unfortunately it didn't miss the rear window of a car that was driving away from the scene. And as she heard the splintering of glass, Lauren knew beyond a shadow of a doubt that the universe hated her.

The driver slammed on his brakes and jumped out of the car. But it wasn't his rage Lauren was worried about. No, she was too focused on the two strong hands that gripped her arms from behind and practically threw her onto the hood of a nearby police car.

"What is it with everyone throwing me around tonight?" Lauren knew she should have kept her mouth shut. She wasn't a troublemaker, and she definitely wasn't someone who disrespected authority. But since she had already accidentally become both in a matter of minutes, she decided to roll with it.

"Keep your mouth shut," the cop ordered as he called for a female officer to come over and search Lauren. "You have anything sharp in your pockets?" he asked her.

Just my machete and my hunting knife. "Not last time I checked," she responded dryly.

"Listen up, honey. Being a smartass really isn't in your best interest right now. You're in deep shit, so maybe you should be a little more cooperative."

"What are you doing to her?" Lauren heard a wasted Quinn ask. "You can't grab her like that!" Quinn was approaching full-blown hysterics.

"Ma'am, back up before you get yourself in trouble."

"Why? We haven't done anything wrong. Let go of her right now."

"It's okay, Quinn. Just do what he says." The last thing Lauren needed was to be responsible for getting one of her best friends arrested.

"Thatta girl. You just follow your own advice, and we'll get along just fine," the cop said to her.

Lauren had had enough of being patronized. "We'd get along better if you'd get your hands off me."

Lauren felt the cop tense. But she really didn't see how things could get much worse. Then he cuffed her, and she suddenly saw things a little more clearly. A female officer arrived and patted Lauren down as the other officer rattled off her charges. "Public intoxication." *Okay, I can't argue that one.* "Disorderly conduct." *Eh, probably no defense against that one either.* "Propulsion of a missile." *Wait . . . What?*

"Did you just say 'propulsion of a missile'? What am I, an AH-64 Apache helicopter? You're kidding, right?"

The cop stilled for a minute before finally speaking. "You watch a lot of action movies I see, uh—" He looked down at the ID the female officer had withdrawn from Lauren's pocket. "Miss Hastings. But no, I'm not kidding. Keep it up and I'll tack on inciting a riot."

"First of all, I'm not a complete idiot. I didn't learn the name of the helicopter from movies. I learned it from my brother, who did two tours in Afghanistan." Lauren wasn't sure why she felt such an intense need to share that information. Maybe it was because she felt insulted by the cop's insinuation that she wouldn't be informed enough to know the name of the most common type of assault chopper. Maybe it was because such an insinuation felt like a slap in the face because Lauren made sure she knew *everything* that even had the slightest bit to do with Cooper. Or maybe it was because he only saw her as a drunken moron, and was therefore probably making all sorts of negative assumptions about her upbringing and family. Whatever the reason, it was important to Lauren that he knew at least that one bit of truth about her. "Second of all, the window was a complete accident. Maybe you should go talk to the jerk who put his hands all over me in the bar. That's what caused this mess in the first place."

"Josh touched you? I'll kill that motherfucker." This time, it was Simone's voice that echoed in Lauren's ears, and she couldn't help but smile. Her girls always had her back.

The cop jerked Lauren's handcuffed wrists, spinning her around to face him. He was older, maybe the same age as her father, and looked weary as all hell. He probably had to deal with shit like this all of the time: self-involved twentysomethings who didn't have the sense God gave them. Lauren found herself feeling a bit of remorse that she was the one causing all of this chaos. He looked at her for a beat, as though he were trying to figure something out about her. When he finally spoke, his voice was low. "Do you want to press charges on someone, Lauren?"

Lauren felt her chin quake the slightest bit. The emotion of the night rolled itself into a ball and settled in her throat. She took a deep breath, forcing the tears down. She wouldn't cry. Lauren hated girls that used emotion to get out of things. She was better than that. Stronger. If she had broken the law, then she'd accept the consequences for it. "No."

He leaned slightly toward her, his voice softening. "Are you sure?"

The truth was, other than grabbing her arm and making her uncomfortable, Josh hadn't done anything to her. Not really. Ultimately, she'd been the one who'd kicked *his* ass. Not the other way around. "Yes. I'm sure."

"Okay, then," the officer sighed. "I'm going to put you in the back of this car, and then you'll be taken to the station."

Lauren nodded her head and let the officer put her in the cruiser. The fight had drained out of her. All that was left was overwhelming exhaustion.

"Don't worry, girl. We'll bust ya out!" she heard Cassidy yell through the window.

Lauren turned her head and offered them a weak smile before the cops pushed the girls and the rest of the crowd away from the vehicle. She suddenly felt embarrassed. She was too old to be behaving this way. She may have still technically been attending a college, but that didn't mean she had to act like a college kid. She sat in the backseat for about ten minutes before the officer who had cuffed her climbed into the driver's seat.

As he got settled and turned the ignition, Lauren found herself speaking. "You want to do something for me?"

The officer sighed heavily. "Nothing would bring me greater joy," he responded.

Lauren couldn't help the laugh that burst from her.

"What?" the officer asked.

"Turn on the lights and sirens. If I'm going to get arrested, I want to at least look like a badass doing it."

The cop shook his head. "Kids," he muttered. But as soon as he pulled away from the curb, he flipped both on.

Lauren was processed and then put in a cell with a middle-aged woman named Eleanor. Eleanor was evidently a *huge* fan of bath salts and tequila. After she tried to climb the wall, exclaiming that she was Spiderwoman, the cops came in, strapped her to a chair, and wheeled her away. Unable to resist, Lauren had uttered, "Bye, Eleanor. Make good choices," which earned her a stern look from one of the officers and a "fuck off" from Eleanor.

Lauren spent the night sitting on one of the cement bunks, her back pushed against a wall. With Eleanor gone, the night passed with alarming slowness. Finally, at what Lauren figured had to be the next morning, the officers wheeled a TV into her cell.

"Oh man, you're not going to attempt to brainwash me by making me watch religious programming, are you?"

The officer tried to suppress the quirk of his lips, and Lauren felt a little more like herself.

"No," the officer responded. "We find it easier to bring the judge to you, rather than taking you to the judge." He turned the set on and then left the cell, locking it behind him.

"Lauren Hastings," the judge began. "This is not your hearing. This is your arraignment. You're being charged with one count propulsion— Wait a minute. Does this really say propulsion of a missile?"

Lauren flapped her arms and nodded her head in a that's-what-I-said gesture.

The judge looked annoyed, but continued. "Anyway, you're also charged with one count of public intoxication and one count of disorderly conduct. You have a right to an attorney. If you cannot afford an attorney, one will be provided to you free at the cost of Fairfax County. The officer is going to give you a copy of your affidavit of probable cause as well as instructions for how to apply to the public defender's office. Bail in this matter is being set at ten thousand dollars unsecured. Your preliminary hearing has been set for three days from today."

And then he was gone. Lauren couldn't help but compare the man to the Wizard of Oz. *Maybe I should've asked him if he had a gift for me, like common sense.*

"What does it mean if bail is unsecured?" Lauren asked the officer when he returned a few minutes later to get the television.

"It means you get to leave without paying anything as long as you show up to court."

"Well, thank God for that." Lauren sighed, relieved.

The officer continued, "I'll get your affidavit, and then we'll get you out of here. You need to call anyone to come pick you up?"

"Yeah, I do. But I can wait 'til I'm released. Thanks." Lauren had called her mom right after she'd been brought in the previous night but told her not to bother coming down to the station until they let her go.

The officer came back a short while later with the necessary paperwork and then led Lauren out of her cell. Once she had retrieved all of her personal belongings, she dialed her mom from her cell phone.

"I'm guessing you've been sprung?" her mom said as a greeting.

"Yup, I'm a free woman."

"Okay, I'll be right there."

Lauren sighed. "Thanks, Mom."

"Oh, anytime. It's not every day I get the pleasure of picking my only daughter up from jail. I'm planning on taking some pictures of you out front, so be prepared."

"You're a riot," Lauren replied drolly.

"No, I think I'll leave the rioting to you."

Lauren hesitated for a second. "That was a good one."

"I know. I'll be there in ten minutes."

Lauren ended the call, walked outside, and sat down on a bench to wait for her mom. She pulled up soon after, and Lauren trudged toward the Explorer.

"There's my little criminal. How was the joint? Get any tattoos?"

"Yeah, my new bitch Eleanor inked a skull and crossbones on my back. She was going to add a teardrop on my face, but she was transferred to the psych ward before we got to it." Lauren reclined in the seat. "I'm freakin' exhausted."

"Yeah, well, jail will do that to you."

"You speaking from experience?" Lauren asked.

Her mom smiled. "Wouldn't you like to know."

They drove in silence for a few minutes before her mom spoke. "Mickey called us this morning."

"Oh yeah?" Lauren asked tentatively.

"You caused quite a bit of damage to his place, Lauren."

"I did not *personally* cause any damage to his bar. Some guy's rear window, yes. The bar, no."

"Yeah, well, that's not how he sees it. He said that he won't press charges if you agree to pay him for the repairs."

Lauren rubbed a hand over her face. "Any idea how much money we're talking?"

"Not yet. He said he'd get back to us once he assessed all the damage. Oh, and he doesn't want you in there anymore."

"Ha, that'll really show me. That place is a hovel."

"Lauren." Her mom's voice was serious. "Despite how minor some of those charges are, you still caused some trouble. I understand that this was all a big misunderstanding, but you're still going to have to suck it up and face the music."

Lauren turned in her seat to face her mother. "I know. I get it. I messed up. I'll pay him for it." Lauren was supposed to be doing an internship at the Inova Fairfax Hospital during the spring semester. She would be working in their mental health facility to get some real world experience before finishing up her master's. In order to take extra credits in the fall and carry a lighter load during her spring internship, Lauren had worked her ass off at H and M all summer and saved just enough to pay the semester's rent for her studio apartment that she'd had since she'd enrolled at George Mason. Thankfully, her dad owned the property, so there wouldn't be any unforeseen housing costs. And she highly doubted that he would kick her out if she was late with rent one month. Still, the whole situation felt shitty. Even though she was technically living on her own, still having to rely on her parents as a safety net was something she'd been working to get away from. "I'll figure it out. I'm sorry you and Dad got dragged into this. Maybe I can get my job back at the mall or wait tables at night or something."

"I may have a better solution." Lauren looked at her mom, whose eyes were shining with something Lauren was sure she wasn't going to like.

Chapter 2

Arrhythmia

After Lauren got back to her small apartment, she took a scalding shower to wash the scuzz of the past twelve hours off herself. She knew her parents wouldn't get too bent out of shape about her arrest. They knew her well enough to understand that her shenanigans were always rooted in her trying to do the right thing. It just blew up in her face sometimes. After she forced herself out of the shower, she threw on her pajamas and climbed into bed to sleep the rest of the day away. She had sent a text to the girls on her way home, and then settled in for the good night's sleep she had missed.

But her much needed slumber didn't last long before it was interrupted by a piercing ring. Lauren picked up the phone and put it to her head cautiously, acting as if the thing were a bomb. "Hello?"

"Lauren? Hey, it's Sam."

Sam had never called her before. *He must be really worried.* Despite that, Lauren couldn't help giving him a hard time. "Sam who?" Lauren asked with a smile.

"Uh, Sam Brooks?"

"Are you asking me if that's your name, or telling me?"

Sam let out a huff, but there was humor in it. "You're such a ballbuster."

Lauren thought for a second. "You know, that may be an appropriate nickname for me after what I did to Josh last night." Lauren laughed, but stopped abruptly when she didn't hear a reply. "Sam? You still there?"

Sam's voice was gritty when he finally spoke again. "That asshole did something, didn't he?"

"No, not really. Nothing I couldn't handle," Lauren said, trying to reassure him.

"Some help I am," Sam said bitterly.

Lauren let out a short laugh. "I'm not your responsibility, Sam. You were working. You shouldn't have to worry about me and my nonsense."

"Yeah, but the person whose responsibility it is isn't here to do it, so I should've done a better job. Done the job like he would've done." Sam's voice was laced with a swirl of emotions: anger, sadness, disappointment, frustration. Hearing him like this broke Lauren's heart all over again.

"I'm twenty-six. I shouldn't need a big brother to take care of me." Lauren's voice was small, affected.

Now it was Sam's turn to laugh, though it was pained. "It would've been his pleasure, Lo."

A tear slipped down Lauren's cheek when she heard Sam use the nickname Cooper had for her. "I haven't been called that in a long time." She released a sigh, then a chuckle in an attempt to shift the mood. "But I guess it's better than ballbuster."

Sam laughed too. "Yeah, I guess it is."

Lauren fidgeted with her fingernails as she tried to think of something else to say. This was the most Lauren and Sam had talked in almost six years. It was comforting and disconcerting, all at the same time. "Thanks for calling. It means a lot."

"It's the least I could do," he replied simply. "Well, I guess I'll see you around."

"Mmm, probably not. I've been banned from Mickey's. Seems as if I'm a bit of a troublemaker."

"You? Never," Sam replied, and Lauren could hear the smile in his voice. "Listen, Lo, I know I'm not Cooper. But if you ever need anything . . ." He let the sentence hang there, unfinished.

"You'll be the first call I make," Lauren finished for him.

"Good. I'll see ya."

"See ya, Sam." Lauren disconnected the call and plopped back on the bed. The conversation with Sam, despite its brevity, had caused a welling of emotions in her. She'd never felt particularly close to Sam, even when he was at their house all the time, hanging around with Cooper. He was the opposite of Cooper in every way: quiet to Coop's outgoing nature, reflective to her brother's impulsive behavior. But Lauren didn't question the veracity of his words for a second. If she needed him, Sam would be there in an instant. Not because he loved her, but because he loved Cooper. And now his love had nowhere else to go.

The next two days passed without Lauren requiring police intervention. She spoke with her family's attorney, and he assured her that this would be no big deal. Maybe some small fines, but nothing that should wind up on her permanent record.

On Tuesday, Lauren showed up to court and prepared herself for her day of reckoning. Mickey hadn't shown up since they had already come to an agreement about Lauren paying him back. The owner of the car Lauren vandalized didn't show either. The girls had told her that as soon as the cops approached him to ask about the damage he'd jumped back in his car and sped off. It seemed Lauren wasn't the only one who was on the outs with the five-o that night. The only person who appeared in court was the arresting officer, who read the eyewitness accounts and his own observations of the ordeal.

Lauren's attorney explained that she would get what was called a "summary disposition." This meant she'd plead guilty to the minor charges, and the rest would be dropped.

The judge ended things by offering his sentence. "All other charges are dismissed in lieu of restitution to the victim. Summary fines will be paid to the court in the amount of two hundred and thirty dollars for each offense. Stay out of trouble, young lady."

"Yes, Your Honor," Lauren replied before being ushered out of the courtroom by her lawyer.

Once they were in the hallway, Lauren's lawyer turned to her. "So, Lauren, do you have plans for how exactly you plan to pay for your fines and restitution?"

"Yes. I'm going to work with my *mother*."

Trinity Hospital wasn't as large as Inova Fairfax, but it was close to home and her mom's boss had agreed to help her out. He'd agreed to pay her a small salary that would go toward her fines and paying Mickey back.

Thankfully, even though Lauren was taking a heavy

course load, she'd still managed to squeeze all of her classes into three days. So, she'd spend Monday, Wednesday, and Friday at school, and Tuesday and Thursday at the hospital. But since school didn't start for a week and a half, Lauren had opted to spend all of the following week working with her mom. Mickey's insurance covered most of the damage, but he was requiring Lauren to pay his deductible, as well as the amount insurance wasn't going to cover. The whole situation sucked. If Lauren had a real job like her friends did, paying Mickey back wouldn't be such a production. Lauren hated that her life wasn't where it should have been by that point, but there wasn't much she could do about it. She had spent the past several years working as hard as she could to make up for her major screw-up at Dartmouth. At least this time she didn't need to leave the state to escape her problems.

Dr. Jacobs had offered to pay Lauren eleven dollars an hour, and she'd agreed to a nine-hour workday. The only thing that hadn't been discussed was what Lauren would actually be *doing* at the hospital. Dr. Jacobs was a general practitioner who was based out of the hospital but also had a satellite office in the area.

But as she and her mom walked through the hospital lobby the day after her hearing, Lauren figured she'd find out soon enough. Her mom took her to security and got her a badge before they headed up to the third floor, where Dr. Jacobs' office was.

As soon as they entered, Lauren's mom began introducing her around. All of the nurses and receptionists seemed pleasant enough, though Lauren noticed that they were all closer to her mom's age than her own. Not that it mattered. Lauren had just been hoping that there'd be someone around her age that she could maybe have some fun with—help the time pass more quickly.

No such luck, Lauren thought.

Scott had been behind all morning. It only took one chatty patient to throw off his entire schedule. He'd now be forced to cut other appointments short so he could get back on track. Scott loved his job, and wanted to make sure that every person who came through his office received the same level of attention as everyone else. But with his schedule backed up, he'd be hard-pressed to do that.

And the fact that it was Pam's delinquent daughter's first day didn't help his mood. He didn't know why he let himself get talked into these things. What the hell did he care if some spoiled brat had legal problems? That had nothing to do with him. But he liked Pam and wanted to help her out if he could. Though he swore to himself, if this girl had piercings all over her face or some kind of weird hair color, she'd have to go. Scott couldn't have his patients made uncomfortable because some rebel without a cause didn't know how to behave in public. He avoided hiring young people for exactly that reason. They were unpredictable and self-absorbed. Never mind that Scott was just twenty-nine himself. He was more mature than most. *Driven.* He didn't have time for childish bullshit.

He stopped around the corner from the main nurses' station, looking at a patient chart, when he heard Pam introducing her daughter to the other women. Scott took a deep breath and rolled his eyes. *May as well get this nightmare over with.* With disinterest and haughty body language, he rounded the corner.

And then he saw her. His feet immediately cemented themselves to the ground and his arms fell to his sides. *No way. That can't be Pam's daughter.*

He took in the girl, older than he'd expected. Of course he hadn't asked her specific age. Pam had said she was finishing up her degree, which he figured put her around twenty-one. But this girl looked older than that. Her light brown hair fell past her shoulders, and she wore a blue and purple silk scarf as a headband. She was petite, maybe five three, with small but perky breasts that complemented her thin frame perfectly. And her eyes. God, he thought he'd never seen anything so blue. But as they locked with his, he found that he momentarily did.

"Oh good, there you are. This is my daughter, Lauren. Lauren, this is Dr. Scott Jacobs."

Lauren approached him calmly, looking completely comfortable in her skin. Her confidence threw him. Scott was used to having a certain influence over women. He was handsome, athletically built, and a doctor. Women usually fawned all over him, batting their eyelashes and pushing their breasts out. But Lauren did none of those things, and it turned him on more than he could've imagined.

"Hi, Dr. Jacobs. Nice to meet you." Lauren extended her hand to him, keeping her eyes on his. She noticed what an interesting shade of green they were, almost emerald. He was gorgeous. And she realized as soon as she saw his cocky stance and condescending smirk that he was well aware of that fact. Lauren loved interacting with guys like Dr. Jacobs. All arrogant and superficial. She had learned early that guys like him were easily thrown by girls like her. Girls who weren't impressed with shiny cars and perfect smiles. And as she watched his eyes appraise her, not registering her outstretched hand, she knew that she was going to really enjoy working at his office.

"You want me to Purell first?" she asked him.

"Uh," he said, narrowing his eyes at her, "what?"

"Before you shake my hand. Do you want me to sanitize or something?"

Scott shook his head, seemingly embarrassed. "No, sorry." He steeled his face and shook her hand firmly in his before releasing it abruptly. "And it's Scott."

"Excuse me?"

"My name. I go by Dr. Scott. Not Dr. Jacobs."

"How pedestrian. I go by Lauren."

Scott seemed taken slightly aback by her response. Like he was surprised she'd poke fun at him. She'd said it playfully, but she began to wonder if he was capable of taking a joke.

"If you don't mind me asking, Lauren, how old are you? I should've asked before I agreed to let you work here. I can't have teenagers running around the place. You understand."

Lauren felt her lips quirk—an involuntary response to his obvious insult. She hadn't meant to be rude when she'd commented on his name, but he seemed to be on the offensive now. *Shit.* When would she learn to stop putting her foot in her mouth?

"I'm twenty-six. So no worries about me—uh, how'd you put it?—oh yes, running around."

"Hmm, twenty-six and still in college? Ah, well, academics aren't everyone's strong suit."

Lauren didn't even bother correcting him by saying

that she was finishing her graduate degree. She wanted to let him build his own house of assumptions so she could watch them crumble around him over the next few months. "Yes, and sometimes they're the only thing a person is strong in," Lauren replied in an overly sweet tone that told him she knew he was intentionally baiting her, and that she was game. Lauren never backed down from a verbal chess match. That was something she prided herself on. "How old are *you*?"

"Lauren!" Pam scolded her, but Lauren never faltered.

"What? He asked me first." Her eyes had yet to leave his.

Her prolonged eye contact seemed to make him tense, which made Lauren want to hold his gaze even longer. "Twenty-nine," he replied.

"And you already have your own practice. Very Doogie Howser of you." Lauren could barely contain her grin, knowing that such a phony pop culture comparison would zing Scott's ego.

"Well, I didn't exactly start the practice. My father started it and left it to me when he died." Scott stopped suddenly and averted his eyes toward the ground. Clearly, Lauren had hit a nerve she hadn't meant to touch. And she empathized immediately. After a few moments, he seemed to collect his thoughts enough to change the subject.

But she noticed the change in his posture. He looked . . . uneasy. "Well, I arranged for you to go up to Pediatrics this week. They can always use the help, and since your addition to my office was somewhat sudden, I'm still working out what exactly we'll be having you do here."

Lauren had a sneaking suspicion that he had done this

less out of the goodness of his heart and more to get a potential criminal out of his office while he could sort out whether he was comfortable with her being there. But as he walked away quickly without another word, she had a feeling she had already begun to make him uncomfortable in all the right ways.

Chapter 3

Narcissistic Personality Disorder

Lauren had spent all morning in the Pediatric Unit and had had a blast. Her proclivity for nonsense and random silliness meant that she was a breath of fresh air to the unit of sick kids. She hadn't realized how much time had passed until one of the nurses stopped her from bouncing between rooms like a tennis ball and told her she could take lunch. Lauren hadn't even noticed how hungry she was, but the mere mention of food caused her stomach to rumble.

Lauren walked back to Dr. Scott's office to pick up the lunch her mom had packed for her. A lesser woman might have felt like a child—having her lunch packed for her by her mommy. But Lauren didn't have that issue. If her mom wanted to pack her a lunch, far be it for Lauren to argue. She walked in and was surprised to find the office empty of patients. "What happened? You guys chase everyone away?" Lauren asked the receptionist, Carla.

"Ha, I wish. We close from one to two for lunch."

That hadn't occurred to Lauren, though she wasn't sure why it would have. She continued around the desk and walked into the back office where the refrigerator was. The other nurses, her mom included, were gathered around a table eating. "Hey, Laur. How's Pediatrics?"

"Freakin' awesome. You guys are missing out working down here. They have Legos," Lauren said with a smile as she grabbed her lunch and began to walk back the way she had just come.

"You want to eat with us, sweetheart?" her mom asked.

"Ah, so now I'm sweetheart again. Just a few days ago I was a felon, and now I'm sweetheart. You are a fickle woman, Pamela Hastings. But no. I'm going to go down to the cafeteria and make some phone calls. I'll see you wonderful ladies later."

The women all said their good-byes as Lauren left the office and made her way back to the elevator. She hadn't spoken to Cassidy, Simone, or Quinn much since her unfortunate brush with the law, and she needed some gossip therapy with her besties.

Scott didn't normally go down to the cafeteria. He didn't quite fit in around the hospital, being too young to really bond with any of the attendings but finding himself often annoyed by residents. Even the two other physicians in his own practice avoided him at all costs, which was just fine with Scott. He had a job to do, not friends to make. But when he had overheard Lauren say she was going down to the cafeteria, he suddenly wanted to go too. He told himself that he was simply interested in figuring out what kind of person she was before he gave her permission to work in his office, but he knew that was bullshit. Mostly since he'd already granted her permission to work there, but also because he couldn't deny that he found her intriguing. Not to mention sexy as hell.

He tried to act natural, taking his time choosing his lunch so that he could watch where she sat without being obvious about it. He waited until she took a seat and pulled out her phone before he paid and walked to a table directly behind her. He could hear her perfectly as she began talking.

"Hey. What's going on?" Lauren said into the phone. "It's going well so far. I spent the morning up in Pediatrics and had a blast. It sure beat hanging around my mom's office. I'm going to be bored out of my mind spending the next few months there."

Scott couldn't help but feel a twinge of disappointment at her words, but he quickly reminded himself that her opinion didn't matter. He wasn't interested in her opinions. He was interested in getting her beneath him on the desk in his office. Though being interested in it and doing it were very different things. Scott knew better than to get sexually involved with anyone who worked for him. Since the relationships he preferred were typically short-lived, he didn't need the awkwardness of seeing the other person every day after he broke things off.

"Well, now that you mention it." Lauren lowered her voice so that Scott had to lean back slightly in his chair to hear her. "The doctor who owns the practice, Dr. Scott"— he ignored the snotty tone she adopted when saying his name—"is megahot. Like off-the-charts eye candy. He's tall, though everyone is compared to me. I'd say about six foot. It was hard to tell just how ripped he is under his white coat, but I could definitely tell he keeps himself in pretty good shape."

Scott wanted to turn around and ask her if she'd like to find out for herself just how in shape he was, but he was too fascinated by her conversation to interrupt her.

"And his face. Listen, Cass, he's straight-up gorgeous. Bright green eyes, short blond hair—just long enough to run your fingers through and give a good yank—square jaw. I think I saw a dimple in his left cheek. Really just surface-of-the-sun hot."

Her comment about his hair caused his dick to jump in his pants. She wasn't inhibited; that much was clear. And that held definite possibilities for him. *If* he had been interested in acting on his baser urges. Which he wasn't. Not really.

"Uh, no," Lauren giggled dryly. "He may be hot, but his personality negates most of it. You know the type: rich, good-looking doctor. He's totally used to women falling at his feet. He probably has some serious control fetish that women think is hot because of Christian Grey."

Goddamn it. Not that bullshit. Granted, Scott had some control issues, but she'd only spent three minutes with him. Scott hadn't even begun to figure Lauren out and she almost had his number; it was starting to annoy him.

The person on the other end of the line said something before Lauren spoke again. "No, he's definitely not interesting enough to be into all that whips and chains shit. Probably just gets off on telling girls what to do. And I bet there are a ton of them more than willing to do whatever he says."

It seemed to Scott that Lauren thought she held the

upper hand with him, thought she knew exactly what type of man he was. She wasn't wrong when she said that he liked to be in control. But Lauren's assessment of him, her keen perception, made him feel very *out* of control. He needed to take charge, restack the cards in his favor. So, before he could give it much thought, he stood and walked around her table and sat down across from her. "I figured that since you were talking about me anyway, I may as well join the conversation."

Lauren's eyes widened a fraction, showing her shock at seeing him. But instead of becoming embarrassed, she simply smiled and continued her conversation. Scott found himself surprised by Lauren. Again.

"He just sat down across from me actually. Seems we have quite the eavesdropper on our hands." Lauren relaxed back into her chair, making it plain that Scott didn't intimidate her. Quite the opposite. "He isn't saying anything really. Just kind of staring."

Scott kept his face neutral to show that he was just as calm and collected as Lauren was. "Is staring a crime?" he asked.

"No. It's just super weird," she said with the same playfulness he'd observed when he'd met her.

"Would you rather I not look at you at all?" he countered.

"No, I like a little attention as much as the next girl. As long as we're clear that it's just looking and no touching." Lauren leaned forward in her chair, pulling up her free forearm to rest on the table.

Scott leaned in as well, making it easier for him to hear the person Lauren was talking to. "Laur, you want to call me back?" the voice asked.

"Not sure. Let me ask Dr. Scott." She tilted her head slightly, directing her attention at him. "Is your interruption something that requires my undivided attention, or can Cass continue to listen in?"

Scott darted his tongue out over his bottom lip. Lauren's eyes snapped to his mouth, lingering there for a moment before drifting back up to look at him. "I think you'd better call her back," he rasped.

"My boss has spoken, Cass. I'll have to call you back."

Lauren hung up the phone without waiting for a reply, and Scott knew he had her where he wanted her. Well, maybe not *right* where he wanted her.

"So, are you always so strict about your looking-but-no-touching rule? I think that line could get a little blurred when dealing with drunk frat guys." Scott's eyes bore into hers. It was like a game of chicken, each one refusing to look away before the other.

Lauren smirked. "You're right. As I found out last weekend, it is evidently a difficult rule for some guys to follow."

Scott's brow furrowed. "So you're speaking from experience. Tell me what happens when someone doesn't follow your rule."

"Past history would indicate that I go to jail."

Scott straightened. *Was she saying— Was that why she was arrested?* He willed himself to appear relaxed, but he couldn't help the slight tightening of his jaw. He wasn't sure what caused the protective feeling he was experiencing, but the thought of someone putting their hands on Lauren when she didn't want them there made him want to put his fist through something. Finally, he realized that she was waiting for him to say something, a curious expression on her face. "Is that why you're having legal trouble?"

She looked thoughtful for a moment, choosing her words carefully. "Indirectly, yes."

"Did anything happen to him?" Scott wasn't sure why he cared about any of this, but he did. Fiercely.

Lauren huffed out a laugh. "Yeah, I kicked the shit out of him."

Scott startled slightly. "You . . . really?" He didn't mean to doubt her, but Lauren was a small girl. If she kicked the shit out of some guy, he must've been a real pussy.

Lauren smiled, a genuine one that lit up her eyes. Damn, he liked that smile. "I'm more than just a pretty face, Dr. Scott."

"Clearly," he replied matter-of-factly, making his comment lose some of its complimentary appeal. He figured Lauren's words had been meant as a joke—an attempt to poke fun at her actions. But Scott couldn't help but acknowledge the obvious truth in her statement. "Who was this guy? A blind midget?"

Lauren sat back in her chair again, appraising him. Scott didn't like it. It was almost as if she could see through him, into the very essence of who he was.

After a few tense seconds, she spoke. "You don't believe me," she observed. "I'm a lot of things: free-spirited, maybe a little crazy and impulsive. And I'm definitely smarter than you think. But one thing I am not, and have never been, is a liar."

"Good to know," Scott replied, his voice deep, seductive. He meant what he said. Because the more he talked to Lauren Hastings, the more he wanted her. And the types of relationships he engaged in required complete honesty. On both parts. *Stop thinking like this, Scott. Pursuing this girl will blow up in your face like napalm.*

"Look, let's cut the bullshit," Lauren said. "I don't have a skewed self-image. I've gotten my fair share of male attention ever since I hit high school and traded in my Coke-bottle glasses for contacts and track pants for skinny jeans. But I did all of that to feel good about *myself*. Not so some guy could feel that it's his right to say and do whatever he wants to me."

Scott wanted to interject, but she was on a roll. And damn if it didn't turn him on.

"So if you think the low voice, the heated gaze, the sexual body language impresses me, you're wrong. It may give me something to gossip about to my friends, but that's all it is. Beauty's only skin-deep. I'm interested in what's under all of that." Her voice never wavered. It remained even and calm. But there was fire behind her eyes. Scott could see it.

"How profound," he replied.

Lauren stood, plastering a smile on her face. "Almost as profound as a man who tries to act unaffected, all the while gripping something in his pocket for the duration of our conversation. Enjoy the rest of your lunch, Doctor."

Scott watched her leave before he looked down at his hand. He'd dealt with uncomfortable situations the same way now as he had when he was a child. It was the reason he normally kept that silver dollar in his pocket. How the hell had she known what he was doing? He'd almost convinced himself that he'd won that round, but how wrong he'd been. Lauren was proving quite the worthy adversary. Scott would need to up his game.

Lauren plopped down into the booth and slid over to make room for Quinn to sit beside her. Cassidy and Simone sat across from them, eyeing her intently. Cassidy had arranged this impromptu dinner after overhearing part of Lauren's conversation with Scott.

Lauren picked up her menu and studied it, trying to ignore the blatant stares from her friends. Finally, she put the menu down and looked back at them. "What?" she asked.

"Oh, you know what," Cassidy replied with a huge smile. "Spill it. What happened with Dr. Scott after you hung up on me?"

"I didn't hang up on you. I told you I'd call you back."

"Which you didn't," Cass added.

"Only because you sent out a text to meet you here."

"Girls," Simone interrupted. "As fascinating as it is to hear about who called who, can we please get to the part where Lauren bangs a smoking hot doctor?"

Lauren's eyes flew to Cass'. "You told them I banged him?"

Cass looked thoughtful. "I think I phrased it in the future tense."

Lauren opened her mouth to argue, but Quinn spoke first. "Lauren. Doctor. Explain."

"There's nothing to explain. My mom works for a doctor who's a total dipshit, and I plan on spending my time there driving him insane. End of story."

Simone let out a laugh and shook her head. Lauren's friends were all used to her antics, but they also knew that she'd never made anyone miserable, not for a day in her life. If she were going to drive her new boss insane, it was most likely because, on some level, he'd enjoy every second of it.

"But he's good-looking?" Quinn asked. Her dark red hair and smattering of freckles over her nose appealed mostly to mama's boys, so she had thankfully escaped the dating cesspool relatively unscathed. Lauren knew that wouldn't be the case if Quinn ever shacked up with Dr. Scott.

"Sure, in a Godlike kind of way. I have a feeling he's got the complex to boot," Lauren replied dryly.

"Don't most doctors have a God-complex though?" Cass asked, clearly implying that allowances should be made for him.

"I wouldn't know." Lauren started picking at the bread that was on the table to try to keep herself occupied. What she didn't want to tell her friends was that she'd been thinking about Scott since lunch. And not in a negative way. The exterior of him was polished, refined—like a work of art. But she knew there had to be more beneath all of that. It made him appealing to Lauren in ways she couldn't even begin to explain.

She wanted to get to know him better—to see what was hiding beneath his facade. She would bet almost anything that she'd be a different person at the end of it, and she wasn't completely sure whether that would be a good or a bad thing. But what she did know was that, if the opportunity arose, it was a gamble she was willing to take.

"Since you're going to be a doctor someday, are you

going to get one of those complexes?" Simone asked with a smirk.

"I sure hope so," Lauren replied with a smile before throwing a piece of bread in her mouth and deciding that she was probably already more like Dr. Scott than she was comfortable with.

Chapter 4

Spastic Paraparesis

As Scott waited in line at the Starbucks in the hospital lobby on the way into work, he wondered what the day ahead held for him. A part of him was happy that Lauren would be spending the day in Pediatrics—mainly because he didn't know quite how to act around her, what to say. And that uncertainty threw him. Confidence was something he prided himself on. Scott always knew the right thing to say and how to say it—especially around women.

But Lauren Hastings was an enigma. One that made him uneasy. It was as if he'd finally met his match in her. Right when he thought he'd said something that would throw her a little off-balance and give him the advantage, she'd hurl a comment right back at him. But before he could think about it much longer, a familiar voice interrupted him.

"What'll it be today, Dr. Scott? Try something new for a change?"

"What do you have in mind, Cheyenne?"

"How about something sweet? Caramel flan latte?" The heavyset black woman smiled as she waited for Scott's answer.

"Well, you know I can't turn down something sweet," Scott said with a wink. "You know, they should really give all of you a raise down here. Taking care of all of us like this," he called to all of the workers as he pointed to the line of doctors and nurses behind him. "I'm basically useless without my daily jolt of caffeine. You guys don't get the credit you deserve."

The baristas rolled their eyes and chuckled at Scott's compliment, but seemed flattered all the same. "Don't I know it," Cheyenne replied.

To those who didn't know him, Scott's comment may have seemed gratuitous or perhaps even patronizing, but anyone who'd spent any amount of time with him knew he meant every word. Scott appreciated little things, and the way in which he interacted with people let them know his words were genuine. "How's Jeffrey's cold, by the way? He feeling better?" Scott asked as he handed the woman a five and told her to keep the change.

"Much better, thanks. Little guy slept it off the last few days and is back to being the little spawn of Satan that he is.

Scott smiled and fixed his tie. "Glad to hear it," he said before grabbing his coffee and turning toward the door. "See you ladies tomorrow."

Lauren strolled into Pediatrics Thursday morning excited to get the day started. A handful of sick kids would be just what she needed to take her mind off of Dr. Scott. After her conversation with the girls, she couldn't help but let her thoughts drift to him. Admittedly, he was hot. There was no denying that. But was she really contemplating digging beneath that? And after her tirade yesterday, was *he* even willing to let her try?

Thankfully, as she spent time coloring pictures of Disney princesses and playing video games, the morning passed quickly, and it was easy to focus on something other than Dr. Scott. Finally, lunch rolled around, and it couldn't have come at a better time because Lauren was starving. She said her good-byes to the kids and the staff and headed downstairs to grab her lunch.

"What are we feasting on today?" Lauren asked her mom with a laugh.

"I just packed ham and cheese sandwiches and some fruit. Nothing special. I'm happy you're planning to eat with us today." Pam handed Lauren her brown bag and took a seat at the table in the middle of the small office kitchen.

"Actually," Lauren hesitated as she took her lunch from her mother, "I was thinking of heading downstairs again. I brought my laptop so I can look up what books I have to get for the new semester. I plan to head over to school after I'm done here for the day to pick them up. This whole working professional thing is cramping my academic style," Lauren said with a smirk.

"Fine, fine," her mother said. "I see how it is. I provide you with proper nourishment and you leave me for bigger and better things."

"Well, as long as you understand what's happening. Glad to see we're on the same page." Lauren laughed. "See you in a bit. Thanks for the, uh . . . nourishment," she said holding up the brown bag before giving her mom a peck on the cheek and hurrying downstairs toward the cafeteria.

For the second day in a row, Scott found himself in the cafeteria. Well, he didn't so much *find* himself there as he actively sought it out. He'd seen Lauren exit the office, lunch in hand. And as if by instinct, he'd left the Thai food he'd ordered sitting out on his desk. Instead, he'd filled his cafeteria tray with a grilled chicken salad and an apple—the healthiest option the hospital provided. It was bad enough he'd come downstairs to eat. He didn't want to be subjected to whatever slop the cafeteria passed off as appetizing cuisine.

As he paid for his meal and picked up some napkins and a fork, he scanned the cafeteria inconspicuously for her. He hoped if she'd been looking his way, she wouldn't notice how his eyes surveyed the tables, taking in each diner at rapid speed.

Thank God. His vision was momentarily obscured by an elderly man walking in front of him, but the quick glance he'd gotten of Lauren had been enough to confirm it was her—the way her soft brown hair fell against her back, the way she sat confidently with her posture straight and her shoulders back.

Lauren had chosen a seat near the center of the cafeteria, her back conveniently to Scott. He was thankful because it gave him ample time to appraise her. She'd probably decided to sit away from the windows to cut down on the glare as she studied her laptop intently, jotting down notes as she scrolled. *Jesus, even* that's *hot. What's the matter with me?*

After a few moments, Scott made his way toward Lauren's table, but paused behind her to see what she was doing on her computer. *Probably tweeting some meaningless quote or something*, he thought. But to his surprise, the screen held a course list from George Mason University. *Advanced Psychology of Intimate Relationships. Interes—*

"Are you gonna stand there all day looking over my shoulder like some middle school stalker, or you gonna have a seat?"

Lauren hadn't even turned around to look at him, and the assertiveness with which she spoke only further impressed Scott. The girl was good. No doubt about that. Momentarily caught off-guard, he slid into the seat next to her and spoke, embarrassed at how uneasy his voice sounded. "How did you ..."

"Reflection in the screen," she said, never taking her eyes off the computer.

Despite her slight smile that served to ease his nerves, he couldn't help but feel like Lauren had one-upped him once again. And he was eager to get back on top. Trying to ignore all the images the phrase "on top" conjured, he set about attempting to make her as uncomfortable as *he* had just felt by saying, "Do you always let your mommy pack your lunch for you?"

She took her hand off the mouse and lifted her eyelids so that her dark blue stare fixed on Scott's. "Yes," she replied simply. "Do you always eat like a woman?"

Scott was careful not to let her comment affect him as his eyes bore into her. "I eat lots of things." *Let her interpret that however she likes.*

He knew his comment had the desired effect when Lauren shifted uncomfortably in her chair and returned her gaze to the computer without so much as a word.

Scott enjoyed the silence—a rare sign that he'd gotten to her—and then he finally spoke again, hoping to rattle her further. "You know, I can help you with that," he said, lowering his voice and leaning toward her.

Scott noticed Lauren shiver as he spoke. "Help with what?"

"The Psychology of Intimate Relationships." Scott was still positioned well within Lauren's personal space.

"I doubt that," Lauren answered quickly. "You can't even find friends to sit with in a cafeteria." There was humor in her voice, but Scott couldn't deny that there was definite truth to her statement. After all, he'd come downstairs twice now, and he'd sat with her both times.

Scott leaned back in his chair, relaxed as he took another bite of his salad. "I'm sitting with a friend now, aren't I? Besides, isn't that class about sex? I'm sure I could help—"

"Just so we're clear, sex is just one of the topics covered in the class. It's more about the dynamics of how people relate to one another when they're in a relationship."

Scott took a bite of his salad before responding. "Oh well, that's way less interesting than I thought. Sex, I do. Relationships, I don't. So maybe you're right about me not being any help to you."

"No relationships, huh? Good to know," she added with a sly grin.

Scott shook his head. "They're too . . . messy. And since you brought it up, I'll admit it. I don't really have any friends here. But that's *my* choice, not *theirs.* I don't make a habit of hanging out with people from work, especially people who are so much older than I am." He motioned to a table full of gray-haired men in white coats a few tables over. "It was either them or you. And if you ask me, it's much more enjoyable to look at you than it is to stare at Harry Giles as he scrapes the salt off his crackers one by one."

Despite Lauren's eye roll, a smile played on her lips. "You basically just told me I look better than a sixty-year-old. I would think someone with your intelligence and charm could do a little better than that."

Scott rubbed a hand across his face and sat back in his chair, clearly satisfied with the direction the conversation had taken. "Did you just call me charming and intelligent?" He raised his eyebrows to let Lauren know he was pleased with her compliment—even if she hadn't meant for it to be one.

"It's not much of a secret, is it? You're clearly confident around women. Unless, of course, I'm some sort of anomaly. And obviously you're intelligent. In order to run your own practice at twenty-nine, you would've needed to graduate high school at what? Thirteen? Were you even old enough to—"

"Sixteen."

"What?"

"I was sixteen when I graduated high school. Twenty-three after med school. Twenty-six when I completed my residency. And twenty-eight when I took over my father's practice." Lauren hadn't said a word as Scott rattled off his accomplishments, and he began to sense that he may have come off a bit arrogant, even for him. "What?" he shrugged lightheartedly. "Boy genius, remember? You said so yourself. You weren't that far off with the Doogie

Howser reference. I just don't keep a diary on some archaic computer program."

"So *you* say," Lauren teased.

Scott's face grew serious. "What *I* say is all that matters."

Scott had spent much of that evening replaying his conversation with Lauren in his head. He'd seemed more open than he meant to come across. All his talk of sex, relationships, and then an explanation about why he had no friends at the hospital. In only a few short minutes, this girl . . . this *woman* had gotten more information out of him than his therapist had in the first three months he'd seen her.

Something about Lauren made him feel comfortable and uneasy at the same time. There were some things that were better left unsaid. But around Lauren, he felt like he might say anything. And that was a new feeling for him. She made him lower his guard in ways he wasn't sure he ever had. Definitely in ways he never *wanted* to.

Friday morning played out like most others. Scott saw some of his regulars first thing in the morning at his satellite office and made a few phone calls about test results. In the afternoon he'd planned to check in on some of his patients who had been hospitalized. He'd felt busy all morning, but by noon, he didn't feel like he'd gotten much done. He'd almost decided to skip lunch and run a few errands, but a better idea occurred to him. He needed to discuss next week with Lauren. She'd be starting Monday, and they still hadn't talked about her job description. But he couldn't bear a third day in a row of cafeteria food.

At twelve forty-five he headed outside to pick up lunch from his favorite food truck, and by one o'clock he was sitting at a cafeteria table eating and checking his stocks on his phone. He'd fully expected Lauren to come downstairs for lunch again, but by one-thirty she still hadn't arrived. Or at least he hadn't *seen* her arrive. *Maybe she stayed upstairs*, he thought. *Or went* out *for lunch*. It wasn't like they had plans to meet.

He was startled out of his internal monologue at the sound of her voice. "Are you pretending to look busy so no one sits with you?" she asked with a smile as she gestured toward his phone and tossed the brown paper bag on the table.

"If I am, it clearly didn't work," he replied without looking up. "Is that what you were doing yesterday?" Scott hoped Lauren didn't pick up on the fact that his disinterest was intentional.

Lauren sat back in her chair, clearly exhausted from an exceptionally tiring day in Pediatrics, and began pulling items out of her lunch. "If I was, it clearly didn't work," she quipped.

Scott didn't know how to respond, but thankfully Lauren continued speaking so he didn't have to.

"Can I interrupt your intense game of Flappy Bird for a little adult conversation?"

Finally, Scott raised his gaze to meet hers and hit the button on his phone for standby. "Flappy Bird, huh? I'm guessing that's some kids' game you've been playing with your new friends on the seventh floor." Scott knew exactly what Flappy Bird was. In fact, he had it on his phone, though he'd never admit that to Lauren.

"Don't try to pretend that you're too old for Flappy Bird," Lauren said, taking a bite of her salad.

"I was starting to think you weren't coming down for lunch," Scott said, suddenly needing to change the direction of the conversation to a subject he was more comfortable with.

"Why wouldn't I? Isn't this, like, our *thing*?"

Scott eyed her intensely. "I didn't know we had a *thing*."

"Well, now you know." She pulled one side of her hair back behind her shoulder, and Scott found himself imagining what it would feel like gripped between his fingers.

"Well, now that you're here, we should discuss the details of next week."

"Okay. I was wondering when you were going to clue me in on what I'd be doing while I'm holed up in your office. I'm sure it'll be thrilling," she joked.

"I guess we should start with defining what appropriate attire is for an office setting." Scott let his eyes roam Lauren's body.

"Oh, this?" Lauren said, pulling at her T-shirt with the hospital logo on it. "Pediatrics gave this to me when one of the kids threw up on my outfit, because they ran out of scrubs. Rough morning. That's why I was late getting down here." She shrugged. "But don't worry. I promise to wear my Sunday best next week."

Scott shook his head and let out a soft laugh. "Good," he said with a slight nod as he looked at his watch. It was already almost two o'clock. He'd left for lunch early and he didn't like taking a longer lunch than he allowed his employees to take. It set a bad example. "Let's go," he said suddenly. "I want to check in on some patients this afternoon. We can finish this discussion upstairs in my office since I need to show you what you'll be doing anyway. I'm not sure I'll have time Monday morning, and I'm assuming since you took a later lunch you still have some time before you need to go back for your afternoon playdate," he said with a smirk.

Scott's urgency took Lauren by surprise. But she followed him toward the elevators without question. She leaned her back against the wall of the elevator, directly across from Dr. Scott. *Shit.* His intense stare and the silence between them made her feel vulnerable, exposed even. Though she wasn't sure why.

They arrived in the office as the women were finishing up with lunch. From the hallway on the way to Scott's office, Lauren could hear her mother and a few others laughing as they exited the kitchen area.

"Second door on your right," Scott directed. "I'll be there in a moment."

No elaboration, just clear and to the point, Lauren thought as she walked briskly through the doorway to his office. Most of the room was exactly how she'd imagined it would be. Though before she entered, she hadn't even realized she'd had an expectation for how Scott's office might look.

A long mahogany desk stood facing the door, and Dr. Scott's large black leather chair behind his desk sat noticeably taller than the two in front of it. It didn't surprise Lauren that Scott felt the need to be above everyone in all aspects of his life. Literally.

Lauren's eyes scanned the dark beige walls: various degrees and awards hung behind his desk, several pictures of him with other people Lauren assumed were equally as important, a few photographs of different places around the world. Though she'd never been to any of the locations, Lauren recognized the Grand Canyon, a Venetian gondolier, and a lion that looked to be sprawled out on the dry, sunny landscape in some part of Africa. All of the pictures were artfully taken, with special attention paid to lighting and focus. She wondered if Scott had taken them himself. *God, does he have to be good at* everything?

As she made her way around the room, Lauren stumbled upon a photo that surprised her completely. It was of a tattoo on a man's lower back. *What guy gets a tramp stamp?* The tattoo was of an arrow pointing toward his ass. Above the arrow, scrawled in playful script, was the phrase, "Dr. Scott saved my ass." Wondering if the tattoo was real, Lauren moved closer to study the photo. *Why the hell would anyone get* that *tattooed on them?*

But when she saw a note framed next to it, she understood.

> *Dear Dr. Scott,*
>
> *If it weren't for your insistence that I see Dr. Sweikert, I would have just attributed my colon cancer to some kind of minor stomach problem. You really pay attention to shit. Literally.*
> *Thanks for saving my ass, Doc.*
>
> *Bill Burgess*

Scott rounded the doorway to his office to the sound of Lauren's soft laughter. He didn't know why, but hearing it made his head fuzz with pleasure. He paused, leaning against the entryway momentarily as he studied the way her tight kid-sized hospital T-shirt rode up to reveal her lower back as she held her arms up to snap a picture of Bill's tattoo with her phone.

Involuntarily, he gripped the files he'd been holding harder. His hands really wanted to grab Lauren's waist and pull her hips into him so her ass ground against his crotch. The thought made his already semierect cock stiffen further against his pants as he stepped toward her quietly. "See something you like?" he asked.

Scott could tell that she hadn't heard him approach, but he could see her body react at the sound of his low voice. She spun around, putting their bodies mere inches apart. Her eyes seemed to search his face as she inhaled deeply, as though she was trying to breathe in more of his scent. "Sorry," she muttered, a faint blush spreading across her cheeks. "I was just—"

"Taking a picture of someone else's property?" Scott could tell she was caught off guard to have been discovered inspecting his things so closely. Seeing this side of her—a more demure, vulnerable side—turned him on even more.

Lauren tried to take a step backwards, but she'd evidently forgotten about the small table against the wall behind her. Her back arched as she lost her balance when her thighs hit the table's edge.

Without thinking, Scott placed his free hand around Lauren's lower back, pulling her hard against him to steady her in one fluid movement. He could feel her heart pounding so hard against his chest, it almost felt as if it were his own. She opened her mouth to speak, but before she could, Scott's lips crushed against hers. Had he given it more thought, he probably could have come up with a hundred reasons for why it was a bad idea. But in that moment, he felt that thinking was grossly overrated. Until his tongue found Lauren's, Scott had no idea just how badly he'd wanted to taste her—to feel her body pressed to his while his cock stiffened against her firm stomach.

She didn't protest as he dropped the file that was in his hands so that he could slip one hand up the back of her shirt, his fingers tracing delicate designs on the skin just above the waistline of her pants. And when he brought the other to tangle in her hair, she released a throaty moan that caused him to kiss her with even more fervor.

That was when his brain caught up with how far everything was going. Granted, he wanted Lauren, but was that really a good idea? The indecision that was racking his brain caused his assault on her lips to slow, and then stop completely. As his eyes opened, he watched as Lauren put her hand to her mouth. Whether it was out of shock or the sudden need to wipe away what they had just done, he wasn't sure. And not knowing just about killed him. His body tensed as he started second-guessing everything with a slight sense of panic.

Fuck, Scott. What the fuck did you just do? You kissed one of your employees. The daughter *of one of your employees, to be exact. You don't fucking do this.* Scott forced himself to say something, to do something that would undo what he'd just done. "Sorry," he blurted out, a tense look on his face as he backed away toward the door and ran a hand through his already rumpled hair. "I swear I brought you up here to show you what you'd be doing Monday. I . . . fuck."

Scott Jacobs took pride in maintaining his composure

in all aspects of his life. He did not unintentionally kiss a woman and then apologize.

Except . . . he just had.

"So that's what I'll be doing Monday?" It was a poor attempt to lighten the mood.

"No, Jesus, I just meant—"

"Relax, I'm kidding. Besides, it's not like I didn't enjoy it."

"What?" The question shot out of Scott's mouth before he could stop it. "It doesn't matter if you enjoyed it."

"Well, I beg to differ," Lauren said casually as she made her way toward the door. "And just for future reference, Doctor, you probably shouldn't make it a habit of kissing women if you don't think they'll enjoy it."

Chapter 5

Farsightedness

Lauren had replayed her kiss with Dr. Scott all weekend. Not in an obsessive way, but in an I-bet-he's-freaking-the-hell-out-wish-I-could-witness-it kind of way. She had seen the torn look on his face, a cross between horror and wanting more.

Her ability to read people made her a natural when it came to her psychology courses. It was part of the reason she'd switched her major. The main reason, however, was something she didn't really want to think about. What Cooper had gone through impacted her decision more so than anything else, though she'd never admitted that to anyone. But Lauren knew that the people close to her understood, so she had the support system she needed. And that's all that mattered.

Classes didn't start for another week, but Lauren sat with her textbooks sprawled in front of her on her bed anyway. Despite her laid-back personality, Lauren was diligent when it came to her studies. Not to mention that she found her classes fascinating. She had just begun taking notes on the first chapter of her Advanced Psychology textbook when her phone chirped with an incoming text. She didn't recognize the phone number, but the content of the text let her know who had sent it.

> Since we didn't get to have our talk Friday, I thought I should make you aware that your shift will be from 9-6. A task sheet will be awaiting you when you arrive.

Lauren couldn't help the smile that overtook her face. Scott clearly couldn't resist making first contact, putting things back on terms he was comfortable with by discussing work. She couldn't help it; she had to fuck with him. How'd you get this number?

His reply came back quickly: It was in the paperwork you evidently had your mommy fill out.

A laugh burst from her. The truth was, her mom *had* filled out her employment paperwork while Lauren was up in Pediatrics. Lauren hadn't asked her to but was glad she did. Filling that crap out was the last thing Lauren had wanted to do. So, other than signing her name in the spots her mom had marked with Post-its, she hadn't had to fill out a damn thing. So did you make a special trip back to the office to peruse my personnel file, or did you do it before you left Friday?

Lauren wasn't playing fair, but she couldn't bring herself to care. *God, Sam was right. I really am a ballbuster.*

Scott's response didn't come as quickly that time, and Lauren mentally high-fived herself for flustering him. Finally her phone chirped again.

Wouldn't you like to know?

Lauren grinned again. One thing was for sure: Dr. Scott had a playful side. A side Lauren found incredibly attractive.

Her phone sounded again before she had formulated a reply. See you tomorrow.

He was dismissing her, ending the conversation on his terms. But Lauren just couldn't allow that.

I do have one question for you before I start my employment, Doctor.

Yes?

Lauren smiled mischievously as she typed. You gonna kiss me again?

His response was quick this time. Have a good day, Lauren.

Lauren dropped the phone on her bed before throwing her hands in the air as a celebration of her victory. She hadn't felt this giddy in quite a while. Though she convinced herself it had to do more with her baiting of the man, rather than the actual man himself.

Lauren had never been more excited for a Monday to get under way. Her mom opened the office and prepped for patients, so her shift began earlier than Lauren's, which meant their carpooling days were over. Though Lauren did hope that her mom had still made her lunch.

She walked into Dr. Scott's office just before nine.

There were a few patients in the waiting room, and Carla was behind the check-in desk. "Good morning, everyone," Lauren called.

The patients barely looked up at her, but Carla grinned fully. "Morning, sweetie. I see you've decided to stick it out with us."

"Yeah, well, what can I say? I'm a glutton for punishment."

Carla laughed as Lauren walked around her and made her way to the back room. Her mom wasn't there, but Stella, the accounts manager; Phyllis, the office manager; Tammy, who worked alongside Carla; and Betty, a nurse, were all working—or at least looking busy. "Okay, I'm here. Put me to work," Lauren declared as she entered the room of women.

Phyllis, who bore a striking resemblance to Bea Arthur, perked up at Lauren's voice. "Hi, Lauren. Nice to see you again. Your desk is right over there. I believe Dr. Scott left you a list of things to get you started. You'll sort of be his personal assistant."

Oh I will, will I? Lauren thought with a smirk.

"His normal days here are Monday through Thursday," Phyllis continued.

"Sounds great." She plopped down into her chair and opened her bottom drawer to drop her purse inside before looking over the list. Lauren was immediately surprised by Scott's handwriting. She knew that doctors were notorious for their illegible script, so as she read Scott's neat block letters, she couldn't help but shake her head. *Even the man's handwriting is perfect.* The list was full of menial tasks: making calls to medical suppliers, pulling patient files, following up with specialists. There was also a "pick up dry-cleaning" on the list, but Lauren crossed it out. First, because she figured it was a joke. And second, well—if it wasn't—she had no intention of doing it. Lauren was just about to get started making phone calls when she heard him.

"Morning, ladies. Lauren."

She tried to bite back a smile at his subtle dig. She was glad they didn't have to waste time with pleasantries since he'd already thrown the gauntlet by implying that she was not a lady. She threw up a hand at him, refusing to turn toward him.

"You all good to get started?"

Lauren jumped when she heard him directly behind her. She hadn't heard him approach. *Stealthy bastard.*

"With this detailed list you provided, how could I be anything less?"

He let out a mocking gust of air and she felt him lean over her shoulder. "You already managed to get my drycleaning?"

She could hear the glee in his voice. She turned her head around to look up at his beautiful, chiseled, glorious face. His perfectly tousled sandy blond hair gave his masculine features a slightly boyish quality that made him inexplicably sexier. Lauren was conscious of the fact that her expression might have betrayed her. So she took a second to compose herself and hoped that her comment might conceal just how affected she was by Dr. Scott. "Nope," she replied, popping the "P" for effect. Then she turned back toward her desk and began looking at the spreadsheet she'd opened on her computer that would show the phone numbers she needed.

He didn't move from behind her, and she could practically hear the cogs in his brain turning.

Thankfully, Tammy saved him from having to think of a witty comeback. "Dr. Scott, your first appointment is here. He's in Four," she said, referring to the exam room's number.

"Thanks, Tammy." Despite Tammy's words, Scott didn't move. Instead, he leaned over Lauren to retrieve a pencil from the other side of her desk. His arm brushed her shoulder as he reached for it.

Suddenly, in a way Lauren wasn't able to explain, the air seemed to change. It became thicker, and goose bumps popped out across her skin. She let out a shaky breath and silently cursed herself for doing so. She didn't want Scott to realize how much he affected her, though she was sure he already knew. Lauren knew she was more than capable of holding her own against him when it came to exchanging words, but she worried that his ability to use his charm to get whatever he wanted far surpassed hers. She felt on edge as he grabbed the pad of paper from in front of her and added to the bottom of the list.

Lauren sat ramrod straight in her chair, casting her eyes down at the paper only when Scott backed away from her slightly. "What's that?"

"What I'd like for lunch. I'd like it waiting for me in my office after I see my last patient of the morning."

"So I guess this means you won't be barging in on me in the cafeteria today?" Lauren's voice was husky. She cleared her throat and shifted in her chair, angry at how quickly her body had responded to him.

"No, not today. I have a phone conference at one-thirty. Which you'd know if you'd bothered to look at my schedule. Enjoy your day, Lauren."

And with that, he quickly turned and walked away from her.

Scott's morning, like most, was hectic. He'd bounced from room to room, performing two physicals then diagnosing several sinus infections, a sprained ankle, a case of bronchitis, and a case of it-may-feel-like-appendicitis-but-it's-really-just-gas. He hadn't even had time to stop in the office and bother Lauren. Or even sneak a quick peek at her, for that matter.

As he assured his last patient, sixty-seven-year-old Thomas Chonsky, that he wasn't having a stroke but rather his arm had simply fallen asleep while he lay in bed the previous night, Scott was grateful that it was almost lunchtime. All the running around that morning had left him famished.

"You're sure that's all it is?" Mr. Chonsky asked. Scott could hear the nervousness in the man's voice. Thomas had lost his wife two years earlier to a massive heart attack, which she'd had in her sleep. Thomas had gone to bed a happily married man, and woken up a widower. Ever since, he'd become a slight hypochondriac.

But Scott got it. He knew what it was like to lose someone you thought you had all the time in the world with. He put his hand on Thomas' shoulder as they walked toward the waiting area. "Tell you what. Why don't you go grab some lunch in the cafeteria, relax for a little while, and then come back when we reopen at two and I'll check you again? You may have to wait a few minutes for a break in my schedule, but I'll get to you as soon as I can."

Thomas stepped slightly away from Scott so he could extend his hand. "I'd appreciate that, Doc."

Scott accepted the outstretched hand and offered Thomas a slight smile. "My pleasure. See you in an hour or so. Carla," Scott said, shifting his attention, "Mr. Chonsky is going to come back in a little while. Can you have someone let me know when he's here?"

"Absolutely," Carla replied cheerily. "You can take care of your paperwork when you come back, Mr. Chonsky."

The older man nodded and shuffled out of the office. Scott turned around to walk toward his office, but stopped abruptly as his eyes landed on Lauren. She was watching him, a warm expression on her face. Their eyes met for only a few seconds before she walked back into the office, leaving him alone in the hall. He was again overwhelmed by how deeply she seemed to see him. When she looked at him, she seemed to be dissecting him—as if she were trying to fit pieces of a puzzle together. It surprised him how badly he wanted her to figure him out.

Scott shook his head slightly to clear it. Feelings like that weren't what he wanted. He had crafted his world carefully, with precision and clarity. He didn't need some woman trying to get under his skin. No, what he needed was someone he could have a few weeks of purely sexual pleasure with and nothing more. No emotions. No ties. No relationships. It just wasn't how Scott was wired.

But as he walked into his office and saw the chicken salad wrap he'd asked her to get, complete with a bottle of water and a note that said *Guess this one's on me,* he couldn't help thinking how useless it was to try to keep her from getting to him. She already had.

*   *   *

Lauren felt . . . Well, she wasn't really sure how she felt. Just when she thought she had Scott all figured out, he'd reveal another layer to her. Not that she was surprised. She had known from the first day in the cafeteria that there was more to the man than he let on. But the way he interacted with his patients, how sympathetic and kind he was—that threw her. She expected him to be good at his job, but she thought his diligence would stem from some innate need to be better than everyone around him. But now she wasn't so sure.

"How is everything going?"

Lauren startled. She spun around to see Phyllis towering over her. "Oh, uh, fine. I finished with Dr. Scott's to-do list and started looking over his schedule for the next couple of days."

"Wonderful. I'll check in with the doctor in a bit and see if he'd like to create a master list of duties for you or if he'd prefer to prepare one for you each day you're here." Phyllis turned to walk away as soon as she'd finished speaking.

Lauren bit on her lower lip. When she had looked over Scott's schedule that morning, something had popped out at her that seemed strange. She debated for half a second over whether or not to ask before deciding that she couldn't resist. "Phyllis?"

The woman turned around and raised her eyebrows, prompting Lauren to continue.

Lauren looked briefly back at her computer screen, then back to Phyllis. "I noticed that Dr. Scott is in his other office on Fridays, and that's the only day the other two doctors are here. Is that . . . normal?" It certainly didn't seem normal to Lauren. If Scott was in the hospital, the other two doctors were at the satellite office. And if the other two were at the hospital, Scott was at the other office.

Phyllis looked at Lauren for a moment, her face remaining expressionless. "No," she replied simply. Then she proceeded to walk out of the office without any further explanation.

"Okay then," Lauren muttered as she turned back to her computer and tried to figure out how she was going to keep herself entertained for the next four hours until she could go home.

Lauren lasted about five more minutes before she was up and roaming the office halls. She found her mom at the nurses' station.

"Come here often?" Lauren said with a smile.

Pam looked up from the chart she was studying and grinned at her daughter. "That line ever work for you?"

"All the time. Whatcha doin'?" Lauren leaned against the counter so she could see the chart her mom was looking at.

"Trying to figure out how the lab lost three vials of blood. Mrs. Waters isn't going to be happy if she has to have more drawn. What about you?"

Lauren put her index finger to her chin. "Well, let me see. It's been such a frantic day I hardly know where to begin. I made some phone calls, stared at a computer screen blankly for about an hour, made some more phone calls, fetched the good doctor his lunch, watched him be surprisingly compassionate to a patient, and then stared at the computer some more." Lauren bent over and rested her arms on the counter, hoping her mother would latch onto the bit of information Lauren desperately wanted to talk about.

"Why would it surprise you that Dr. Scott's compassionate?"

Bingo! "I dunno. He seems pretty . . . cocky."

"I guess he can come off that way." Pam hadn't looked up from the chart, and Lauren was thankful for it. She stood a better chance gleaning information if her mother was somewhat distracted.

"That's the impression I got," Lauren prompted even though she wasn't being entirely honest. It was the impression Scott *wanted* to give, but she saw beneath that cavalier bullshit almost immediately. But Lauren sure as hell didn't want her mom thinking she was asking for any other reason than vague curiosity.

"Hmm."

Lauren widened her eyes and stared at her mother. "Hmm? That's all I get?"

Pam's lips quirked slightly. "Why are you so interested?"

Busted. Lauren should've known that her mom would see through her feigned disinterest. She'd really have to stop underestimating the woman. "Because I have to work for him for the next few months. I'd like to know who I'm dealing with."

Her mom closed the chart and appraised Lauren for a second. Anyone observing them would have instantly recognized where Lauren got her shrewd observational skills. Mother and daughter stared into each other's eyes, searching for the words neither of them were saying aloud. "Scott cares more about his patients than any doctor I've ever worked with. And considering I worked for his father, that's really saying something." Pam began to gather her things, but Lauren wasn't finished with her yet.

"So Scott's dad was a good doctor?"

"He was a great doctor. And an even better man. Scott inherited both traits from him, even if he likes to keep that fact hidden sometimes."

"Pam, Mrs. Barton is here."

Lauren had been so focused on her conversation with her mom that she hadn't even noticed Betty approach.

"Thanks, Betty," Pam called as Betty kept moving down the hallway. "Back to the grind. I'll see you later, sweetheart."

But before her mom could make it two steps, Lauren stopped her. "Why are the other doctors in the practice never in the same place Scott is?"

Pam stopped, but didn't turn around. She let out a breath before responding quietly. "Because jealousy makes some people downright ugly." Then Pam moved toward the waiting room to retrieve her next patient, leaving Lauren standing there wondering why the thought of people being ugly to Scott made her want to bitch slap them.

Lauren was sitting at her desk, head propped on her hand, staring at the clock on the computer screen. Ten more minutes and she could get out of there. Almost everyone had already left for the day. Only Lauren, Betty, Tammy, and Scott were left. The rest of Lauren's day had dragged after she'd finished the menial tasks Scott had assigned to her. She considered going and asking him what else she could do, but he was in with patients all afternoon and she hadn't wanted to bother him. Phyllis had told her that Scott would have a list of things she could do waiting for her each morning when she arrived. But Lauren couldn't bear another day like today, so she'd fired off an e-mail to Scott requesting a larger list. She bit back a smirk when she signed it: *Sincerely, Your Office Maid.*

He hadn't replied, which disappointed her. If she couldn't bicker with him in person, she had at least hoped she could get some kind of cyber banter going. But so far, no such luck.

Lauren opened her desk drawer and started gathering her things so she could slip out of there as soon as the clock struck six.

"Excuse me, but is Lauren here?"

Lauren knew that voice. *Cass.* She jumped out of her chair, grabbed her purse, and practically sprinted toward the front desk.

"What are you doing here?" Lauren felt excitement bubble under her skin as her eyes took in the sight of Cassidy, Simone, and Quinn.

"We thought we'd take you out to dinner after your first official day," Simone responded.

Lauren wasn't falling for it. She knew damn well that her girls wanted to know all about her first full day with Dr. Scott. Lauren hadn't told them about the smoldering hot kiss in his office on Friday. It wasn't like Lauren to hold out on them, but she hadn't felt right talking about it. She wasn't exactly sure why. But she held it back all the same.

"Awesome. I'm starving," Lauren said. "Oh, and Tammy, these are my friends: Cassidy, Simone, and Quinn. Girls, this is Tammy."

They exchanged pleasantries, and then Tammy excused herself by saying that she had some things to take care of in the office before she could leave for the day, though Lauren knew she was trying to give her some space to talk freely with her friends.

Cass spoke up. "So, you ready to go?"

Lauren looked at the clock on the wall. "I still have five minutes until my shift ends. Wouldn't want my liege to get bent out of shape about me leaving early."

"Your liege, huh?"

As soon as Lauren heard his voice, she closed her eyes and took a deep breath. Of course he was standing right behind her. Where else would he be? She watched her friends' eyes widen as they took in the deliciousness that was Dr. Scott. She huffed out a small laugh as she smoothed down her skirt and turned to face him. "Yup. My feudal superior was *quite* specific in our text message correspondence. I am to stay under his rule until six, lest I be taken to the stockade for failure to comply." Lauren was rambling again, but she couldn't stop herself. She wasn't caught off guard by *what* he'd heard as much as the fact that he *kept* overhearing her talk about him. He probably thought she discussed little else. The only way she knew how to deflect her discomfort over the whole "liege" thing was to act cool and unaffected, and yet she was doing the exact opposite.

As she finished speaking, her eyes locked with Scott's, and in an instant she watched his normally bright green eyes morph into a stormy forest color. And it did things to her that made her glad she'd worn underwear.

"Well, I'm sure he wouldn't mind you heading out"— Scott looked down at his watch—"three minutes early. My office maid can finish up any work she didn't get to when she comes in tomorrow."

She saw a glint of humor spark in his face. *He really*

thinks he's something else. "Are you done for the day?" Lauren asked Dr. Scott as she rounded the reception desk and moved toward her friends, looking back at him once she reached them.

Scott appeared taken aback by her question. "Yeah, I just have some notes I need to write. Then I'm done."

"Can that wait until tomorrow?" Lauren asked.

His eyes narrowed at her as he seemed to try to figure out where her line of questioning was heading. "I suppose."

"Then hang up your white coat and let's go."

Scott stared at Lauren for a minute. He looked at her friends, who looked riveted by the interaction in front of them, and then back to Lauren. "Why would I go out with you and your friends?" he asked, his voice revealing his confusion.

"Dr. Scott, if you really think they're here to see me, you're not nearly as intelligent as I thought. Hurry up. We'll wait for you."

Scott stood there for another few seconds. Lauren could tell he was trying to figure out the best way to play this situation. If he declined, he'd show that he was too good to hang out with her beyond work, effectively putting her in her place. But she knew he wanted to accept her invitation. Otherwise he wouldn't have hesitated. He probably wanted to give her a little taste of the real Scott Jacobs: man on the prowl. And part of her also believed that Scott wanted to know Lauren beyond the office walls, see what made her tick. She knew she was right when he plastered a broad smile on his face and replied, "Just let me get my things and tell Tammy I'm heading out for the day. I'll meet you ladies in the hallway."

*   *   *

Lauren wasn't sure what the hell prompted her to invite Scott. Well, that wasn't entirely true. She had wanted to wipe that smug look off of his face. Which she had. Until he accepted her invitation. Then his Prince Charming facade flew up like a shield as he prepared to win over the damsels in sexual distress. Her girlfriends were already practically drooling, and he hadn't even spoken directly to them yet.

"Lauren, I swear to God, if you don't jump on that like a trampoline, I'm going to have to rethink our friendship," Simone threatened.

Lauren quickly ushered her friends out of the office. She figured that Scott had said he'd meet them in the hall because he didn't want Tammy to know that he was leaving with them. And she was more than willing to comply. She didn't want to become the subject of office rumors. Nor did she want that to happen to Scott. "Whatever," she replied with an eye roll, hoping it came across as nonchalant, though she felt anything but. Lauren knew damn well that she wanted on Scott, like yesterday. But part of her—a large part—had liked it when he had initiated their contact in his office. She figured she'd leave it to him to do all the jumping.

Scott came into the hallway wearing his black slacks and a light blue button-down. He loosened his tie, and Lauren's eyes were drawn to the way the fabric of his shirt clung to his strong, defined biceps.

"Ladies, shall we?" Scott asked as he extended a hand toward the door.

Lauren's friends were reduced to giggling schoolgirls as they exited the office. Lauren couldn't help but smile as she shook her head at them. She craned her neck to look back at Scott. "So *now* I'm a lady, huh?" referring to his jibe from that morning.

"If we're using a very broad definition, then yes. Especially if we're pairing it with other words like bag and cat."

"Your wit is astounding," Lauren replied dryly.

Scott leaned closer to her as the office door shut behind them. "It's not the only thing about me that's astounding."

She felt his breath hit her ear as he spoke, and the feeling caused all of the synapses in her brain to fire rapidly, sending messages of pleasure throughout her entire body.

Which gave her an idea.

Lauren quickly walked a few more steps before stopping dead in her tracks, causing Scott to barrel into her back. He reached his hands around her abdomen to catch her, squeezing her tightly to his muscled chest. Lauren couldn't resist. She pressed her ass into him slightly, letting him know that not only could two play that game, but she was as willing to play as he was. She felt his body tense and his breathing hitch. *Mission accomplished.* Then she quickly began walking again, breaking free of his arms and trying to catch up with her friends.

She arrived at the elevator just behind them. Her friends jabbered away as Lauren leaned against the wall next to the elevator door, trying her damnedest to act casual. Scott made his way toward her, his mouth in a taut line, his eyes unwavering from hers.

He stopped beside her, leaning in slightly, but not enough to draw attention. "You do that again, and I'll have you bent over in front of me. And I don't care whether your friends are watching or not."

Lauren tried to return his glare with cool impassivity, but there was no chance at success. She was practically panting as he maintained his proximity. The elevator dinged, signaling its arrival. Her friends walked on, oblivious to the sexually charged exchange that was happening not three feet from them. Once they had boarded, Lauren leaned into Scott, pushing her small, perky breasts into him. "Don't make promises you can't keep, Doctor." Then she slid past him and stepped on the awaiting elevator, feeling incredibly pleased with herself.

Only a block away from the hospital, The Curveball was a loud sports bar that had been recently renovated in an attempt to deter the seedier crowd it had previously attracted, and instead lure doctors and nurses looking to unwind after a long day at the hospital. Though Lauren didn't recognize anyone there, it was clear by the few nods Scott directed at various people that he did.

They were shown to a rectangular table against the far wall that had a giant baseball diamond painted on it. Scott hung back and allowed the girls to sit first. Lauren tried to covertly control the seating arrangement so that she was on the opposite side of the table from Scott. She had an overwhelming need to watch him interact with her friends, to observe every facial tic, smile, tremor, and eye movement.

Simone took the open seat on the end, so Lauren quickly threw herself into the chair beside the one Cass was claiming, forcing Quinn to move to the other side next to the only other open seat. Scott lowered himself into the chair and smiled at the four pairs of eyes that were trained on him. Lauren watched as he leaned back slightly so that he could slide his hand into his pocket. She hadn't noticed him do this since she called him out on it. Evidently, though Dr. Scott oozed confidence, there was still a hint of discomfort beneath it.

"This place has great burgers. I always get the mushroom and Swiss," he said as he began leafing through a menu.

"Then why do you need a menu?" Lauren hadn't even realized she was speaking until she heard the words.

"I like to know my options," Scott said with a sexy smirk that made all the blood in Lauren's body flow south.

Lauren tried to bite back a smile. *Well played, Doctor. Well played.*

"So, has our little Lauren been a stellar employee so far?" Cass wasted no time steering the conversation in the direction that suited her interests. Namely, Scott and Lauren fucking like rabbits in his office.

Lauren wondered if Cass would have been so forward if she knew all that had transpired with Scott last Friday.

Scott huffed out a laugh, his eyes trained on Lauren. "She's had her moments."

Quinn dropped her menu on the table and shifted in her seat to angle herself toward Scott. "Laur tells us you're really young. You must be some kind of medical prodigy to have your own practice while still in your twenties."

Lauren drew in a silent breath. She anticipated the comment before it even left his lips.

"Ah, so *Laur's* been talking about me, I see." Scott's emphasis on her nickname made it plain that he was on a mission: to infiltrate Lauren's core group of girlfriends and use their idle chitchat against her.

"Only under duress," Lauren replied as she took a sip of the water the busboy had just come over and filled.

"So Laur, huh? That's the best nickname you girls have for her?"

Simone snorted. "The only one we'd tell you." Her voice was sweet, but the message was clear: there'd be no further breaking of girl code at this table. Even if it meant they had to gag Quinn with a napkin.

"Aw, come on, ladies. We're all friends here." Scott let loose with a full, panty-dropping smile, but to no avail. Lauren's girls weren't dishing. "I'll just have to come up with my own then. Let's see," he tapped his chin with his index finger. "How about 'Lo'? Don't people use that as a nickname for Lauren?"

Lauren tried not to visibly react, but she couldn't resist her hands flying to the table to grab her napkin and pulling it into her lap, almost as if it were a Kevlar vest that would protect her from the memories that nickname conjured. Her friends all looked at her, sympathetic expressions marring their faces.

"Uh, Lauren doesn't really like that nickname," Simone softly informed Scott.

Lauren lifted her eyes to look at Scott. She saw the furrow of his brows, the concern etched on his face, the playboy facade gone, and she suddenly was overwhelmed with the desire for him to call her that again. It felt . . . right. That nickname had been special to her for most of her life. And she wanted it to feel that way again.

"I'm sorry," Scott said. "I won't call you that if—"

"No," Lauren interrupted. "It's okay. You can call me Lo."

A moment passed between them as they gazed at

each other. An understanding that they both had pasts they'd rather not share. And they'd just . . . let it be.

"Okay then. Lo it is," Scott confirmed with a strong nod of his head before looking back down at his menu.

The atmosphere at the table had shifted, and Lauren needed to get it back to a more jovial place. She just wasn't sure how the hell to go about it.

Thankfully, Lauren could always count on Cass to swoop in and rescue a conversation. "So, Scott—you don't mind if we call you Scott, right? We don't need to address you as Dr. So-and-So?"

Scott smirked and shook his head.

"Good. So, Scott, there's a very important question that we absolutely *must* get an answer to."

Lauren felt a twinge of nerves as she anticipated where Cass could be taking her line of questioning, but she also couldn't help but grin slyly. Whatever Cass was going to ask, Lauren would bet her last dollar that it'd fluster him.

"What's that?" Scott responded with an easy smile as he crossed his arms and set them on the table.

Lauren noticed his hands close into fists and then purposefully release, tension still there even though he no longer hid them in his pockets.

Cass leaned in. "Are you single?"

Lauren snorted as she tried to resist laughing, but the rest of the girls sat there intently, their eyes boring into Scott as they awaited his answer.

Scott was unaffected by the question. He seemed used to women asking him that. "Yup. Why? You interested?"

Lauren knew Scott could probably flirt in his sleep. If

her friends thought they were going to intimidate him simply because they outnumbered him, then they had another thing coming.

"Baby, you couldn't handle me," Cass said dismissively.

Lauren knew Cass' words were bullshit; she suspected that between the five of them at the table that Scott would be the one who'd be the hardest to handle.

"But," Cass continued, "I will admit you're a good looking guy. Successful. How do you manage to stay unattached? Oh my God! I'm sorry. I didn't mean to ... You're gay, aren't you?"

"Cass," Quinn hissed as a reprimand.

"I'm really wondering," Cass replied simply.

Scott quirked an eyebrow, clearly entertained by Cass. "Are all gay people single?"

Cass pondered that for a moment. "No, but my question stands."

Scott laughed and leaned back in his chair. "No, I'm not gay. And I'm single because I prefer to be. Does that answer your question?"

"So you're a player then?" Simone added.

Scott shook his head in delighted disbelief. "You ladies are a real trip. I see why all of you are friends. Whole group of ballbusters."

Lauren grinned widely. It was the second time she'd been called that in less than two weeks. And she considered it a compliment each time.

"To answer your question, I'm very upfront about what I want. I don't lead women on, and my goal isn't to get every woman I meet into bed. However, when I'm seeing a woman, I'm monogamous with her until we decide that it's time for us to move on. Also, it's clear from

the beginning that eventually—sooner rather than later—
we *will* move on. I'm not looking for a girlfriend or a wife.
I'm looking to satisfy a need that we both have as often
and as completely as possible. And I don't try to hide any
of these facts. So, no, I don't think I'm a player." Scott was
answering Simone's question, but his eyes drifted to Lauren during his explanation. He was putting it out there for
her. If she was in, so was he.

As the waiter took their dinner plates away, Scott briefly
surveyed the women at the table with him. He'd actually
learned a good deal about them over dinner. Where they
had gone to college, their majors, and their current employment status. Quinn was a writer at a local magazine,
Simone was working in an art gallery in downtown Falls
Church, and Cassidy was trying to work her way up the
ladder in a major Virginia PR firm. He had to admit he
liked Lauren's friends. Not simply because they were hilarious and interesting, but because they were obviously
great friends to Lauren. Why that was so important to
him, he'd rather not ponder. But the fact remained that
no matter how he tried to wheedle information out of
them about Lo, they were a tight bunch who had one
another's backs. Scott knew the value of that. He may
not have had a ton of friends, but the ones he did have
were loyal to a fucking fault. *Speaking of that . . .* "We've
got to get you ladies together with my buddies some-
time. They'd be all over you. Though I have a feeling that
all of us together may get a little rowdy. All kinds of
chaos would ensue."

"Lauren's great at causing chaos, aren't you, Laur?"
Cass shot Lauren an overly sweet smile.

"I curse the day you were born," Lauren muttered as she took a sip of her beer.

"Is she now? I find that hard to believe." Scott's eyes were twinkling at the prospect of getting some juicy gossip about Lauren.

Lauren set her drink down and her lips quirked into a small smile. "You don't get arrested for encouraging peace and quiet."

Scott's eyes widened. He'd been wondering about her legal troubles since she first mentioned them to him, and he was desperate to know the details. "You know, I've been thinking about this. I believe that, as your employer, I have a right to know exactly what caused you to turn to a life of crime. Spill it."

Lauren was opening her mouth to respond when Quinn interrupted. "Wait. I have a great idea. Let's all go around the table and say a few words about all the stuff Lauren did to get herself arrested, and then let Scott try to put it together."

Lauren infused as much excitement into her voice as possible. "That sounds like," then let it all fade away, "a horrible idea."

"No, no, I like where her head's at on this one," Simone added. "I'll start. Fire alarm:"

"I object. That's already inaccurate. I didn't pull a fire alarm," Lauren protested.

"But you were the reason it was pulled, were you not?" Simone countered.

Lauren let out a huff and waved her hand, signaling the girls to continue.

Scott was riveted. He knew from Lauren's drooped

shoulders that she really didn't want to get into all of this. Which made him want to know every detail about it.

"Broken car window," Cass chimed in.

"Inciting a riot," Quinn quipped.

Scott's head bounced from girl to girl like a ping-pong ball as they added words like fights, trashed bar, kicking ass and taking names, screaming, trampled patrons, sassing law enforcement, propulsion of a missile, drunk in public, and banned from a bar.

"Okay, Scott, now put it all together. What do you think happened?" Quinn asked.

Scott brought his elbows to rest on the table and propped his chin on his steepled hands as he appraised Lauren. She had been smiling slightly throughout the game, but he could tell that she'd rather not rehash the details of the night. But as she sat there waiting for him to share his version of what may have happened, she lifted her eyes to his and held his gaze. And as he watched her, he suddenly realized why she kept him so off balance. She was simply . . . *different*.

Lo's friends were all similar to her, but they *weren't* her. Not by a long shot. None of them saw Scott like she did.

Lo saw right through all the bullshit. She had been watching him engage with her friends all night, dissecting his behavior. And the only times she fully participated in conversation with him had been the few times he'd dropped the act and been real. She saw beyond the bright lights and fanfare that Scott wrapped around himself like a defense system, and right into the haze beneath. It scared the fuck out of him. But it also turned him on.

He suddenly realized that he'd prefer to get to know Lauren and her story on his own terms, without her girlfriends' interferences.

"I think I get the picture," Scott said, never breaking eye contact with Lauren.

Lauren tilted her head, showing just how surprised she was that he wasn't going to push this issue any further.

Scott accepted that look as his first victory. He'd finally surprised Lauren Hastings. And he had a feeling that there was a lot more where that came from. When the waiter dropped the bill off at the table, Scott reached for it and pulled out his wallet. Knowing Lauren would remember using the same words, he looked at her and said, "It's only fair. This one's on me."

The five of them left The Curveball and walked back toward the hospital. When they reached the main entrance, they all said their good-byes as the girls walked toward Quinn's car, which they had parked in the visitor lot, while Scott and Lauren entered the employee lot.

"You really don't need to walk me to my car. I'll be fine," Lauren griped.

"Shut up," Scott responded playfully. Had he bet money that she'd have some kind of sarcastic reply, he would have lost.

"That's me," Lauren said, pointing to a green Cabrio.

Scott had been walking with his hands in his pockets, but as Lauren unlocked her car and pulled the door open, he quickly propped his hands on the roof, caging her in.

She stood stock-still. She didn't turn around to face him. It was as if she was waiting to see what he'd do next before she moved.

"I meant what I said, Lo."

"About what?" Her voice was low, husky.

"I don't do relationships. At least not in the traditional sense. I'm not going to lie: I want you. So if you decide to walk down this road with me, you need to know that there's no happily ever after at the end of it. No love or prolonged commitments. It'll be raw and consuming, but eventually it'll be over. Can you handle that?"

Lauren started to turn around but Scott pressed himself against her, putting a stop to her movement. "Don't answer me right now. Think about it. I need you to be sure. The last thing I want is to hurt you, Lo." He pressed a soft kiss to the nape of her neck that was somehow both innocent and filthy. "I'll see you tomorrow." And with that, he pushed off the car and left, hoping like hell her answer would be yes.

Chapter 6

Impulse Control Disorder

On Tuesday morning Scott opted for an extra shot of espresso in his coffee. He knew he'd need it because he'd been kept awake much of the night because he couldn't stop contemplating what he may be getting himself into. Never had a woman caused so much turmoil in his life. Shocking, considering he'd only known Lauren for a few days and hadn't even slept with her yet.

Yet. As he made his way up to his office, Scott repeated the word in his mind over and over. And he hoped that his silent mantra would be correct. He'd left Lauren the previous night with a clear proposition. He wasn't normally so concerned about getting a woman to be with him. If it wasn't them, it'd be someone else. *But what the fuck is it about this girl?*

With Lauren, it was different. In fact, *everything* with her was different. That's what caused him to break his own rule about not getting involved with anyone from work. Rules and routines made him feel in control. But just like every other day since he met Lauren, he was feeling a complete and utter *lack* of control.

Still, he took comfort in the fact that he was still doing things on *his* terms. I'm *the one breaking the rules. My own rules.* Plus, he justified his decision by telling himself that even if things between them got awkward after the sex ended, that awkwardness would only be temporary. After all, Lauren would only be in the office two days per week, and her time there had a definitive end date.

When Scott arrived in the office, he found his newest patient in the waiting room. Scott greeted him with an outstretched hand. "There he is. Sayid, good to see you out of the gym."

Sayid rose to shake his hand. "Thanks for fitting me in, Dr. Scott. I know it was short notice."

"Anything for the guy who taught me how to kick anyone's ass," Scott replied with a smile. "Just give me a few minutes and I'll be right with you."

"Take your time, Doc. I don't have any classes until this afternoon."

Tammy looked up from her desk. "I was wondering how you knew him," she said to Sayid as Scott flipped through Sayid's records from his previous doctor.

Sayid tilted his head slightly, clearly not understanding Tammy's remark.

"Dr. Scott's highly requested. He only accepts new patients who know him somehow. The maître d' at his favorite restaurant, the guy who fixes those midget cars he races, his Krav Maga instructor," she said, gesturing to Sayid with a smile.

"Ahh, I had no idea. When I told him my back's been

bothering me for a few weeks, Scott just told me to come in first thing Tuesday morning."

Tammy shook her head and laughed. "Yup, sounds like Dr. Scott. He usually keeps Tuesday mornings open for new patients or anyone he tells to just 'pop in,'" she said, using air quotes. "I think you're actually his only patient this morning."

"As it should be," Scott chimed in. "This guy's spent hundreds of hours helping me perfect my counterattack. One appointment's the least I could do. Come on back, Sayid. Pam will be in to take your vitals, and I'll be back in a moment." Scott pointed Sayid in the direction of Exam Room Three before turning his attention back to Tammy. "Lauren should be here at nine, Tammy. When she gets here, can you please let her know that I've e-mailed her a list of tasks for today."

"Absolutely," Tammy replied.

Lauren strolled leisurely into work despite the fact that she probably should have felt slightly anxious about how her interaction with Scott might go. She had to admit, she was intrigued.

From the moment Scott had made his offer, Lauren knew what her answer would be. She wasn't someone who slept around, but she never shied away from sexual encounters she wanted. Lauren believed in partaking in every experience that allowed her to live more fully, more honestly, and more happily. Maybe it was because Cooper hadn't gotten to do any of those things that pushed her to confront life that way. Whatever the reason, diving into things that scared her was liberating, and Lauren loved the feeling.

"Hey, Tammy," Lauren said with a smile as she made her way behind the reception desk and toward her own.

Tammy turned to address Lauren. "Morning." She took a sip of her coffee and winced when it burned her mouth. "Oh, before I forget, Dr. Scott e-mailed your to-do list to you."

"Thanks." Lauren smirked as she wondered if he'd put his own name on the to-do list. She took a few minutes to put her lunch away, pour herself a cup of coffee, and start up her computer. Once it was loaded, she clicked into her work e-mail that had been set up for her yesterday.

Dear Office Maid,

I'm assuming by your title that you don't mind cleaning the bathroom a little. It can get messy in there due to some of the patients' incontinence, but I'm sure you'll figure it out. Don't forget to wear gloves.

Dr. Scott

P.S. Just kidding about cleaning the bathroom, but I do need you to do a little organizing in the filing room. Most of our patient files have been transferred to our computer system, but we still need to keep the hard copies. It's kind of a mess in there, and I hate messes. I'd like you to go through the stacks of files that are sitting out, cross-check them with our electronic database, and then file the ones that are already digitized in the cabinets according to last name. If they

haven't been entered into our system, please let
Carla know. Have a good day.

Lauren clicked out of her e-mail, unsure of what to
think. Scott clearly had a sense of humor. That she already knew. But the second part of his e-mail had been
direct and professional. And he'd closed it out with
"Have a good day." *Will I not see him today? He's always
in this office Tuesdays.* She didn't know why she even
bothered to dissect his final sentence. She wasn't one for
overanalyzing things. But with Scott, she found she had
a certain curiosity about his underlying motives.

She sat back for a moment, her hands crossed calmly
in front of her before opening her e-mail back up and
typing a quick response.

Got it, boss. Just wanted to check to make sure
it's ok if I listen to music in the file room while I
work. I know some employers are strict about
that sort of thing.

See you when I see you,
Lo

She had considered not even signing her name at all.
After all, Scott would know who'd sent the e-mail. But
for some strange reason, it felt almost as good to *write*
that nickname as it had to hear it when Scott had said it
the previous night.

Lauren trudged into the file room and spent the next
fifteen minutes flipping through the folders that were
placed in stacks and scattered around the small room.

Scott wasn't kidding. The place was a disaster. A small wooden table had been pushed up against the wall across from the door. It was overcrowded with paperwork and a computer that looked like it could have been made in Steve Jobs' garage. Six four-drawer filing cabinets of various colors were placed haphazardly around the cramped room.

Before beginning Scott's task, she decided that it would be better to at least push the filing cabinets neatly against the wall so she had a space in the middle of the room to work. Then, she retrieved her laptop from her desk—since she was certain the computer on the table wouldn't even turn on—and began separating the files. At 10:13 she heard her Outlook ding: an e-mail from Jacobs, Scott.

Lo,

Music is fine, though I appreciate that you asked my permission. I may be a hard-ass, but not about things like that. Hope you are making a dent in those files.

Scott

P.S. I like it when you call me boss.

Once Scott had finished seeing his morning patient, he had time to catch up on paperwork. And time to think about Lauren being one room over. Alone. As he pushed to his feet, he decided that the patient notes he had sprawled across his desk could wait until later. He heard the muffled words of Sam Smith's "Stay With Me" playing as he approached the file room and his eyes immediately landed on Lauren as she sat on the floor looking over files.

"So I take it you got my e-mail?" Scott asked with a raised eyebrow.

He leaned against the doorframe, hoping he conveyed the powerfulness he was going for. Lauren registered his presence. And as her eyes raked their way up his body before finally meeting his, he was sure he'd been successful.

"Or did you have this playing the whole time?" he continued. Scott took a few steps toward the table, picked Lauren's phone up, typed in the passcode, and turned down the music.

"How did you—"

"Know your passcode?"

Lauren nodded her head in response without standing up.

Scott wore a sneaky grin. "Twelve-twenty. Figured your birthday would be a good guess."

Lauren's eyes narrowed. "I see you've been going through my file again."

Scott moved toward her and extended a hand to help her up off the ground. "Not *again*. Just remembered it from the first time. I'm not one to forget details."

The feel of Lauren's smooth skin on his made his pulse race as he helped her to her feet. But instead of letting go when she stood, he lowered their clasped hands between them, his warm palm still holding hers. Finally, he let her hand drop, but not before it was obvious that the prolonged contact had been intentional. "So how's your morning been?" he asked, hoping she'd feel the heat from his intense gaze.

"Pretty uneventful," Lauren replied, a slight hesitation in her voice.

Scott swept his tongue across his bottom lip and tilted his head to the side slightly. "Hmm . . . I'm not a fan of *uneventful*." He was daring her to make the first move, and he wondered if she could feel the obvious flush to her cheeks.

"Neither am I," she said before pushing the door closed softly and pressing the lock behind her—silently answering the question that Scott hadn't wanted to actually verbalize. She wanted him, and he'd be damned if he wasn't going to act on her desire. The moment the door latched behind her, Scott pressed Lo up against it with his hips—one hand roughly massaging the back of her neck as it tangled in her hair, the other resting firmly against the door just above her head.

As Lauren let her eyes linger on his, he saw her breathing hitch. She already knew him so much better than most of the women he'd been with—waiting for him to kiss her, knowing that *he* was going to take control. But he was excited to show her all the things she didn't know too.

Scott struggled to restrain himself. He wanted to throw her legs around his waist and fuck her against the door. *That'll have to be another time*, he thought. *A time when I don't have to hold back.*

"Are you gonna kiss me again?" Lauren whispered.

As soon as the question left Lauren's mouth, it was as if Scott had caught it with his own. He'd needed his lips on hers. Needed to feel her want him back this time.

When he'd kissed her before, it had been so sudden, so unexpected. For both of them. But this time was different.

This time Lauren was his to devour, and the way she surrendered herself to him as he slid his tongue forcefully inside her mouth made him want to lick more intimate parts of her.

Lauren tugged on Scott's white coat, her mouth parting just enough to allow Scott to suck hungrily. His teeth clamped over her bottom lip, just hard enough to make her wince slightly. But she didn't try to pull away. Instead, she let her head tilt back, giving Scott access to her neck.

But he withdrew for a moment, his tone brusque with need. "I wasn't done with your mouth yet," he said, his forehead pressing against hers. "And if *that* tastes this fucking good, I can't wait to find out what your pussy tastes like. I bet you'll be like vanilla ice cream—sweet and creamy when you melt against my tongue." Scott didn't wait for Lauren to respond before he captured her mouth in his again to continue his erotic assault.

She let out a soft moan and the vibration caused Scott's cock to grow from stiff to rock hard instantly.

The hand that had been grasping the back of Lauren's neck skated down her throat to her chest. In seconds, Scott had some of the buttons of her white satin blouse undone and was slipping his hand beneath the fabric to pull on the taut nipples above the lace of her bra. She arched her back to give him better access, her right breast fitting perfectly in the palm of his hand as he roughly massaged it.

But again, Scott pulled back, knowing he'd leave Lauren breathless and wanting at the absence of his lips on hers. "Don't stop," she pleaded.

God, did he want to comply. It took everything he had not to pull those tight black pants of hers down and bury himself inside her. "I need to let you know," he began, "what I want to do to you. I can't do that here . . . now."

"Why?"

It was a simple question. But one that was difficult to answer. So Scott chose his words carefully. "Because when I finally get to have you, I want *all* of you. I want my fingers and tongue tracing every inch of your body inside and out until you beg me to fuck you. And when I do, I want to know how loud I can make you scream."

Lauren hesitated a moment before responding. "How about I get that now? And I'll save the screaming for later," she replied with a playful smile.

She moved to kiss him again, but he put two fingers over her mouth to stop her. "There's one thing I need you to understand. *You* don't call the shots here. *I* do. If we're going to do this, that's how it'll be. Are you good with that?"

Lauren nodded her silent affirmation, and Scott slowly removed his hand from over her mouth. "Good. Now get on the fucking table and spread your legs."

It took Lauren a few moments to compose herself enough to force her legs to move. Since the moment Scott's lips had touched hers the first time, she'd fantasized about him taking things further. And until now, the image had only been that—a fantasy. But the reality was even hotter than what she'd envisioned. And it made the slickness between her thighs increase steadily with his every word and touch.

Though her legs felt like freshly cooked noodles—hot and limp—she somehow willed them to walk backward toward the table. Scott's eyes never left hers as they followed her gradual movements. Then she leaned back against the table's edge and shimmied up onto it, expecting Scott to come toward her. When he didn't, she knew why. He was waiting for her to follow his orders. But knowing that Scott would probably appreciate a little teasing, she kept her knees locked together as she brazenly rubbed her hands up and down her thighs.

Scott stood where he'd been, arms crossed, waiting patiently for her to comply with his request. Lauren's nipples hardened further when she saw one side of his lips twitch a bit. Teasing Dr. Scott was going to be more fun than she'd expected.

She let her gaze drift below his waist to see the tip of his hard length straining against his gray slacks. Involuntarily, her tongue swept across her bottom lip with the urge to take him inside her mouth.

But before she had time to do anything else, Scott was on her, his strong hands gripping her thighs, roughly jerking her legs apart and yanking her quickly toward the edge of the table and settling himself intimately against her. She was surprised at how much she liked being handled so roughly.

"So we're going to tease each other, are we?" Scott rasped, his eyes speaking just as clearly as his words. "I'm pretty sure that's a game you'll lose."

Lauren inhaled a sharp breath as Scott's hands slid up her thighs to grab under her ass. Then he pulled her up his legs, his pants straining until his cock pressed perfectly against her aching clit, causing another rush of moisture to work its way onto her thong. "I think you're right," she replied, her voice low with need.

Scott's deep growl was his only reply as he shifted her up and down slowly against his shaft, his fingertips digging harder into her ass with every caress.

With Scott lifting her hips off the table, Lauren was at his mercy. And as she lay back and let Scott rock into her, taking each thrust he gave, she decided there was nowhere she'd rather be. She knew better than to say she wanted him inside her. And she was enjoying the feel of his dick stroking her toward orgasm way too much to ask him for anything else anyway.

Scott choked back a groan as he spoke. "Are you loud when you come?"

Lauren was caught off guard by his question. She had never been asked something so directly personal. "Sometimes," she answered honestly.

"Sometimes means yes. You won't be this time. Remember that."

"Okay." It came out a breathy moan, which made Scott increase the speed and pressure against her clit. It had only been a few minutes and Scott wasn't even inside her, but she was dangerously close to the edge.

And she had a feeling Scott was too. His breathing had quickened, and she could see a hint of sweat on his hairline. He leaned back slightly as his pace grew faster. "Take your shirt and bra off."

The way Dr. Scott told her exactly what to do, exactly what he wanted, made her that much closer to climaxing. Lauren's fingers fumbled with the buttons on her shirt that Scott hadn't already undone until she was able to let it fall off her shoulders, followed quickly by her bra so Scott could see her breasts.

Scott's forest green stare felt hot on her skin as he looked her up and down. "God, Lo. They're fucking perfect," he said as he rolled his hips in delicious circles. Lauren locked her legs tighter around him, writhing in pleasure beneath him. "I'm gonna make you come while I watch you play with your nipples."

That wasn't something she normally did. But she was willing to do things for this man—for herself—that she hadn't done before. This experience with Scott would be about exploration and self-discovery. She needed to step out of her comfort zone.

So with only slight hesitation, she softly let her fingers travel across her breasts until they reached the hard peaks of her nipples.

Scott watched her touch herself tentatively for a minute before speaking. "Don't be so gentle," he said brusquely. "*I* wasn't." He slowed his movements gradually, making Lauren want to buck against him. "Seeing you do that to yourself . . . God, it does things to me. All I can think about is how soft your tits will feel when I get to rub my cock between them."

"Oh *God*, Scott." Lauren's fingers squeezed her nipples, pulling them more roughly than she was used to. "Please . . . keep going."

"If I keep going much longer, I'll come in my pants." His eyes narrowed slightly at Lauren before he spoke. "But I think that's what you want, isn't it? To feel me fucking lose it while I grind against you and make you do the same? Tell me, Lo, is that what you want?"

Lauren was practically panting with need, her orgasm only seconds away if Scott would pick up his speed. "Yes. Yes, that's what I want. Please, Scott."

At Lauren's desperate pleading, Scott thrust harder, grunting softly as his hips moved in smooth circles. The steady motion had Lauren struggling to suppress a moan as waves of pleasure coursed through her at the feel of Scott's hard length. She didn't know an orgasm could feel that good without anything inside her. A few seconds later, Scott followed with a groan and she felt his cock twitch against her sensitive clit, only prolonging her own climax.

When the aftershocks of their orgasms subsided, Scott placed Lauren down on the table and fixed his clothing without saying a word.

"So that was . . . different," Lauren finally said, needing to break the silence.

"Different good?" Suddenly the powerful Scott had vanished, and in his place stood a man who seemed concerned, maybe even a little vulnerable.

"Different . . . unbelievable. And you barely even touched me."

Relief seemed to wash over Scott's face at her confession. "I couldn't do everything I wanted to." He stood rigid, his gaze holding hers when he spoke. "I have a feeling that when I touch you, really touch you, I won't be able to stop," he said simply, before leaving the room and shutting the door softly behind him.

Chapter 7

Migraine

Scott experienced the next twenty-four hours as if he was in a fog. Lauren had gotten to him. Again. All he'd done was dry-hump her on a table, but the bliss that had ensued was consuming. His desire for her made him feel vulnerable and self-conscious. And he fucking hated it.

He also hated how he was completely unable to stay away from her. No matter how much he told himself that a little distance would go a long way, he only made it until lunch the next day before he was tracking her down like a lovesick bloodhound.

"Ah, so you're not purposefully ignoring me?" Lauren playfully scolded when he sat down across from her in the hospital cafeteria.

"Did you say something?" Scott asked with a smirk as he bit into his turkey club.

"Ha, ha, very funny. Busy morning?" Lauren tried to sound nonchalant, but Scott could hear the uncertainty in her voice. After their romp in the file room, he'd gone almost totally MIA. He couldn't blame her for wondering what the hell his problem was.

"Pretty typical, I guess." Scott knew that his answer wouldn't put her mind at ease, but he didn't want to lie to her. He hoped that she'd accept that response and they could move the conversation along to topics that didn't make him want to grip the silver dollar in his pocket for dear life. "Did you finish in the file room?"

Scott had never wanted to take words back so badly in his life. *So much for changing the subject, asshole.*

Lo cocked her head, clearly trying to bite back a smile. She set her yogurt down and rested her head on her hand. "Why yes, Doctor, I did." Her eyes danced with delight. All Scott could do was stare back at her, a slight grin twitching at his lips.

"Okay, smart-ass, calm down. I know I walked right into that one."

"You really did." Lauren burst out in the laughter that she couldn't hold back any longer. Thankfully, once she calmed down, she answered his real question. "Yeah, I finished yesterday afternoon actually. So today I've been doing the scintillating job of talking to pharmaceutical reps and requesting samples. Thanks to you, I may never talk on the phone ever again."

"Somehow I doubt that."

Lauren quirked an eyebrow as she resumed eating.

Scott watched her for a moment. One thing was becoming overwhelmingly clear to him: he wanted to *know* Lo. Not just sexually, but personally. Wanted to know what made her tick, what her aspirations were, what made her who she was. All of it. And though he chalked it up to basic human curiosity, he knew that wasn't quite it. He didn't want to think about what it *was* though. "So why are you still in college when all your friends have graduated?" The question spouted from him like water from a fire hydrant.

She stared at him curiously for a second before scraping her spoon against the inside of the yogurt container. "Guess I'm just dumber than them," she retorted playfully.

Scott set his sandwich down again and looked at her intently. "No, really." Despite how haphazardly the question had left his mouth, he did want the answer.

"Well, I'm in grad school, not college."

"Wait. Why didn't you tell me that when we met and I asked how old you were?"

"I hate to ruin a chance at a good first impression," she retorted with a quirk of her eyebrow.

Scott laughed but still looked at her expectantly. "But seriously, you're almost twenty-seven. I'd think you'd be working in your field by now."

Lauren took a deep breath and crossed her legs, as if she were preparing herself for a story she wasn't too thrilled with sharing. But Scott knew she would. "After I graduated high school, I went to Dartmouth for two years. I got into a little . . ." she hesitated, seemingly searching for the right word, "drama up there. So I took some time off to get myself back in order. Eventually, I enrolled in George Mason. But since I switched majors, I lost some credits, and it put me a few years behind."

Scott was intrigued. He could tell by the way her face scrunched up that there was a story there. And he was determined to know it, even if he had to chain her to his desk and torture it out of her. "You? Drama? I don't believe it."

"I know. It's so unlike me," Lauren joked before staring at him silently for few seconds. "You're dying to know what happened, aren't you?"

Scott let out a laugh. "I am."

"It's really not that interesting of a story." Lauren thought for a moment. "I take that back. It's pretty fascinating." She laughed, and Scott was momentarily distracted by how much he liked the sound.

"Now you *have* to tell it," he prompted.

"Fine. I kind of had a stalker. Well, not really a stalker. Kind of like an overzealous admirer." She paused for a moment before continuing. "Whom I was also sleeping with."

"You were sleeping with your stalker?" Scott's eyes widened in shock, and he felt his mouth gape open. He wasn't sure what he thought Lauren's story would involve, but it wasn't that.

"I said he *wasn't* a stalker," Lauren defended.

"Can you please tell me the difference between a stalker and an overzealous admirer?"

Lo thought for a few seconds, tilting her head back and forth. "No," she finally answered before laughing again. "He didn't start out as a stalker. He just got . . . really attached."

Scott could see how such a thing could happen. *Am I really sympathizing with a stalker?* "How did he start out?"

Lauren clearly tried, and failed, to fight a grin as she lifted her water bottle to her lips. "As an Intro to Philosophy professor," she said over the rim before taking a sip.

Scott nearly choked on his drink. "You're shitting me!"

Lauren slowly shook her head.

Scott slouched back in his chair. "That's so cliché."

Laughter burst from Lauren. "I know, right?"

"What, do you have a thing for authority figures?"

She shrugged her shoulders as she let her eyes roam overtly over Scott's body. "Maybe," she joked. "But in my defense, he wasn't *my* teacher, and I didn't even know he worked at my school when he took me home from the bar." She hesitated a moment, seeming apprehensive, which was in contrast to the Lauren he was getting to know.

"Man, where were you when *I* was in college?" Scott joked, hoping to bring back the lightness of their conversation.

"Probably riding the bench on my seventh grade basketball team, Doogie."

Scott glared at her, causing Lauren to burst out laughing. "So you were, like, into him?" he asked when she finally calmed down.

"He was a nice guy," she said simply. "I was going through some stuff and he was a welcome distraction. I thought we were on the same page, but we clearly weren't."

"On the same page about what?" Scott was fascinated.

"I was looking for casual, something completely devoid of messy feelings. I was dealing with enough of that already. I just wanted . . . an escape, a chance to forget the shitstorm that was my life at that time." Lauren hesitated for a moment. "I had . . . my brother had just passed away. I needed something to get my mind off of all that I had just lost." Lauren sighed heavily before seemingly shaking herself free of her thoughts. "Anyway, I thought he was on board with what I was after."

Scott vaguely remembered when Lauren's brother had died. His father had been really upset by it. Scott wanted to ask her more about it, but it wasn't really his place. However, he did find himself empathizing with Lauren. He knew what it was like to want a break from his emotions—to check out from real life and just let sex be sex. He was relieved that she could relate. "But he fell for you?"

"I don't think it was love or anything. I mean, he thought it was. But it wasn't."

"He didn't . . . hurt you, did he?" Scott didn't want to ask this question, but he had to know. Though he was pretty sure he'd be going to prison for a very long time if she answered in the affirmative. Scott had no tolerance for men who felt it was okay to put their hands on women.

"No, he just tried to get involved in every aspect of my life. Started talking to my professors, trying to get them to give me grades I wasn't earning, cornering my friends and asking how I was. Just weird shit that made my life there really difficult. In the end, it was easier to just leave and start fresh back here."

"Has he tried to contact you since you left?"

Lauren shook her head. "My dad threatened to expose him to the university. I think he threatened a little more than that, but I never asked and he never told. Now *that* was an awkward conversation, telling your parents that you were being hounded by one of the professors, who you willingly engaged in sexual relations with. I swear, nothing fazes my poor mom and dad anymore. I've completely numbed their ability to be shocked about anything." Lauren laughed again, her eyes crinkling in amusement. Then she looked down at the table, her face morphing into ill-concealed sadness.

Whatever prompted her to get further involved with someone even after she found out he was a teacher had been rooted in something dark, painful. He could see that much. However, there was one bit of information Scott did need to know more about. "So," he motioned between the two of them, "our situation isn't all that new for you?"

Lauren smiled again. "Well, I hope it's a little different. I'd really prefer to not have to have my dad threaten to break your legs."

Scott shook his head. "I don't mean in that way. Just," he lowered his voice so that only she could hear him, "the no-attachments aspect."

Lauren tilted her head in what looked like mock sympathy. "Is this your way of making sure that I'm not going to fall hopelessly in love with you, Dr. Scott?"

Scott didn't know how to respond, so he didn't.

Lauren still smiled, but her eyes lost the crinkle at their edges. "Relax. We're on the same page. We both want the same things from this. I'm not going to fall in love with you. I promise."

Her words did relax him. For reasons he couldn't explain, he trusted Lo. He knew that she was as good as her word. That would have to be enough.

To Lauren's disappointment, Dr. Scott didn't make any more office advances, but he stopped actively avoiding her there after she subtly called him out on it. In fact, on Thursday Lauren noticed a shift. Scott started to initiate more physical contact. Small touches, ones that she was sure no one even noticed, and if they did, they wouldn't think anything of them. It was a touch to her elbow as he squeezed past her, a hand on the small of her back as he let her walk through a doorway first. But he was ever the professional, never engaging in personal conversations in the office. Their daily lunch meetings were another story.

They never left the office together, but always met up in the cafeteria, with Scott arriving a few minutes behind Lauren. They'd begun sitting at the same table: one in the corner of the room that allowed them relative privacy. Lauren was surprised by their easy conversation. For a man who, at times, seemed hell-bent on not forming any lasting ties to her, he often said things that implied the direct opposite. Whether it was asking her about her friends, her family, or her plans after college, it all gave the appearance of something very close to friendship. And despite herself, Lauren found that she very much wanted to be friends with Scott.

It was with all of this in mind that Lauren sourly began her Friday. Scott would be spending the entire day at the satellite office, while the other doctors in the practice would be at the hospital. She had missed out on meeting them last week, due to her stint in Pediatrics. And while she was interested to see what the other doctors, Florence Atler and James Prescott, were like, she already kind of hated them. Phyllis and her mom had implied all Lauren needed to know: they didn't like Scott. This made them automatic assholes in Lauren's book, and she didn't care how immature that made her.

Scott had sent her an e-mail the previous night, letting her know what she could spend the day doing. So she quickly immersed herself in what Scott had affectionately begun calling her "Housekeeping List." She had just begun typing Scott's schedule for the following week into his Outlook when she heard a throat clear behind her.

"Well, well, who do we have here?"

Lauren spun around to see an older gentleman, perhaps in his late fifties, appraising her with patronizing eyes. "Oh, hello. I'm Lauren." Lauren stood and stretched her hand toward the doctor, who lifted his hand as though he were too good to even be conversing with her, let alone touch her.

"So you're Pam's daughter? The one Scott decided to hire on without consulting the rest of us?"

Lauren's face contorted in annoyance before she had time to stop it. Not that she would have. This guy was a Grade A prick, and Lauren didn't care if he knew exactly what she thought of him. Especially since *he* didn't bother concealing what he thought of *her*. "One and the same," Lauren replied in a cheery voice that didn't match the look she was giving him.

"Hmm." Dr. Prescott stared at Lauren for a minute, obviously either trying to intimidate her, make her uncomfortable, or both. "Guess we'd better give you some *real* work to do then. You can start by vacuuming and dusting the waiting room."

Lauren stood up a little straighter and returned the glare. It was in this moment, staring into the blank eyes of Dr. Prescott, that Lauren figured out a little more of the Dr. Scott puzzle. Scott pretended to be like this asshat when Lauren first met him—like he was cool, calm, and detached. But there was a light in his eyes that was unmistakable. She'd bet anything that Scott was a better doctor than the man who currently stood before her. He was obviously a better person, for that matter. It's what drew Lauren to him even when she shouldn't have been. Lauren found that she missed Scott more than she should.

"James, you going to see some patients today or stand there staring at the new piece of eye candy?"

Lauren's eyes darted to the source of the voice that had interrupted her staring contest with Prescott the Pretentious. *This woman's one to talk*, Lauren thought as she took in the thin, athletic-looking woman with short blond hair. She looked about the same age as Prescott, though without the weary countenance.

The woman was already in her white coat, looking over a patient's file, ready to begin her day.

Without so much as a hello, Dr. Atler only nodded her head at Lauren before addressing Prescott. "You have a patient waiting in Two." Then she stalked back the way she came. Prescott followed close behind.

Lauren allowed her body to drop into her chair. She hadn't been that tense in a long time. If that encounter was any indication of what the rest of the day would be like, Lauren was going to need a stiff drink later. Or maybe twelve. She already had plans to go to an exhibit at the gallery where Simone worked, so at least there would be some free wine waiting for her at the end of the day.

Lauren settled into her work, pushing all thoughts of Prescott and Atler from her mind. About an hour later, her desk phone rang. She answered it quickly, not taking her eyes off of the computer in front of her. "Hello, Jacobs' Family Practice, this is Lauren. How can I help you?"

There wasn't a response from the calling party, though Lauren thought she heard the rustling of papers.

"Hello?" Lauren asked. "Can I help you?"

Lauren heard a throat clearing before it actually spoke. "Sorry, Lo. It's Scott."

"Scott? Christ, you sound out of it. Are you okay?"

"It's great to hear from you too," Scott replied dryly. "Listen, I have an awful migraine. I need you to tell Atler that she needs to come over here and cover my appointments. The majority of them have seen her at one time or another, so she's the better choice. I thought I'd be able to make it through the day, but I can barely open my eyes. I would just cancel everyone, but I have a few patients who absolutely need to be seen today. Just tell Tammy to reschedule who she can from Atler's patient list today, and reassign the rest to Prescott. He normally runs light in that office anyway.

"Sure, no problem, I'll tell them right now. Are you going to be okay?"

"Yeah, I just need to sleep it off. I'll be fine."

Lauren had a twofold reason for the next words out of her mouth: one was that she had no desire to be left in the office alone with Prescott all day. The other was slightly more confusing, but no less pressing to her. She knew that Scott lived alone, and the thought of him being on his own when he wasn't feeling well gave her an odd pang in her chest. "What's your address? I'll come bring you lunch."

"What?" Scott sounded truly confused. "No, that's okay. I don't need you to bring me lunch. I'm not even hungry."

"Aren't you a doctor?" Lauren asked accusingly.

"Obviously."

"Then you should know that it's important to eat when you're sick."

"And where did you get this expert medical advice, the back of a Campbell's Soup label? It's a headache, not the flu. I don't need anyone to take care of me. I've done just fine on my own for the past ten-plus years."

The thought of Scott being on his own with no one to take care of him for the extent of his adult life didn't sit right with Lauren. Not that she'd have told him that. "Listen, if you think I'm going to let you trap me in this office with Prescott all day, then you've got another thing coming. Now what is your address?"

"He was a dick, wasn't he?" Scott sounded angry and apologetic at the same time. How he managed it with a voice that sounded exhausted, Lauren didn't know. But it warmed her to her toes.

"No, he *is* a dick. And if you force me to stay in this office with him, then there's a good chance I'll be back in jail by lunch. Address, Scott."

Scott sighed before rattling off his address to her. "And Lo," he said just as she'd been about to hang up. "I like Lipton's Chicken Noodle Soup." And with that, the line clicked dead.

Lauren wasn't sure what she was more perturbed by: the fact that Scott had basically dismissed her after placing his soup order or the fact that she'd still stopped and gotten it for him. She walked into his apartment building, her eyes immediately landing on the security officer dressed in a burgundy suit jacket with the apartment complex name embroidered on the breast. *Of course the bossy bastard lives in a guarded fortress.*

"Can I help you?" the large older man asked cordially.

Yeah, you can talk some sense into me. "Yes, I'm here to see Scott Jacobs. My name is Lauren Hastings."

"Ah yes, Miss Hastings. He told me to send you right up. Just take that elevator to the seventh floor. Take the hallway to the right and his apartment is the very last one."

Lauren's eyes followed where the man was pointing and then she nodded at him before setting off for the elevator. As she boarded, she couldn't shake the feeling that she was willingly walking into the dragon's lair. But before she could get too anxious at the prospect of ending up burned by him, she remembered that more often than not, the dragon was the one who got slayed. And my oh my, how she wanted to slay Dr. Scott.

She followed the security guard's instructions and found herself in front of Scott's door. She knocked softly, not wanting to make his headache worse. She was about to observe Scott in his natural habitat. The thought gave her a sudden urge to adopt an Australian accent and invite a camera crew to document the experience. She waited for a bit, and when he didn't answer she knocked again, louder this time. Again, there was no response. She stepped closer to the door to listen for sounds from inside. Nothing. She knocked on the door again and this time spoke loudly. "Scott, if you're making me wait out here as some kind of weird show-her-who's-boss thing, you're really missing the mark."

Finally the door swung open, and she was greeted by

a weary Dr. Scott as he walked away from her. "It was open," he said gruffly.

"Oh, sorry. I'll add mind reader to my list of skills to brush up on." Scott plopped down on his couch and covered himself in a thick blanket. Lauren looked him over as she walked into his apartment. "You look like hell."

Scott glared at her. Or at least she thought it was a glare. It lacked the ferocity she was sure he intended.

She continued toward him and sat in a chair next to the couch. "Did you take anything?"

"Are you really playing doctor with me right now?"

"Not if you're going to be such a shitty patient," she replied calmly. "I brought you your soup. Do you want any?"

"No," Scott said as he closed his eyes and curved his body into the fetal position.

"Aren't you supposed to keep your strength up?" she asked, unable to keep the slightly patronizing tone from her voice.

Scott's eyes flew open. "Aren't you supposed to be at the office working?"

"Nope. My boss lured me to his apartment so I could take care of him."

"I somehow find that very hard to believe." Scott winced suddenly, reflecting how much pain he was actually in. Once he seemed able to speak again, he continued. "I don't need anyone to take care of me. I'm fine."

"Clearly." She took a moment to take in his apartment. It was . . . expensive looking. The wall behind the couch was made up almost entirely of windows and offered a great view of Fort Taylor Park, a historic site in Falls Church. The brick wall behind where Lauren sat led all the way to the exposed beam ceiling that betrayed this building's original use as a factory of some sort. His dark-stained wood floors complemented his gray furniture and black accessories. It was very masculine-chic. When Lauren looked back to Scott, his eyes were shut again and his breathing had evened out. "Guess I'm great company," Lauren muttered to herself as she set off for the kitchen. The apartment was an open-concept, the living room separated from the kitchen only by a breakfast bar with stools. She dropped the grocery bag that contained the soup, a couple lemon-lime Gatorades, and a liter of ginger ale on the granite countertop and began looking for a pot to boil water.

Ten minutes later, she was carrying a bowl of soup and a glass filled with ice and Gatorade into the living room. She set them on the coffee table and sat down on the edge of the couch beside him. Pushing his sweat-slicked hair back, she brushed her hand against his forehead again.

"It's a crime to molest the unconscious." Scott's voice was weary.

"Well, since you've obviously developed a brain tumor overnight, I doubt I have to worry about you ratting me out." Lauren let out a gentle sigh. "I made you soup. And brought you some Gatorade. Which do you want first?"

"Neither," he muttered before dimming the lamp beside him.

"That wasn't one of the choices."

"I make my own choices."

"Not today, you don't," Lauren informed him. "Gatorade it is. Sit up."

Scott gripped the blanket tighter.

"Scott, stop being a baby. If you drink it like a good boy, I'll give you a lollipop." Lauren's voice was playful, but her eyes were trained on him, letting him know that he wasn't going to win, so he may as well give in.

"Ugh, fine." Scott propped himself up on his forearm and took the glass from her. The exasperation in his voice didn't faze Lauren in the least. He eyed her over the glass as he took a sip. "Don't you have somewhere to be? Like anywhere other than here?"

"No, Doogie, I don't. Now shut up and have some soup while you're up."

Scott swallowed a few spoonfuls before declaring that he was done and falling back onto the couch. He was asleep before Lauren could nag him to drink more. She watched him curl into himself again, a frown marring his beautiful face. Pulling the blanket up to his neck, she walked over to where she'd dropped her purse and fished out her phone. Looking briefly back at Scott, she typed a quick text to the girls, telling them that something came up and that she'd have to bail on the art exhibit that night. Thankfully, no one pressed her for details.

Then Lauren sat back in the chair she'd occupied earlier and settled in for a long night of watching Scott sleep.

Scott awoke and looked at his watch. *Shit, it's almost midnight.* He didn't remember much of the past twelve or so hours, probably because he slept through most of it. He vaguely remembered Lauren showing up and forcing Gatorade down his throat, but that was about the extent of it. He assumed she'd gone home hours ago, but a quick glance around the room proved otherwise. There she was, curled up on his oversized club chair, sleeping soundly.

He couldn't resist staring at her for a minute, taking in how beautiful she was: her soft brown hair flowing over her shoulders, the steady rise and fall of her chest, the peaceful, almost angelic, look on her face. She'd taken care of him. Stayed with him on a Friday night so he wouldn't be alone. *Who does that?* Though that answer was simple: the baffling, stubborn, intelligent, gorgeous girl sleeping in front of him. Before he could get carried away thinking about just how much he liked having her in his space, he sat up, rubbing his hands soothingly over his face. The movement made Lauren stir.

"Hey," she murmured. "You okay?"

"Yeah, I'm feeling a little better." Scott rested his arms on his knees and raised his head to look at her. And as his eyes locked with her brilliant blue ones, he felt his breath catch slightly. "You stayed," he said so softly he wasn't even sure she heard him.

"You were really out of it. I didn't want to leave you like that. Hope you don't mind."

"I never mind when you're around, Lo. Thank you." Scott wasn't sure where the admission came from, but he was glad he'd uttered it, if for no other reason than it was the truth. But now that he'd put it out there, he was growing increasingly uncomfortable. "You're the one who should mind. You probably had plans." He started to get up.

"Nothing important. Do you need something? I can get it."

"Nah, I'm just going to go to the bathroom and get some more medicine. Go back to sleep."

Lauren nodded and closed her eyes again, settling back into the chair.

Once Scott was done in the bathroom, he wandered

back down the hallway. When he came to his bedroom, he thought about how it probably made more sense for him to sleep in there. He'd be able to stretch out on his bed *and* put some distance between him and Lauren. But as he walked into his room and grabbed the afghan from the foot of his bed, he realized that he didn't want to be a room away from her. He carefully walked back into the living room, covered her with the afghan, and before he could talk himself out of it, placed a soft kiss to her forehead. "Sleep well, Lauren."

As the morning sun streamed in through the windows and shone on Lauren's pale skin, Scott decided she was simply too tempting. That's the only excuse he could think of as he began leaving a hot trail of kisses down her exposed neck. He'd woken up an hour ago, feeling almost completely back to normal. He'd puttered around for a bit, brewed some coffee, taken a shower, and watched Lauren sleep. But now it was almost eight a.m., and he'd had enough watching.

Lauren grumbled, causing him to laugh softly as he kept up his assault. Pressing soft kisses to her smooth neck, then graduating to nipping and sucking when she refused to respond.

"Are you serious right now?" she finally groused. "Aren't you supposed to be sick?"

"All better. And I have a debt to repay."

"You can pay it later," she groaned, still not opening her eyes as she tried to pull the blanket up higher.

"No can do. I am not one to put off until later what I can do right now." He slipped a hand under the blanket and rubbed along her ribs.

It didn't take long for Lauren to begin moving into his touch. And as a gentle moan left her mouth, he knew he had her. Her hands came up and pushed into his hair, the movement causing the blanket to fall into her lap. "Did you cover me last night?" she breathed.

"Yeah. Figured it was the least I could do. At least right at that moment. I can do a lot more now." Scott sucked on her collarbone that was blessedly exposed, thanks to her tank top. "Is this what you wore to the office yesterday?"

"I had another shirt over it. But yeah. Why?"

"I was just thinking that I may need to change our dress code policy. This shirt gives me perfect access to your breasts," he said as he nuzzled lower.

Lauren released a giggle that quickly morphed into a moan as Scott's hand rubbed along the waistband of her pants.

"These pants on the other hand," he said as he kissed along her jaw, "are really starting to piss me off. They've gotta go."

Lauren hummed her assent, but Scott quickly realized that the chair wasn't the best place for what he intended. In a quick but fluid motion, he stood, lifting her with him easily.

Lauren squealed with the unexpected shift in position, but instinctively wrapped her legs around Scott's waist, her arms draped around his neck, hands still in his hair as he continued to kiss her on every inch of skin his mouth could reach.

He walked her to his bedroom as she sucked languidly on his ear. He wanted nothing more in that moment than to slam into her, burying his cock so deep that it was unclear where he ended and she began. But he wouldn't. She'd selflessly taken care of him the previous day, and he'd be damned if he couldn't do the same.

He dropped her onto his bed, causing a quick laugh to burst from her. Taking a moment to look at her for a second, he watched as she bit her bottom lip, reclined back on her arms, and stared up at him like she wanted to devour him. *Jesus Christ, has a sexier woman ever walked this planet?* He leaned over her, supporting himself with one hand on the bed as his other deftly popped the button on her pants and dragged the zipper down. He rubbed his hands around to her ass and lifted her a little so he could slide her pants and thong down her legs. Once he had them off, he tossed them to the floor behind him and sunk down to his knees. His bed was the perfect height for having her this way, and he silently congratulated himself on the fact, even though it had never crossed his mind until that point. He lifted her leg and placed her foot on his shoulder, pressing kisses to the tender flesh of her shin. Then he let his lips roam up her leg, getting closer to their destination with every lick, suck, and peck.

"Scott, what are you doing?" Lauren was breathless.

He darted his eyes to catch a quick glimpse of her. She was looking down at him, entranced by what he was doing to her. "I told you. I'm repaying a debt."

"Fuck," she said on a sharp rush of air. It sounded appreciative, almost reverent, and it fueled him.

He lifted her other leg onto his other shoulder and pressed a wet kiss to the inside of one of her thighs before settling between them. Scott didn't go down on women often. But holy fuck did he want to taste Lauren.

He had a sinking suspicion that one taste would hook him and then he'd never get enough. But that didn't stop him from flicking his tongue over her clit and then shifting even closer so he could give it the attention it deserved.

"Scott," Lauren moaned.

Hearing her say his name made his cock harden even more than it already had. He was pretty sure he would burst out of his sweatpants if he got any more turned on. He continued to lavish her with his tongue, pushing a finger in to fuck her while his tongue worked her toward bliss.

Lauren began writhing, pushing ever so slightly against his face, clearly trying to deal with all of the pleasure he was unleashing on her body. The gasps and murmurs that left her mouth made him want to both hurry to push her over the edge and slow down so he could relish in what he was doing to her.

"I'm so close," she groaned, pushing a hand through his hair as he worked her.

Scott pushed another finger into her and felt for that place inside of her that would make her go . . .

"Fuck, Scott. Right there."

Two more licks of his tongue had her convulsing around his fingers, her entire body quaking as her orgasm hit her full force. He could feel how wet she was making his fingers, and it made him want to lower his mouth to her again and start all over. He pressed a kiss to her inner thigh before looking up at her. What he saw was earthshaking. Lauren lay there, sated and relaxed, her eyes shining brightly, the slightest smile on her lips. She was looking at him like he was the king of her universe. And even though it caused anxiety to spark low in his gut, he also reveled in it.

"Come here," she said softly.

He shifted and slowly slid up her body, using his hands to support his weight, but allowing their bodies to touch, connect. He rested his head in the crook of her neck and enjoyed the citrusy scent of her as she tightly wrapped her hands around him.

After a few minutes of comfortable silence, Lauren spoke. "Once you're back at full strength, I'm thinking I'll have to make a list of all the other things you owe me for."

Scott's body shook with a chuckle. He pulled back so he could look at her face. "And just what would be on this list?"

"I'm not sure. But to get you to do that again, I'm not above making shit up."

They looked at each other for a moment before both erupting in laughter.

"Just so you know, I'm pretty sure you owe me for a few things too," Scott joked.

Lauren's smile morphed, easing into something more seductive. "I know. And trust me, I fully intend to pay up."

"I'll hold you to that," Scott replied as he eased away from her. Almost every cell in his body begged him to collect right then, but he didn't. They were in a different place in that moment. What she'd done for him—caring for him like she had—it hadn't been part of their deal. And while it may have sounded silly, he would've felt like a prick for having sex with her right then.

*   *   *

Once Scott managed to force himself away from Lauren, he offered to let her use his shower. He expected her to pass, preferring to leave instead. But she didn't. And the fact that he wasn't annoyed surprised him.

"Sounds great," she replied before turning and heading toward his bathroom.

He followed her, got her an extra toothbrush, showed her where the towels were, and summoned every fiber of his being to allow himself to walk out of there without pushing her against a wall and taking her any way he wanted. "I'll grab you something to wear," he said softly as he pulled the door shut behind him.

Scott leaned back against the closed door for a second. He wasn't sure what the hell his problem was. Normally he couldn't get women out of his place fast enough. But with Lauren he was actually searching for ways to make her stay. *Isn't this some shit.* He reasoned that it was their friendship that made the difference. He liked hanging out with her, just like he enjoyed spending time with his other friends. It was no different. So what if she was sexy, and witty, and genuine. That in no way factored into his decision to cook her breakfast to try to delay her departure. Not at all.

Scott pushed off the door and returned to his room, rummaging through his drawers until he found an old pair of track pants that hadn't fit him since college and a tank top he'd worn for Halloween one year when he'd dressed up as a sorority girl. It was a little stretched out, but it would have to do. He knocked on the bathroom door.

"Come in," Lauren called. She was already in the shower, but poked her head out when Scott entered.

"Here are some clothes. They'll be big obviously, but they should be okay for you to just hang around in."

"Thanks."

And there it was again—that smile. Scott was more than a little worried about what that smile could get him to do. "I'll make us some breakfast. Anything you don't like?"

"I don't like you out there while I'm in here."

And he was hard again. "I don't care for it much either. But I'm not a hundred percent. And when I finally get to fuck you, I intend to be." That wasn't the complete truth, but Scott couldn't risk sounding like a jackass by telling her he was trying to be a gentleman. For once.

Lauren's eyes widened. "Gotcha."

"I'll be in the kitchen." Scott dropped the clothes on the counter and left the bathroom.

Lauren joined him about ten minutes later, looking way too cute in his oversized clothing. "Do I want to know why you own a shirt that says 'I only bang football players'?"

Scott barked out a laugh as he explained the shirt's original purpose.

"Well, that's reassuring. I really didn't want to be wearing the clothing of one of your late-night conquests," Lauren teased.

"I don't keep trophies," Scott quipped.

"Or girls."

Scott sobered slightly and looked at her intently. "Nope, don't keep them either."

Lauren leaned on the countertop next to where Scott was scrambling eggs. "I bet there's an after-school-special-worthy story behind the reasons for that."

She was probing, but Scott wasn't biting. "Thankfully for us, we're both too old to still be in school. Oh, wait . . ."

"You're a real comedian." Lauren must have clued in to the fact that Scott wasn't interested in continuing that conversation because she let it drop. "So you seem almost . . . *sprite* this morning. How is that possible? I thought you were a goner yesterday."

Scott went to the fridge and pulled out a carton of orange juice before turning to get two glasses out of a cabinet. "Because I know doctors that prescribe good shit. Here, make yourself useful," he added as he handed her the glasses and juice.

"Where are the plates?" Lauren asked after she'd finished filling their glasses and returning the carton to the refrigerator.

Scott nodded with his head toward a cabinet by the stove.

Lauren set the breakfast bar while Scott finished cooking. He set the pan down by their plates and slid onto a stool beside Lauren. They talked casually until both of them had finished eating.

"That was really good. Your list of talents just keeps growing," Lauren said with a smirk.

"Baby, you haven't even seen the half of them."

"So you keep saying. I'm starting to think you're all talk."

Scott simply quirked his eyebrows at her before rising to clean up. Lauren moved to help him, but he stopped her. "Go snoop around or something. I got this."

She briefly looked like she was going to argue, but ultimately decided against it and walked over to look out his wall of windows.

After he finished putting the dishes in the dishwasher, he joined her, walking up behind her, standing close behind her without touching.

She took a deep breath in. "This is a really amazing view."

Scott pushed his hands into his pockets. He looked down at the back of her. "Yeah. It is."

After a few more minutes of quiet window gazing, Lauren turned toward him. "What are you up to today?"

He shrugged. "Just hanging around, I guess. I should probably take it easy, make sure the migraine is gone for good."

"Sounds exciting." She walked around him and made her way toward his coffee table, letting her hand brush over the magazines he had there. "Want company?" She said it casually, as though she didn't really care about the answer.

But Scott knew it for what it was: she didn't want to leave any more than he wanted her to. "I wouldn't mind."

She looked up at him. "Okay." Then she flopped down onto the couch and reached for the TV remote.

Scott moved behind her and snatched the remote from her hand. "If you think I'm giving you control over the TV, you're nuts. I have no interest in watching the latest drama on *Teen Mom* or *Keeping Up with the Kardashians* or whatever other nonsense girls your age are into." He was intentionally baiting her. And as her eyes narrowed, he realized that this was the Lo he liked best. The playful, funny one who didn't put up with his taunting.

"When you say stuff like that, you just make yourself sound like a pedophile. And I stopped watching the Kardashians when Kim got with Kanye. That was just weird."

Scott snorted and sat beside her. And that's how they remained for the better part of the morning, arguing over what to watch and making flippant comments to each other. He couldn't remember the last time he'd enjoyed himself so much.

Around eleven, Lauren sighed heavily. "Okay, I can't take it anymore. Let's go out to the movies. Everything on TV sucks."

Out? Is she serious? "I don't want to go out," Scott stated. It sounded too datelike. Granted, Scott liked spending time with Lauren, but he didn't want to blur the lines of their relationship any more than they already were.

"Suit yourself," Lauren replied as she shifted and stood up.

"Where are you going?" he asked. He hadn't anticipated that she'd leave if he didn't want to go with her.

"I just told you. To the movies."

"By yourself?" Scott hated going places alone. It made him feel self-conscious.

"Yup," she remarked as she stepped into her shoes.

"Dressed like that?" he said with a chuckle.

Her eyes darted up to his. "Is there someone there I'm supposed to be impressing?" She grabbed her purse. "I'll bring the clothes back to you on Tuesday. Thanks again for breakfast."

"Thanks for . . . everything," Scott mumbled.

"Anytime." She gave him one of those sincere looks that let him know she truly meant it.

As she made her way to his front door and pulled it open, he heard himself speak before he had a chance to think his words through. "At least give me a second to get changed. We can't both look like we're homeless or they won't let us in." He couldn't miss Lauren's sly grin as he made his way into the bedroom and tried not to berate himself too much for falling right into her trap. He didn't stand a chance.

Chapter 8

Reflux

Scott spent most of Sunday relaxing around the house and recuperating from the remnants of his headache. Though what he really needed to recover from was how he'd been acting around Lo.

Never in his twenty-nine years had he turned down a sexual favor from a woman that he wanted to have sex with. But somehow, allowing Lauren to reciprocate seemed . . . wrong. And that feeling was foreign to Scott. It's not like he only cared about his own needs. But he just hadn't ever *not* cared about them before.

Until the past weekend, that is. And when he'd finally had time to dissect his recent actions fully, he noticed that he'd been acting out of character ever since he'd met Lo. Sometimes he'd find himself at a loss for words with her, and other times he'd divulge personal information that he rarely shared, even with those closest to him. And then Saturday . . . Saturday he'd nearly sprinted after her when she'd said she'd planned to go to the movies alone if he didn't want to go. Scott Jacobs didn't chase *women. They* chased *him.*

All of it was simply too much for him to ponder, so he did his best to refrain from thinking about it more than necessary. And when Sunday night rolled around, he realized that he'd be getting a bit of a reprieve from his Lauren-centered thoughts.

Unfortunately, that reprieve would have to be Susan Jacobs. His mother.

Though Scott didn't especially enjoy spending time with her, he couldn't bring himself to hate it either. Furthermore, after his father's death, he'd come to the realization that time with family should not be taken for granted. Scott was all his mother had, and even if he'd never be able to forgive her for all the mistakes she'd made, and all the hurt she'd caused, he still couldn't abandon her. So if a few hours of his time a couple of Sundays a month were required, well, that was a sacrifice he would have to accept.

Scott reminded himself of this fact as he sat in the quiet booth of the upscale Brazilian steakhouse, listening to his mother prattle on about her latest vacation.

"Scott, it was so beautiful," his mother said in between bites of her lamb. "You can't see the Irish country-side too many times. You just can't."

"Apparently not," Scott replied dryly. "This is, what, your third time there in the last year and a half?" He knew his question sounded accusatory, and he also knew that's how his mother would interpret it. But he couldn't bring himself to care. Ever since his father had died, his mother had toured virtually every inch of the globe. And she'd done so on his father's dime, carelessly spending the money he'd worked a lifetime to earn.

His mother took a sip of the water the busboy had just refilled before she responded. "Honey, you know I've always dreamed of seeing places like that. We've talked about this. I loved your dad. I *still* love him," she corrected herself. "But our entire marriage was based around your father's practice and you and Tim. It's time I focused on the things that I want."

Scott barely controlled the impulse to remind her of the damage her actions had caused. Thankfully she didn't give him time to interrupt her.

"You're a smart man, Scott. But I'm not sure you realize how difficult marriage is. Especially to a man consumed by his career. Love isn't always what it's cracked up to be." Susan lifted her deep brown eyes to look at her son and pushed back a stray strand of her auburn hair so that it fell to her shoulder with the rest. "I just wish you wouldn't make me feel so guilty for doing things that make me happy."

Scott wanted to ask her to clarify if she meant the trips or the affairs she had throughout her marriage, but he managed to refrain. At that point, Scott just wanted to get out of the dinner from hell and go home. So he did what he always did; he told her what she wanted to hear. "You know I appreciate everything you've done. And I know it hasn't always been easy with Dad getting sick and . . . with Tim. I do think you should try to talk to him though. He's doing better, you know. Making a lot of progress. He's not," he lowered his voice before continuing, "he's not the son you remember."

This time his mother was quick to respond. "You're

right, Scott. He's not. The son I remember cooked me a Mother's Day breakfast every year. He had good grades and plenty of girls falling at his feet. The son I remember started varsity lacrosse as a freshman. The son *I* remember would *not* have traded such a bright future for drugs. And the son I remember would have never stolen from his own family to pay for his disgusting habit."

Susan's voice was cold, but deep down Scott didn't doubt that she loved Tim. But that love had become gnarled throughout the years. It had twisted and transformed into something nearly unrecognizable, and definitely not acknowledged. She loved the son she once had. But that son was gone, at least in her eyes. Scott was once again reminded that if a mother's love could change, any love could.

"You can't possibly know what that was like for a parent to go through. And I don't expect you to. To watch your own flesh and blood destroy everything you gave to them, everything you helped them earn. It's a feeling of unbelievable failure." She set down her fork, clearly having lost her appetite. "You're all I have now. That's why I'm so hard on you. *You* are my pride and joy. Tim *had* that chance. He *made* his choice. It's up to you to carry on the Jacobs name like your dad would have wanted."

Scott sat in silence for a few moments, not willing to continue the conversation. He'd known how delusional she was since he was a teenager, and nothing he could say would change the way she saw things. When the waiter returned to ask if they'd like dessert, Scott declined with a polite, "Just the check, please, would be great."

"Are you seeing anyone?" his mother asked once the waiter was out of earshot.

Scott knew the reason for her question. It wasn't just a poor attempt to change the subject. It was a subtle probing into his personal life—a way to find out if Scott would be settling down anytime soon to give her the grandchildren she'd hoped for. Other than that not so minor detail, he'd been the ideal son. Smart, handsome, athletic, driven. A perfect substitute for Tim. Family man was all that was missing from his résumé.

"Mom," Scott replied, a smile playing on his lips in an effort to lighten the solemn mood that had settled over the table, "I think you know the answer to that."

Susan settled back into her chair and folded her hands neatly in front of her. "I think I do too," she said.

Over the course of the next ten minutes, Scott managed to pay the check and have the valet bring their cars around. Thankfully, they had driven separately, limiting the awkwardness as the night came to a close.

Well, that went well, Scott thought to himself as he watched his mother drive away without looking back. But despite his making his mother feel like a callous spend-thrift, Scott couldn't help but laugh that he'd managed to do one thing right. He hadn't thought of Lauren the entire time.

Well, *almost* the entire time.

Chapter 9

Gamophobia

"Be honest. How many of you signed up for this class thinking it would be some kind of sex manual?"

Lauren glanced around the lecture hall to see hands raising as students tentatively searched for others who'd thought the same thing before they'd admit to it. *Seriously?*

"Okay, okay, you can put your hands down," Dr. Peterson said with a corresponding gesture. "Now, how many of you wanted to raise your hands for that question but were too embarrassed?"

A handful of students put their hands up.

"Interesting," he added, running a hand through his salt-and-pepper hair, which was trimmed neatly at the sides and a bit longer on top. "What's even more interesting is that a few of you didn't raise your hands at all. And that could only be because of one of two options." He removed his glasses—which Lauren noticed were trendy for his age—and polished the lenses with his tie before speaking any further. She'd been in enough psychology classes to know what Dr. Peterson was doing. He was waiting to see if anyone would guess the two options. When no one did, he continued. "Option one is the most plausible. Simple psychology really. When I asked my first question, you were embarrassed to admit you signed up for this class hoping to learn about sex. Then, when I asked you a second time, it felt stupid to admit that you didn't raise your hand the first time because you were too embarrassed. After all, what's more embarrassing than admitting you're embarrassed?"

The class chuckled politely, Lauren included. There was something she instantly liked about Dr. Peterson. She wished she'd felt the same about the professor of her previous class. She just couldn't get into a guy who seemed less enthused about teaching Psychology Factors in Aging than she was to learn about it.

Dr. Peterson turned away from the class and walked toward the interactive board at the front of the room. "Option two is that you actually know that this class will be about more than just sex. But I would venture to guess that those of you who didn't raise your hands are in the embarrassed-to-be-embarrassed boat." He paused for a moment to flash a picture of the *Titanic* on the screen. "Well, that boat's sinking, so you'd better jump ship. We'll be discussing some personal and taboo topics in here. So there's no room for embarrassment."

Lauren couldn't stop the disappointment from flashing across her face. She didn't like that he was making assumptions about her and her fellow students. It went against the very discipline he was supposed to be educating her about. Not to mention that she'd spent the entire previous week prepping for this course. *Maybe Dr. Peterson isn't going to be my cup of tea after all.*

But before Lauren could dwell on her train of thought, the professor's voice interrupted her. "Young lady in the purple, third row back."

Lauren sat up straighter and gave a quick glance around the room. *Shit.*

"You didn't raise your hand, and you look a little . . . displeased. Tell me. Do you disagree with my hypothesis?" Dr. Peterson was questioning her, but nothing in his tone or posture was accusatory. He seemed genuinely interested.

Lauren took a moment to formulate a response. She had no desire to offend a man who would be responsible for her grade. Not that Peterson seemed like one for petty acts of vengeance. But she did have a strong feeling that she could learn a lot from this man. He seemed sharp. And she had no interest in getting off on the wrong foot with him. "Lauren Hastings," she started with a slight smile, wanting to identify herself. She cleared her throat before continuing. "And yes, I do disagree."

Her reply caused a steady murmur to roll through the crowd. Dr. Peterson continued to look at her with discerning eyes. "Go on," he prompted.

"I guess I just found your generalization about the non-handraisers a little off-base." *Is nonhandraisers even a word?* "You assumed that most of the people who didn't raise their hand didn't do so because they were embarrassed. That wasn't the case with me. I've already spent some time looking through the required readings for this course. I'm aware of what it's about. That's why I enrolled in it. I'm interested in how people interact intimately, even when sex *isn't* involved. In the psych classes that I've taken, I've learned that everyone has their own individual motives. And in this instance that was the case for myself." Lauren found that she was talking faster now in an effort to justify herself. But the more she talked, the more she wished she could make herself shut up. "Sometimes people fit the mold, and sometimes they don't. It just— The assumptions just rubbed me the wrong way, I guess. That's all."

Then Lauren heard her phone ding for the third time since lunch, only making the moment that much more awkward. She mentally scolded herself for not remembering to silence it. She'd been dodging her friends' questions about Dr. Scott since the weekend. *What's up with you and the hot doc? So, did you play doctor, or what? Has Dr. Scott examined you properly yet?* Lauren hadn't returned any of the texts because she hadn't wanted to disclose what had happened between her and Scott. Though she wasn't really sure why. She never withheld anything from them. Especially details as juicy as the ones she had currently had. She was sure that the sound she'd heard was another text from one of them begging for information.

Surprisingly, Dr. Peterson didn't say anything about the phone, and Lauren was momentarily thankful. "Thank you, Miss Hastings, for your thorough, if not long-winded, explanation." *So much for being thankful.*

Lauren wanted to crawl under her seat and hide. But then, he spoke again.

"Don't worry. I tend to be quite, shall we say *detailed*, when I'm passionate about something as well. Which you'll all soon find out," he said, directing his attention to the class again. "Now, if you're wondering if this course is about sex, the answer is no." There were some loud groans from the audience. "Is it about intimacy? No again. See, sex and intimacy are both mutually exclusive and one and the same. One can't exist without the other, right? Or can they?"

Dr. Peterson put up a picture of a naked couple on the verge of kissing, the man's hands placed lightly on the woman's arms. The background was faded to black, and the couple was positioned vertically in the photo, making it difficult to tell where they were. "What do you think? Is this sex? Is it intimacy? Or is it both?" he asked the class. Take a minute to discuss this with someone nearby."

Lauren turned to the girl beside her, who introduced herself as Miranda. She looked no older than twenty-two. "I think it's intimacy," Miranda said confidently. "Look at the way they're embracing. You can see how gentle he is with her."

"*Sex* can be gentle," Lauren countered. "It doesn't mean it's intimate."

"I agree sex is gentle," Miranda replied.

Lauren didn't bother to correct her and tell her that wasn't what she'd said. Sex wasn't always gentle, she knew that firsthand. Or at least she would when Dr. Scott stopped being an unbearable tease, and now, for the second time today, she found herself thinking about Scott.

"But you don't even know they're *having* sex," Miranda continued. "You can't see below their waists."

"How many guys have you hugged naked and not had sex with?" Lauren quipped.

Dr. Peterson's voice boomed through the room, interrupting the conversations before Miranda had a chance to respond. "Okay, okay, that's enough idle chitchat. I know you're all on the edge of your seats to know the answer." The room remained quiet, and Dr. Peterson continued. "All right, maybe not. But that's probably a good thing because I don't have one for you." A small rumbling overtook the room. Clearly, many of the students were eager to learn if they'd been right in their prediction, Lauren included. "You see, there is no clear answer for the couple in this photo just as there is often no clear answer in real life. The lines between sex and intimacy often become blurred. That's why this is a topic of such controversy. Sex is a physical action. Most people won't argue with that." Many of the students nodded their assent, and "Mm-hms" were heard throughout the room. "Just as most people won't argue that you can have intimacy without sex. Correct?" As Dr. Peterson probably expected, no one contradicted him. "So," he said dramatically, "where's the disagreement then?"

"Can there be sex without intimacy?" a high-pitched voice yelled from the back.

Dr. Peterson pointed to the person who had said it. "Precisely," he said. "Now I'm sure since most of you are in your midtwenties, you'll say, 'But Dr. Peterson, haven't you ever heard of a one-night stand?' Why yes, I have. I know it's hard to believe, but they had them back in *my* day too. We just used the floors of caves instead of beds."

Even Lauren couldn't suppress the laugh that escaped her.

"I actually don't mean to make light of it. It's a good point, the one-night stand argument. But critics would say that sex, in and of itself, is always an intimate act because you are opening up to someone in the most vulnerable way possible. The obvious exception being rape, of course. But for our purposes here, we are speaking only of consensual sex. So I leave the question for all of *you*," he said, lifting his arms out toward the class. "Can sex exist devoid of any intimacy? Think about it, and I'd like a two- to three-page paper with your thoughts next time we meet."

Lauren quickly typed the question on her laptop and then gathered her belongings before heading out the door. When she was finally out of the lecture hall, she reached into her bag to check the texts from Cass, or Quinn, or Simone. She knew it had to be one of them. They couldn't just drop things. But when she pushed the home button, she was surprised to not only see texts from the girls, but also one from Scott. She quickly typed in her code—which she reminded herself should probably be changed to keep certain doctors from accessing her personal information—and clicked into her texts to see his message in its entirety. Good luck on your first day. Although, I guess it's probably almost over by now. Hope you didn't feel too old around all the other students. Learn anything?

Lauren quickly typed her response. Thanks. You don't really learn much on the first day. And no, no one even noticed I was old as dirt. Well, no one except for you. Guess I'll see you at work tomorrow. Hope you're feeling 100% ;) She figured that, being as smart as he was, it wouldn't take long for Scott to pick up on the implication of that last sentence. Satisfied with herself, she quickly shoved her phone back into her bag and headed toward the parking lot.

*   *   *

Scott sat in the hazy lighting of his favorite neighborhood bar, Calhoun's, with his best friends, Alex and Xavier. They had been talking about the Redskins' deplorable preseason for the last half hour, and Scott was growing increasingly depressed as the conversation wore on.

"I'm telling you, the preseason means nothing. Just let them get their rhythm back and it'll be all good."

Alex, ever the optimist. Scott lifted a pint glass of Dos Equis to his lips and took a long sip. He had been participating in the conversation, but his head wasn't in it. No, his mind was permanently fixated on his text to Lauren earlier. *Did I really text her to see how her day was going? Fucking sap.* And then she'd replied with that sexually charged winky face and he had to do everything he could not to jerk off in his office. Everything was becoming muddled. Despite his desire to keep their relationship casual, every one of his actions made it something . . . more. But he didn't want *more*. *More* meant drama, and pain, and sacrifice. And Scott needed to experience those things again like he needed to drive nails into his arms.

"You're dreaming, Alex," Xavier responded. "Speaking of dreaming, what the hell is up with you? Trying to solve discrete geometry problems?" Xavier bumped his elbow against Scott's.

"No, I leave that math shit to nerds like you," Scott replied with a smirk.

"Yeah well, nerds of a feather flock together, my friend."

Scott laughed at their old motto. He had met Alex and Xavier in his freshman year at Brown, and they became immediate friends. It helped that they were all good looking kids with IQs bordering on the obscene. Scott had the same problem fitting in in college as he did at the hospital. But with Alex and Xavier, Scott didn't have to worry about any of that bullshit. It was why they'd stuck together all of these years, both Alex and Xavier taking jobs in Washington, D.C., after they'd finished their graduate work. Xavier worked as a financial analyst, doing something that required the highest level of government clearance, and Alex was a supervisory special agent assigned to the National Center for the Analysis of Violent Crime at Quantico.

"So what's going on?" Xavier questioned.

"Nothing. Just tired, I guess."

"You're such a shit talker, Jacobs. You're sitting there, being all contemplative, while I bash your beloved Redskins. Something is definitely up. Let me guess. Your pretty boy looks are starting to diminish with age and now you're only getting laid every *other* night."

Scott shot him a withering look, to which Xavier simply laughed.

"Okay, I guess that's not it. Any guesses, Alex?"

"You're having a hard time figuring out how to spend your trust fund? I already told you, supporting a charity called Get Chicks Naked is not the best way to build your practice."

"You guys are hilarious. Seriously. You should take your act on the road. You'd make tens of dollars."

Alex and Xavier laughed their reply.

Scott rested one forearm on the bar as he slid his other one into his pocket, fiddling with the silver dollar. Part of him wanted to tell his buddies what was going on with Lauren. How he often had trouble figuring out whether he was coming or going ever since he'd met her. But a bigger part didn't want to seem like a giant pussy, so he changed the subject instead. "Though you may not want to incur any extra income, Alex. It'll only make Tessa take you back to court." Maybe deflecting attention onto his best friend by referencing his messy child support battle wasn't the most thoughtful thing to do, but nothing else came to mind quickly enough.

"Christ, don't remind me," Alex muttered as he took a long drought of his beer. "I swear, she's made it her mission in life to drive me to the brink of insanity. And it's not like I even did anything to deserve it. She left *me*. For her fucking trainer at the gym. She fucked around on me, yet I'm the one getting screwed. Unbelievable." Alex shook his head in disgust before continuing. "And for her to use Nina against me is bullshit. She doesn't have to keep taking me to court so that I'll support my daughter. If she needed something, all Tessa would need to do was ask. I'd give that little girl my right arm if she needed it."

And Scott knew that was true. Alex was an excellent father. And he'd also been a great husband. His world had revolved around the two women in his life since the day each had come into it. And it was infuriating that Tessa was trying to make his life miserable. It reminded Scott why he didn't get involved with women beyond a certain point. It just wasn't worth the hassle. And *kids*? Scott couldn't even begin to imagine himself as a father. Even though he'd had a great role model, Scott liked his freedom. And as much as Alex tried to convince him of the opposite, Scott saw parenthood for exactly what it was: a fucking life sentence without the possibility of parole. *Fuck that*. But even though Scott was thankful for the reminder of why he needed to take an emotional step back from Lo, he still felt like an asshole for dredging all this shit up. "Sorry, man. I'm a dick for mentioning it."

Alex waved him off. "It's cool."

Scott observed Alex stare intently at the TV screen, though Scott was sure he wasn't actually watching it.

Xavier must've noticed as well because he quickly cut in. "So, Doc, it seems you have an admirer." He covertly gestured toward the end of the bar where a stunning brunette was eyeing Scott.

Scott gave her a quick once-over: her brown hair was styled well, with not a single strand out of place, and her makeup was flawless. Her light brown eyes glittered with seduction as she pushed her huge tits forward. *Leading with your best asset. Smart girl.* Scott couldn't deny that the woman was beautiful. She screamed designer clothes and thorough maintenance. But as he looked at her, he couldn't help wishing that her hair fell more naturally around her shoulders, that her makeup was used as an enhancer to her existing beauty rather than as a perfectly applied mask. He wanted her eyes to be more genuine, and still have the ability to see past his mound of bullshit. But what really shook him to his core, was how he wished she'd leave more to the imagination: leave him wanting to unwrap her like a present instead of giving him a sneak peek of the goods before he even got her home. *What the hell is wrong with me?*

Xavier and Alex looked at him, waiting for him to make his move. But instead, he said the only truth he could. "Eh, not for me."

Chapter 10

Hiccups

Somehow Lauren had managed to dodge her friends' probing questions about why she'd bailed on them the previous Friday. She'd texted back that she'd just been busy with school and her new job and would talk to them soon. She'd just neglected to mention the fact that part of what had kept her busy over the weekend was her sexy-as-sin boss. *Lying by omission doesn't really count as lying, does it?*

Unfortunately, on Tuesday, Scott had gone to the satellite office to tie up some loose ends since he'd missed Friday. He had sent Lo an e-mail to tell her that he'd be back by lunch, so she hoped that meant he'd be joining her in the cafeteria. She also hoped she'd finally experience the one thing she'd been waiting for since she agreed to have casual sex with Scott: that they would actually *have* casual sex.

Lauren spent the rest of the morning completing the mindless tasks Scott had instructed her to do as she thought about how awesome it would be to run her tongue over Scott's cock. It was that thought that had her nearly salivating when he finally showed up at noon.

"Hey. Anything going on I need to know about?"

Lauren turned her chair in his direction. "Nope. Just working through my Lauren-Do List."

She saw a sly grin overtake his lips. He moved closer to her. "Am I on that list?" His voice was low, ensuring that he wouldn't be overheard.

Lauren licked her lips. "You've been on that list for quite a while now."

Scott pursed his lips as if he were thinking about the best way to respond. Finally, he straightened and took a step back. "Going down to the cafeteria today?"

"Always do."

Then, with a quick nod of his head, Scott walked out of the office.

What a fucking clit tease.

Lauren continued working for the next hour and tried desperately not to think about Scott. It didn't work. By the time one o'clock arrived, Lauren was so horny she could barely keep herself from squirming in her seat for relief. She quickly gathered her lunch, told her mom and the other women that she'd see them in an hour, and left the office without Scott.

The last thing she wanted was for anyone in the office to find out about her relationship with Scott. Well, that wasn't completely accurate. She didn't exactly have a *relationship* with Scott. Really, the last thing Lauren wanted was for anyone in the office to know they were . . . doing whatever they were doing.

Lauren began her trek down to the cafeteria when she suddenly felt a firm hand on her biceps.

"Let's take the stairs," Scott growled as he pulled her toward the stairwell.

Lauren was so stunned and so ready for him to do what she'd been fantasizing about all morning that she didn't bother to respond. She allowed herself to be led through the heavy steel door. And once it closed behind them, she also allowed herself to be thrust up against it while Scott moved in on her, rubbing his erection into her abdomen.

"So about that list," Scott murmured as he began kissing her neck.

"What about it?" Lauren expelled a gust of air as she twined her fingers in Scott's hair, bringing his lips even deeper into her neck.

"I think we need to check a very important item off of it."

Lauren couldn't find words to reply. It didn't matter that they were in a stairwell where anyone could walk in on them. Actually that fact made it all the more appealing. She lifted her leg over his hip, causing her pink and purple cotton dress to slide up her leg.

Scott's hand was instantly there, roughly kneading the flesh that was so close to where she wanted to feel him most. She moaned wantonly as she let her hand drift down to his pants, unhook the button, and pull down the zipper.

Scott's kisses intensified. His lips pushed into her skin harder, with more fervor.

It was fucking awesome. Lauren dipped her hand into his boxers and fisted his long, thick cock. *Jesus Christ, am I going to enjoy being on the receiving end of this.* She began to work him, dragging her clenched hand over his steely length.

"That's it. That is so fucking it," Scott groaned as he slipped his hand under the material of her dress and pushed her panties to the side. His finger ran over her clit, causing her to dig her heel into the back of his thigh. "Mmm, someone liked that."

Lauren released a shaky breath. "Do it again."

Scott rested his cheek against hers. "Ask nicely," he whispered roughly into her ear.

She didn't care how it made her sound in that moment. Lauren was not above begging. "Please, Scott. Please do it again."

Scott nibbled her earlobe as his finger teased her clit again.

Lauren felt the juices flow to her core. She wasn't sure if she had ever been so turned on before. She continued to jerk him off, increasing her speed as he worked her into a frenzy.

"I need to be inside of you, Lo. Is that okay?"

Lauren couldn't believe he was even asking. She was letting him finger-fuck her in a hospital stairwell for Christ's sake. "Yes."

She felt him reach into his pocket with the hand that wasn't unraveling her, and withdraw a condom. "You want to put this on me?"

Lauren was just about to take the condom from him when she heard voices above them. *Dear God, why do you hate me?*

They both froze and stared at each other with wide eyes. When it became clear that the voices were descending toward them, Lauren and Scott quickly pulled away from each other and set about fixing their wayward clothing.

"Worst fucking timing," Scott grumbled as he buttoned his pants, grabbed Lauren's hand, and yanked her away from the door before swinging it open. "We'll definitely be finishing this later."

Once they were back in the hallway, Scott dropped her hand. "You didn't bring a lunch today?" he asked when they reached the elevator.

"No, my mom said she wasn't packing one for me anymore and I didn't feel like putting anything together."

"Well, if you need some added incentive, you could always pack me a lunch when you're making yours." Scott flashed her his megawatt smile that Lauren couldn't help but return.

"I'll think about it." Lauren and Scott boarded the thankfully empty elevator and began their descent. "So," Lauren said, "when exactly are we finishing what we started?"

Scott smiled again. "Desperate, are we? Don't worry. I tend to have that effect."

"Whatever, narcissist." Lauren rolled her eyes. "How about later tonight? I could come by after work."

Scott groaned. "I can't. I have a meeting for a benefit the hospital is having at the end of October."

"Oh yeah, my mom and I got an invitation to that. It's a children's charity, right? Some kind of gala?"

"Don't feel obligated," he said. "Just a bunch of pretentious ass-kissers flaunting their money and discussing politics. If I wasn't required to go, I wouldn't."

Scott's explanation confused her. The way his eyes darted away from hers made it seem like he intentionally fabricated reasons for her *not* to attend. It wasn't as if they would go *together. Why wouldn't he want me to go?*

But Lauren abruptly halted her overanalysis and decided that the most likely explanation was the one he'd given. *The thing is gonna blow.*

They made their way to the cafeteria and ate their lunches in between jibes and playful conversation. There was one thing Lauren definitely couldn't deny: she really enjoyed spending time with Dr. Scott.

The next day, Lauren was still replaying her encounter with Scott in her mind. Finally she couldn't take it anymore. She had to see him. As she sat at the food court of George Mason munching on a fresh pastry, she snapped a picture of her books spread across the table in front of her before sending Scott a text. Better food, but the company's not nearly as entertaining.

Lauren took a sip of her iced latte before placing her phone inside her bag, certain that Scott wouldn't text back until later. He'd just be returning from lunch, and she figured he probably had a busy afternoon since he'd been out of the office until noon on Tuesday. He'd most likely be catching up on paperwork and phone calls in between patients. So she was surprised when her phone sounded three minutes later. Entertaining, huh?

You seem surprised, she wrote back. Couldn't you tell I was entertained? Don't underestimate yourself, Dr. Scott. Lauren could feel the flirtatious grin spread across her face as she texted back. The three dots on her screen indicated that Scott was writing back. And she had no doubt Scott would reciprocate with his own innuendo.

And he didn't disappoint. I never underestimate myself. And for the record, I "entertained" you more than once.

Yes, you did, Doctor. And I fully intend to even the score. Lauren leaned back in her chair and inhaled a deep breath as she waited for Scott's reply. She could feel a rush of warmth make its way down her core and settle itself between her thighs at the thought of getting to touch Scott's cock, stroke it in her hand, and wrap her lips around it.

This time Scott wasn't so quick to reply, and the anticipation of waiting turned her on more. What happened to you? You still there? she wrote before clicking it to sleep and setting it down beside her.

Finally a message popped up on her lock screen, and she slid her finger across it and entered the code. Sorry. Just trying to figure out how I'm supposed to make it through the rest of my appointments with my cock pressed up against my pants like this.

Lauren knew Scott was playing her game. She doubted that he was actually hard from a few texts, but damn if the possibility didn't make her squirm in her seat a little. Only one remedy I know of to take care of such a condition, she wrote back.

And what's that? He obviously wanted her to tell him what she planned to do to him. But something inside her told her it would be more fun to make him wait. Not sure words would do it justice. How about we meet at your place after you get done with work?

Again Lauren stared at her phone, waiting for Scott's response. But what she saw made her wish she hadn't gotten so excited for it. I can't tonight. It was simple. Direct. Very . . . Scott. But she hadn't expected it. Something else she hadn't expected was the twinge of disappointment that shot through her at the subtle rejection.

OK, she wrote back, not knowing what else to say. Your loss. This time she didn't wait to see if he replied before throwing her phone in her bag, tossing the rest of her pastry and coffee in the trash, and heading to her last class of the day.

"So what's been going on since I saw you last?"

Scott shifted uncomfortably in the dark brown armchair that engulfed his large frame. He had never realized how emasculated he felt by that chair. It was as if the damn thing was swallowing him. *I know who else I'd like to swallow me.* And so went Scott's thought-hemorrhage. He knew exactly what he should talk to his therapist about, but opening up to her suddenly felt like a bad idea. *Did I actually turn down sex for an appointment with a shrink? Should it feel weird to open up to my therapist? God, I'm so fucked up.* "Nothing in particular," he finally replied. He felt himself actively avoid her stare as he lied and wondered if she noticed. When she remained silent, he chanced a glance at her. She was studying him curiously. *Damn it.*

"You sure about that?"

Scott thrust his hand into his pocket, a movement that didn't escape Dr. Specchio's attention. "Yes. No. Ye— Maybe." Scott sounded like a blathering fool and he couldn't do anything to stop it.

Dr. Gwen Specchio, a petite woman who was probably in her midfifties, sat back in her chair, obviously hoping a more relaxed posture would elicit the same response in Scott. Scott knew it immediately for what it was. He'd been in therapy for long enough to know when he was being de-escalated.

"Why don't we start with any new developments in your life since I saw you last?"

How about we not? Scott hadn't been to therapy in a couple of weeks. He normally tried to attend his weekly sessions, but he'd canceled the last few. He told himself it was because he'd simply been too busy to attend. But he recognized the real reason for what it was: he had absolutely no interest in talking about Lauren. "I had dinner with my mom Sunday. She was her normal self. She discussed my brother." Scott knew therapists loved talking about mommy issues, and he wasn't above feigning an Oedipus complex to get out of going where Gwen was steering the conversation.

She typed on her tablet before looking back at him. "How did you feel afterward?"

Scott loved that question. It seemed cliché whenever she asked it, and he almost laughed every time. But that didn't stop him from answering it honestly this time. "Angry."

She leaned forward slightly. "Angry at what?"

"At everything. At the fact that she can't understand that my dad gave her endless chances, but she can't do the same for her own son."

"Why do you think that is?"

"Because she needs to maintain the facade of the innocent victim."

Gwen pondered that for a moment. "Do you think it's a facade or do you think your mother really feels victimized?"

Scott couldn't quite see where this line of questioning was going, but he was sure he wasn't going to like where it ended up. He knew when a conversation was being guided toward an end goal. "I think she's afraid to be judged. By convincing herself that she's the victim, she frees herself from all responsibility in what's happened with Tim. She can neatly transfer all that blame onto him without feeling any herself. And Tim *is* to blame for the choices he's made. But she can't be absolved of all culpability, especially when she deserves it the most."

How many times had she dragged her sons to "playdates" with her lover's children? How many times had she disappeared while Scott and Tim played happily with their new "friends"? And when Tim answered his father's simple question of *How was your day?* honestly, and the truth had come out, it had been Tim who his mother blamed. She had accused him of trying to deliberately sabotage her marriage. And even though his father had forgiven her, even though she continued to be unfaithful, even though *she* had been the one to destroy their family, it was *Tim* who'd suffered the consequences.

"Does it really matter where the blame falls?" Gwen asked.

"It matters to me."

"Does placing that blame on her, does it make you feel better? Do you think it makes Tim feel better?"

"Tim doesn't blame anyone but himself. But we all played a role. His demise was a family affair."

"But Tim's doing well now, isn't he? So there is no demise."

Scott swallowed and rubbed the silver dollar. "He still suffered. And we don't have the relationship I wish we did. That I feel we should have had."

"You were a young child when Tim started using, weren't you?"

Scott hated that Gwen asked questions she already knew the answer to. But that didn't stop him from responding. "I was nine. At least I was when we first found out he was doing drugs. I remember because I spent that summer away at camp and came back to find a strung-out brother and a family with their heads buried in the sand."

"And how old was Tim?"

"Fifteen."

"You weren't even home when things deteriorated with him. So how was your nine-year-old self responsible for any of it?"

"Because I allowed them to replace him with me."

Gwen's head shot up from her tablet. "In what way?"

"In every way. They had high hopes for him: he was going to follow in my father's footsteps. Excel at everything and make our family proud. When he didn't do that, they turned their attention to me. And it was a role I took on without an ounce of hesitation. I never questioned how any of it would make him feel. I made it easier for him to disappear. So he did."

Over the course of Scott's three years with Gwen, he'd discussed everything there was to know about Tim. None of what Scott shared about his family was news to her anymore. But he knew why she asked him the questions, so he repeated his story anyway. There was something soothing about hearing himself say things aloud. It was a therapist's way of getting you to realize things about yourself on your own. To recognize and acknowledge your feelings. And that was something Scott rarely did.

"From what you've told me about your father, he didn't seem like the type to just write off his son."

Scott couldn't help but feel defensive. His mother made his father's life hell whenever he tried to defend Tim, or insist that they do more to help him. Eventually she wore him down and he threw himself more into his practice, hoping that ignoring the problem would make it cease to exist. "He wasn't," Scott finally responded.

"Do you think your father was a good man?"

Scott startled at her question. He was unable to mask his annoyance when he responded. "Of course I think he was. We all have our flaws. He wasn't a bad father. He loved Tim. He just . . . didn't know what to do."

Gwen wrote on her tablet some more before readjusting her position in her seat, seemingly ready to shift gears. "The facade you referred to earlier—do you think your mother was that way before the issues with Tim, or did it surface after?"

Scott thought for a moment, trying to remember if he'd ever felt that his mother was a warm person. If she'd ever seemed real. "I honestly don't remember her any other way."

"So Tim was not the root cause of your mother's veneer? Do you have any idea what may have caused her to be that way?"

"What does it matter what caused it? It's who she is. Analyzing it isn't going to change her. Isn't that what you just said?"

Gwen smiled enigmatically as she set her tablet on the small wooden table beside her chair and looked at him.

Scott suddenly felt that the room was entirely too bright. With the late-afternoon sunlight streaming through the open blinds, he felt like Gwen was able to see him too clearly.

"Scott, how long have you been coming here? Three years?"

Scott thought for a second. "Yes, about that. Why?"

She leaned forward slightly, resting her forearms on her knees, making herself more compact, less intimidating. "Causes for behaviors are always important. It allows us to understand a person better and perhaps effect some kind of change."

"But I don't expect my mother to change," Scott interrupted.

"It's not her I'm talking about."

Scott looked at her in confusion.

"I bring this up because despite knowing you for three years, this is the first time you came here clearly affected by something. No charm, no cocky attitude, no fake smile. I feels like this is the first time I'm actually meeting you, Scott. And I must say, it's about time."

Scott lay awake most of Wednesday night. He wasn't one to overanalyze people's words, especially therapists'. They said all kinds of shit. Some helpful and some not. Normally, he maintained a use-it-or-lose-it attitude about most of Gwen's comments, opting to only focus on the ones he believed would do him some good, while completely ignoring the rest.

Unfortunately, though he knew it did nothing for him to replay her last observation over in his mind, he couldn't stop. And that just wasn't him.

Or *was* it? Gwen had implied he'd put on a facade — an outer shell to mask his real feelings. That the arrogant, charismatic exterior was just that: an exterior. "So what the hell is inside?" he asked aloud as he stepped out of the shower and unfogged the mirror to look at himself.

When the answer didn't come, he finished drying off, running the towel quickly through his hair, over his face, and down his chest. He brushed his teeth, ran a tiny bit of gel through his hair to give it an intentionally messy look, and headed toward his closet to put on his clothes.

There was no denying that Scott felt like a dick. Lauren had offered to meet up the previous night, presumably for a night of uninhibited sex, and he'd turned her down without so much as a reason. He hadn't even bothered to make up a lame excuse for why he couldn't meet her.

And now he'd have to face her at work. Words rolled around in his mind, but he wasn't sure which ones he should choose. Should he act like nothing had happened? Though he supposed nothing *had* happened. In fact, he'd told the truth. Should he tell her he was sorry he couldn't get together last night but was free tonight? *No fucking way.* He wasn't the apologetic type. And it's not like he owed Lauren any sort of an explanation.

So he didn't give her one. He spent his workday doing exactly that: working. He didn't actively avoid Lauren. He just found that between his appointments and Lauren's clerical work, the two of them didn't cross paths in private.

And it was better that way. After their tryst in the stairwell, Scott had decided that mixing work with . . . whatever was going on between them was dangerous.

At quarter to six, Scott hung up his white coat on the rack in his office and began packing up what he needed for the satellite office the next day. When he was finished, he walked down the hall and stuck his head around the corner to Lauren's desk.

She spun her chair around at the sound of Scott's hand hitting the doorframe. He leaned his shoulder against it and stared down, her sapphire eyes wide as she seemed to be waiting for him to speak. Suddenly, his mind was filled with images of those same eyes staring up at him as he exploded in her warm mouth. *How the hell did I turn that down . . . turn* her *down for fucking therapy? I really* am *nuts.*

"Yes?" she asked, and he realized that he'd probably been silently staring at her for an uncomfortable amount of time.

"Just thought I'd cash in that rain check tonight if you're available," he said casually. The left side of his mouth turned up to reveal a hint of his white smile. "Doctor said I am a hundred percent. He actually recommended that I get some physical activity."

Lauren leaned back in her chair, arms crossed as she grinned. "He did, did he?" Scott gave a slight head nod, and Lauren cocked her brow at him. "And which doctor is that?"

Scott pulled on the knot of his tie to loosen it, a gesture he knew women couldn't resist. "The only one that matters," he replied as he stepped toward her.

Lauren was silent for a moment, a skeptical look on her face before she let her expression ease into a more relaxed one. "Well, who am I to argue with a doctor?" Lauren glanced around at her desk, which was covered with papers and her laptop. "Just let me straighten up since I'm not here tomorrow, and I'll meet you in the lobby in ten minutes."

"Sounds good," Scott said with a smile.

"What sounds good?" Lauren and Scott turned toward the reception desk to see that Cass wasn't the only one who'd come to the office. Quinn and Simone flanked her on each side.

"Uh . . . we were just talking about a benefit for the hospital that's in a few weeks. I just told Dr. Scott that I'm going." Scott's eyes narrowed at Lauren, unsure of whether or not she was serious about attending. "I think it sounds like fun," Lauren added without taking her eyes off of him. "And who am I to turn down a chance to help children?"

"Oh yeah, Laur's Virginia's own Mother Teresa. Haven't you heard?" Cass asked Scott without waiting for a reply. Then she directed her attention toward Lauren. "Get your stuff. I think we have some things to discuss."

Lauren looked to Scott, obviously uncertain about how to proceed. Did she ditch him for her friends, or explain that she had plans with him after work? He understood her dilemma, so he did the only thing he could think to do to rectify it. "It's almost six," he said, glancing at his watch. "It's fine with me if you head out early."

"Oh, uh . . . okay," Lauren said, clearly confused. "Thanks. Um . . . have a good weekend. See you next Tuesday."

"See you Tuesday," Scott replied with a polite smile. But inside, Scott felt a pang of disappointment that he wouldn't be seeing Lauren that night. And it had to do with more than just missing out on sex. *So much for feeling a hundred percent.*

Chapter 11

Attachment Disorder

Sitting in the corner booth at McGillen's, Lauren studied the menu in an attempt to ignore the burning stares of her friends. She felt like she'd been employing a lot of avoidance strategies lately, but it was better than facing the questioning squad in front of her. "So what's good here?" she asked.

She could feel six eyes on her, and she lifted her own to look at her three girlfriends. "You know what's good here. We come here all the time," Simone accused. "Now cut the shit. What's been going on?"

"Well . . ." Lauren thought quickly as she tried to think of anything to discuss other than the reason they'd clearly brought her there. "I found a cat the other day, and he didn't even have a tag. Can you believe someone would be so irresponsible?" Lauren knew she was talking at a rapid rate. "School's school. Just trying to get through this last year so I can join the working world and become an actual adult. I have this one class that—"

"Okay, Laur, stop acting like you don't know why

you're here. We don't care about cats or classes. We're worried about you. You've been avoiding us for days now with no explanation." Cass' eyes softened before continuing. "You've only been distant with us one other time." She reached across the table and squeezed Lauren's hand. "We just wish you'd let us help you through it this time."

Lauren returned Cass' sincere expression with her own. "I know," she said, giving her a small smile.

"Really, we mean it," Quinn added. "Cooper was like a brother to us too."

Lauren felt a lump in her throat at the sound of his name, and a pang of guilt coursed through her knowing her friends thought her sudden conspicuous evasion had been due to some renewed sadness over the death of her brother. They had been anxious about her well-being—and with good reason, after her previous bout with depression—and she'd been allowing them to worry needlessly all because she didn't want to tell them about Scott. "You know I would tell you if there were anything to be concerned about. You girls are my first call when I'm upset. You know that. What happened before with me was a one-time thing. Coop had just . . ." she allowed the sentence to taper off, knowing her friends would understand what she couldn't bring herself to say. "I haven't been like that since."

The girls looked confused. Simone spoke up first. "Then what's been going on?"

Lauren crossed her hands in front of her confidently. She wasn't sure how her friends would take the news that she'd been avoiding them because she didn't want to reveal what had been going on with her and Scott. In her mind, it could have gone one of two ways. They might be relieved because they had no real reason to be concerned about her. Or they could be pissed because she'd let them worry for nothing "Well, it's not as serious a problem as you might think. It's actually not really a problem at all. I just didn't . . . I'm not sure why I didn't want you to know."

"Didn't want us to know what?" Cass asked tentatively.

"About Scott."

It took the girls a few seconds to register the implications of what Lauren had said. Then their eyes lit up almost simultaneously. "Oh. My. God!" Simone said, nearly bouncing up and down in the booth. "You had us worried for your sanity, and this was all because you've been screwing your boss?"

"You know that means you owe us. So spill it. Just how good *is* our hot doctor in bed? Spare no details," Cass demanded.

Lauren shrugged. "I wouldn't know." It was the truth. She hadn't had sex with Scott yet, and she was thankful for the chance to be honest without revealing any specifics. Though she knew it wouldn't last long.

The girls looked incredulous. "What do you mean you don't know? You just said you've been avoiding us because of Scott."

"I did. But I didn't sleep with him."

"Okay," Simone said slowly, drawing the word out. "So maybe you didn't bang him. But you definitely did *something* with him. I hope. For the love of God, please tell me he felt you up on an exam table or something."

"But that would be a lie," Lauren said with an intentionally serious expression. Then she let a slow smile creep up her face before speaking. "I do have a pretty good story about getting dry-humped in the file room though." The girls' mouths hung open in shock, and Lauren laughed. "Wow, all these years, and that's all it took to make the three of you speechless. I wish I'd known sooner."

"Funny," Cass said without laughing. "So what else?"

"Nothing. We've just fooled around a few times. That's all."

Quinn folded her arms across her chest and leaned back in the booth. "You're seriously gonna sit here and pretend you fooled around with him a few times and that's it—that nothing else will happen? Like you can just *not* do it again?"

Lauren looked serious. "I didn't say nothing else *will* happen."

Cass' eyes grew wide with excitement. "So you're, like, *dating* Scott then?"

"I didn't say I was *dating* him. In fact, we are definitely *not* doing *that*."

"Stop being so cryptic. This isn't *The* fucking *Da Vinci Code*. If you're not dating and you're not screwing, what the hell *are* you doing?"

Lauren's mind struggled to find the right words. Somehow, though *she* saw nothing wrong with the arrangement she and Scott had, she knew that it wouldn't sound right when she said it aloud. "We sort of have an agreement that—"

"No, you didn't," Simone scolded. It was obvious that she remembered Scott's explanation of why he remained single. "You did *not* agree to sleep with this guy, no strings attached."

Lauren didn't respond, knowing that her silence would be enough to confirm Simone's suspicions.

"Seriously, Laur?" The concern on Cass' face was evident. "It's one thing to bang someone a few times. It's another to have a standing agreement to let your relationship only be about sex. You remember how well that worked out for you last time, right?"

Cass had a point. The decision to have a sexual relationship with the professor had been an obvious mistake in hindsight, but the situation with Scott wasn't the same. "Look, I get why you're worried. But this is totally different. *I* wasn't the one who couldn't do the no strings thing last time. You seriously think Scott will turn into a creeper?" Lauren shook her head. "He can have any woman he wants."

The girls were silent for a moment before Cass spoke quietly. "What if he wants *you*?"

Her question was simple. Luckily so was the answer. "He won't," Lauren replied. "And I won't want him either. Not like that."

The girls looked at her, doubt showing on their faces.

"You don't believe me?" Lauren asked. The girls' skeptical looks answered her question. "Fine. Then I'll just have to let you girls observe us in our natural habitat: the bar." Lauren grabbed her phone and began typing.

"What are you doing?" Simone asked as she tried to lean over and see Lauren's phone.

"I'm texting Scott to see if he and his friends want to come out with us on Saturday. Then you can see how we are together and you'll see that I'm telling you the truth."

"We're not doubting that you *think* you're telling us the truth," Cass countered. "But don't be naive, Laur.

You're playing with fire and you know it. This casual shit *never* works out."

"It can and it will. You'll see."

After Lauren had left with her friends, Scott had stayed in the office. For some reason, going home alone when he was supposed to go home with Lauren didn't seem all that appealing. So he figured he'd order takeout and use the extra time to catch up on some work for a few hours. When his phone dinged after about an hour and a half, alerting him that he had a text, he was more than surprised to see that it was from Lauren.

But his initial excitement quickly dissipated when he saw its content. Was she asking him out on a date? Scott didn't do *dates*. It was one thing to go to the movies or grab a bite to eat on a whim. But it was something else entirely to plan a night out days ahead of time. There was an importance—a formality to it—that didn't sit well with him.

But after he texted back a few vague questions—so as not to reveal his internal panic—he was relieved to find out that she'd just been wondering if he wanted to hang out at a bar with all their friends. That, he could handle.

Sure, you can tell the girls I'm in.

I will when I talk to them. I actually left early. What are you up to?

Scott looked at his desk. *Being a loser,* he thought. But he typed : Still at the office. What about you?

Just heading home, I guess. Unless . . .

He waited for her to finish her sentence, hoping it was going to say what he thought it would.

Unless I can cash in the rain check on the rain check.

Scott shook his head at the cheesiness of her last line, but he couldn't help but smile. I was just getting ready to leave, so I can meet you at my place if you want. So what if it wasn't the complete truth?

Your office is right up the road. I'll come there ;)

The winky face at the end of her text told him the innuendo in her last line had been intentional. And it made his cock stiffen instantly. Having sex with Lauren in his office had been a fantasy of his since he'd met her, but he would never do that during the day with people in there. That day in the filing room had been a momentary lapse in judgment that he'd promised himself he wouldn't let happen again.

But with no one here, he could have her any way he wanted, any*where* he wanted. And he planned to.

Scott didn't even hear her come in when Lauren arrived a few minutes later. "Evening, Doctor," she said flirtatiously, a look of seduction flushing across her face. It wasn't until she spoke to him that the reality of what was about to happen set in. Her sheer cream blouse had already been removed and laid by her feet on the floor beside her. Apparently, Scott wasn't the only one who had fantasies.

He settled back, leaning against the edge of his desk, his arms folded as he appraised her from head to toe.

Her tight white tank top gave him a perfect view of her hardened nipples as they pressed against the thin satin. Scott studied her as she slowly unbuttoned her pants, carefully sliding them down her thighs to reveal the white lace beneath, before she finally kicked off her shoes and removed her pants completely. He could tell how hard he was, embarrassingly so, considering he hadn't even touched her yet. But he wanted his hands on her skin, his tongue inside of her mouth, his cock buried so fucking deep inside her. He'd waited for this moment for much too long. And he was done waiting. "Turn around," Scott said.

When Lauren complied, Scott stalked toward her, his hot stare lingering on Lauren's ass as she pulled her tank top over her head and tossed it beside her. Scott smoothed his hands over the taut flesh of her stomach, allowing himself to feel her sharp inhale.

Lauren ground her ass against him, letting a soft moan slip from her as she pushed against him. Then he spun her around to face him, his lips mere centimeters from hers as he pinned her to the wall next to the door with his hips. "Didn't I warn you about that?" he asked, hoping his voice conveyed the firm playfulness he was going for.

"Yes," she breathed, loosening his tie and pulling it off so she could unbutton his shirt to reveal his bare chest.

He struggled to control his reaction to her, but the feeling of her nails running up and down his flesh caused a small groan to escape his throat. He slipped a hand beneath the lace of her bra, toying with her nipples for a few moments before moving to unclasp the back and slide it down her arms. "And what did I tell you?"

"You said that next time I did that you'd bend me over no matter who was watching."

"That's right." Scott pressed his lips hard against hers, needing to feel the warmth and wetness they provided even if only for a few moments. His hand massaged her breast and caressed her jawline. Then he pulled Lauren away from the wall, holding her hip with one hand and unhinging his belt buckle with the other. "So I'm going to give you exactly what you asked for."

Lauren's "Mm-hm" vibrated against Scott's throat as he led them both across the hall, guiding Lo backward until her thighs hit the edge of the exam table.

They were all hands and tongues, clawing and sucking at each other's hot skin as if the other might be taken away at any moment. Scott reached his hand inside the waistband of his boxers, finally shoving them, along with his pants, down just enough to pull himself free. Lauren's hand instantly gripped around his shaft as she pumped him with varying speeds and movements. She gave a fucking handjob like she did everything else: unpredictably.

When Scott felt himself close to climaxing, he cupped his hand over Lauren's to stop her. Then he reached into his back pocket, unwrapped a condom he'd taken out of his wallet, and slid it over his length. He breathed in slowly, taking a long look at Lo as his fist tangled in her hair. He suddenly found himself a little captivated by her. She really was gorgeous. He was a damn lucky bastard. They'd been working toward this moment since that first day, and he couldn't believe that he finally had her here, waiting for him. *What the hell am I waiting for?*

All of the pent up desire suddenly consumed him and he spun her in one fluid movement.

Lauren immediately bent over the table, moaning in appreciation as she wiggled her ass against him.

Scott gripped both her hips then moved his hands down to massage her ass roughly before pulling one hand away and returning it with a sharp crack. Lauren let out a perfect combination of breathy curses in response. Clearly she was enjoying herself. He moved to the other cheek, alternating several times between the two and rubbing his palm against her in between smacks.

Finally, when Scott didn't think he could get any harder, he jerked her thong roughly to the side, tearing it in the process, before pushing completely into her. The warmth he experienced once inside her was like nothing he'd ever felt—their bodies conducting heat from one person to the other. He slid perfectly in and out, listening to the sound of her moans and heavy breaths as his hands guided her hips to match the rhythm of his own.

"Jesus, Scott, this feels so good. I don't know how much more of it I can take."

Scott leaned down, his chest against her back, as he spoke softly but sternly into her ear. "You'll take whatever I give you."

But Scott wasn't entirely sure how much more he could give. The way her hair fell over her face as it pressed against the table, the feel of her flesh under his fingertips, how fucking tight she was around him . . . it was almost too much. He wasn't sure how long he got lost in the beat of their bodies moving in time to each other. But eventually Lauren's voice pulled him out of his pleasurable trance.

"I'm gonna come, Scott. Fuck, make me come. Please," she pleaded.

Scott sped up his pace at Lauren's request, reaching around to stroke her clit with just the right amount of pressure to push her over the edge. In moments, her body quaked beneath him, her back vibrating as she moaned her release.

He continued to rock his body into hers until he felt his orgasm build uncontrollably. Even though he needed to feel himself let go—needed to feel the relief his climax would provide—he didn't *want* to. He pumped into her a few more times before he felt himself explode. But as much as he enjoyed Lauren milking every last drop from him as he thrust more slowly inside her, he hated it too. Because he didn't want it to end.

It all felt too fucking good.

Chapter 12

Autoimmune Disorder

Nothing Gold was a large bar that took on a club vibe after nine p.m. on weekends. It was one of Scott's favorite spots to pick up women, which made him wonder why the hell he'd decided that it would make a good venue for his friends to hang out with Lauren and hers. Especially after Thursday night. He'd been replaying every detail of their sexcapade for the past two days, and his dick had gotten hard every time. After it was over, they'd put themselves back together, and he'd walked her to her car. Then Lauren had planted a kiss on him that was a promise for more. And Goddamn, did he want more.

"Scale of one to ten, how hot are these chicks?" Xavier asked as he took a sip of his beer.

"Depends on your taste," Scott replied as he covertly eyed the doorway.

"You know my taste."

Alex watched Scott intently, obviously interested in the answer.

"If you care so much, why didn't you ask before you agreed to come? It's a little late to be picky now. Besides, I didn't invite them here for you to try to bang them all. They're a fun group to hang out with."

Xavier looked skeptical. "Fun means ugly."

"Jesus Christ, you really are a bastard. Fine. There are four of them. Quinn is the girl-next-door type, dark red hair, freckles, very pretty. Simone is African-American, taller than the others, and curvy in all the right places. Cass is blond, bold, and beautiful. But she reminds me of a praying mantis: she's awesome to look at, but just may bite your head off after she's done with you. And lastly there's Lauren."

The guys looked at him with expectant eyes. When he didn't continue, Alex spoke. "And Lauren is?"

"Off limits." Scott took a long drink of his beer and looked again toward the door. Thankfully the girls chose that moment to make an appearance, so he didn't have to deal with any shit from Xavier or Alex. He hadn't told them anything about Lauren. When he'd called to see if they wanted to hang out with some girls, they'd both accepted without much explanation on his part. But he also knew that if either of them tried to hit on her, he wouldn't react well, so putting it out there seemed like his best course of action.

Lauren spotted him and led the girls toward them. "Hey," she said as she made her way to him.

"Hey," he replied. Scott looked at her for a moment, probably a second longer than could be considered casual appraisal, before snapping out of it and introducing the girls to his friends.

"Thanks for meeting up with us," Cass said. "I mean,

I'm sure you could've thought of someone else to do—I mean some*thing* else. It was nice of you to include us." Her lips quirked up slightly as she looked pointedly between Scott and Lauren.

Yup, definitely a praying mantis. "What could be better than hanging out with you beautiful ladies?" Scott replied, kicking up the wattage on his smile.

"I bet you say that to all the girls," Cass teased. "Let's find out. Lauren—"

"So what are you guys drinking?" Lauren interrupted, clearly trying to prevent Cass from continuing.

Scott had to admit that he liked Cass the best out of Lo's friends. She was definitely a board-certified cock twister, but she did it in a way that was humorous instead of offensive. *I bet she'd give Xavier a run for his money.* But when Scott's eyes wandered to his buddies, it was Alex who seemed to be edging his way closer to Cass. *Interesting.* "Blue Moon." Scott set his beer down on the high top table they were standing around. "What would you all like? I'll go get it at the bar."

"That's okay," Lauren replied with that smile he couldn't get enough of. "We'll go up. Be right back."

Scott watched the girls walk away before reaching for his beer. When he did, he noticed his friends staring at him. "What?" he asked.

"Nothing," Xavier replied.

"Not a thing," Alex added.

"Yeah, fuck off. Both of you."

Alex and Xavier burst out laughing. Scott knew that, between his warning for them to stay away from Lauren and the way he looked at her, there was no way they weren't on to him.

"You said you work with her, right?" Alex asked tentatively.

Scott knew where he was heading. "Yeah, but not for long. Only until the semester's over."

Scott's explanation didn't satisfy Alex's curiosity. "Nice. Banging a college chick."

The guys kept their eyes on Scott, waiting for him to expand on his single word response. He heaved out a sigh. "She's finishing up her master's this spring. I'm not *that* desperate to go trolling college campuses looking for women."

"It's a little unlike you to shit where you sleep though, buddy," Xavier said.

Scott grimaced slightly at Xavier's choice of words, but understood what he was saying. Scott had never done this with someone he had to see in his day-to-day life. But how was he supposed to explain it to them? Say that Lauren was different? That he couldn't fucking resist her? That would only prompt more questions, and he was over answering their questions when he couldn't even answer his own. "First time for everything," he replied coolly.

"Hey there," a soft, breathy voice said from behind him.

Scott watched Alex and Xavier, who were facing the interloper, reach for their beers and take huge gulps, the international guy signal for "You're not going to like what you see when you turn around." Scott took a deep breath before spinning around. The girl standing in front of him was shorter than Lauren, and not nearly as pleasing to the eye. She was built kind of like a football, with dark-blond curly hair and heavy eye makeup. Scott may have spent many years as a playboy, but he still wasn't a total asshole. While he wasn't into this girl, he had no interest in hurting her feelings. "Hey," he said. "How are you?"

"Better now. I was looking at you from across the bar and my friends finally told me to just come over and introduce myself. I'm Bethany."

Scott stretched out his hand toward her. "Hi, Bethany. I'm Scott. And this is Xavier and Alex."

"Hmm," she purred. "What are a bunch of handsome men like you up to tonight?"

Scott suddenly wondered what the hell was keeping Lauren. His eyes darted toward the bar, where he saw that Lo and her friends had already gotten their drinks and were talking to a few other girls. *Hurry up, Lo.* "Just meeting up with some people. What about you?"

Bethany moved closer to him, which made Scott lean back into the table. "We're just looking for a good time. Any suggestions for where we can find one?"

Fuck, this girl is forward. "Um, I'm not sure," Scott stammered, unsure of how exactly to respond.

Bethany's hand came up and rested on his forearm. "Oh, come on. I bet you can think of something." Her voice had lowered, and Scott assumed she was trying to be seductive, but it just made her sound manly. Like how he imagined a lumberjack or bounty hunter would sound.

He looked back in Lo's direction again, and this time his eyes caught hers. She tilted her head and looked at him curiously, as though she could tell something was off. He widened his eyes and gave a brief look down, trying to signal that her help was needed. *Now.*

She seemed to get the message as she turned to say something to the girls, who then began walking toward the guys.

Bethany's hand started sliding up and down Scott's arm, and he was just about to tell her that the feel of her hand on his skin was about as appealing as getting a mole removed when he finally felt a hand wrap around his waist.

"Hey, baby. Sorry it took us so long. The bar's packed. Who's your friend?" Lauren's voice was sweet and calm.

Bethany quickly retracted her hand and glared at Scott. He gave a brief look around to his friends. Lauren's girls had formed a female power wall around them. Quinn and Simone were flanking Xavier while Cass pressed herself into Alex's side. He also couldn't ignore the shit-eating grin on Alex's face. *He has no fucking game.* "Uh, Bethany. This is Bethany. She came over while we were waiting for you girls to come back. Bethany, this is my girlfriend Lauren."

Lauren stretched out a hand toward Bethany, which the woman reluctantly shook. "Nice to meet you, Bethany. I hope our boys were being nice to you. They tend to get a little flirty with pretty girls."

Scott noticed how Lauren avoided explicitly lying, and he wasn't sure how she managed it.

Bethany's face was a mass of confusion. She clearly couldn't figure Lauren out.

Welcome to the club, Bethany.

But Lauren's smile was genuine, and Bethany seemed to accept her words as a sincere compliment rather than as a sarcastic slight. "Yeah, they've been nice enough."

Scott didn't know how Lauren did it. She was just . . .

so *good* with people. She could've come over and been a catty bitch to get rid of Bethany, but that just wasn't her style. She knew exactly what to say so that the woman wouldn't be defensive or embarrassed. He was in awe of her.

"Well, good. I wouldn't want to have to bitch him out in front of a bar full of people." Lauren smiled at Bethany.

"Don't think she wouldn't, Bethany. Lauren's great at causing a scene," Cass teased.

"It's true," Lauren agreed.

Bethany released a small laugh before she excused herself from them. But as she walked away, she turned and gave Scott a long and indecent once-over. Clearly, Lauren's kindness wasn't going to be enough to deter Bethany.

Once Scott's stalker was out of eyesight, Lauren's hand dropped from his waist. Scott immediately missed it. He leaned down, bringing his mouth to Lauren's ear. "I like when you put your hands on me." His voice was playful, but damn if he didn't mean what he said.

Lauren leaned into him a little. "Oh, really?" she asked.

Scott pulled back slightly so he could look her in the eyes. "Yes, really."

"Trust me, Dr. Scott. I've barely begun to put my hands on you."

And fuck if the entire room didn't fade away with her words. It was like they were the only two in the place, the chemistry crackling between them like a fuse. He wanted her hands on him in that moment more than he wanted his next breath. But he also wanted her to want to keep them there. For a long time. And it was that uncomfortable thought that forced him back into reality. This thing with Lauren could never go there. *Would* never go there because Scott just wasn't that guy. "That's a promise I'll hold you to," he said as he took a step away from her. He turned toward the table to pick up his beer and was surprised to see Cass and Alex engaged in conversation. *Maybe the old boy does still have a little something up his sleeve.*

They all spent the next hour or so bullshitting. The liquor was flowing, and Scott watched as Lauren's face took on a tipsy glow. He was surprised by how great things were going. Their friends got along well and had a good time sharing outrageous stories about one another.

Then some song by Justin Timberlake came on and Simone yelled that it was her "jam" and that they needed to go dance.

The guys stayed rooted to their spots, but the girls headed off toward the large dance floor. They found an open spot and began moving their bodies in ways that should be illegal. Especially Lauren.

Scott watched her. She had rhythm—that was for sure.

"You got it bad."

Scott turned around to stare at his friends. "What do you mean?"

"You can't take your eyes off her," Alex said.

Scott turned back around. "You know how I am. Once I see something I want, I don't sleep on it."

"Yeah, I guess that's true," Xavier chuckled. "Just seems that you might want to keep this one around for a while."

Scott steeled his voice. "Not sure why you'd think that. I'm going to get another beer. You guys need anything?"

The guys said that they were good, so Scott took off

for the bar. As he waited for the bartender to bring him his change, he felt a body brush next to him. He looked down. *Shit.*

"Just thought I'd stop by and see if you changed your mind," Bethany said in her scary, deep voice.

"About what?" Scott replied shortly. His tolerance was quickly waning.

"About having a girlfriend."

Scott huffed out a laugh. "No, I don't think so."

"Pity," Bethany said with mock sincerity. "It seems that she's changed her mind about you."

"What are you talking about?"

Bethany turned and looked at the dance floor. Scott's eyes followed her line of sight. And what he saw made his heart hammer in his chest and his blood boil. Lauren was still dancing with her girls, but a group of guys had moved in on them. And one of the pricks had his hands on Lauren's hips, trying to pull her closer to him.

Scott didn't say anything more to Bethany. He was moving before he even realized it. Reaching Lauren, he grabbed her waist more roughly than he intended and pulled her to him so quickly that she collided into him, her hands hitting his chest to brace herself against the impact. He half expected her to be pissed at his harsh handling, but he relaxed when she registered what had happened and slid her hands over his pecs and around his neck. Scott pulled her closer to him and rested his chin against her temple. "Move on," he barked at the guy behind Lo.

"What was that about?" she asked so softly, he barely heard her over the music.

"Bethany came back. I had to set her straight." Scott

couldn't admit the real reason he'd barged over there and virtually pissed on Lauren's leg to mark his territory.

"She's still looking at us. You'd better watch your back. She looks like the type to peep in windows and make voodoo dolls."

Laughter rumbled in Scott's chest. "Then I guess you should watch your back too."

Lauren laughed too, and the two of them continued to move to the music. It was an up-tempo song, and they ground into each other with quick movements, though they kept each other close. They stayed that way for two more songs, bumping, grinding, and laughing. Scott couldn't remember the last time he'd had such a good time.

Then the DJ played a song Scott had actually heard before: Clean Bandit's "Rather Be."

Just as it started, Quinn came up behind Lo. "Come on, we're all hot. Let's go get a drink."

Lauren peeked around Scott's arm. "Your stalker's gone. You can probably safely make it back to the guys now. I'll meet you back at the table."

There was a disappointment in her eyes that he'd never seen before. He wasn't sure what had sparked it, but he did know that he fucking hated it. As he watched her start to walk off the dance floor, Scott suddenly couldn't help himself. He took two steps after her and grabbed her wrist. He didn't pull her toward him. Rather, he just held it, and waited.

Lauren wasn't sure what she saw in Scott's eyes. She was usually so good at reading him, but right then, she was lost. Her wrist burned where he touched her, and the feeling quickly spread throughout the rest of her body.

She never wanted him to let go. And even though she knew that he would sooner rather than later, in that moment she refused to think about any of that. Instead, Lauren focused on how badly she wanted his arms back around her. Focused on how much Scott probably wanted the same thing. Why else would he be standing there, letting his eyes blaze into hers as he gripped her wrist? It was no longer a choice. She couldn't have followed her friends even if she had wanted to. Screw how they interpreted things between them. She wanted him. So she moved back toward him slowly, allowing him to pull her closer than she thought she'd ever been, and resumed their sexy sway to the music. It was beautiful and expressive and fucking filthy. It was the most fulfilling dance experience Lauren had ever had. And as the words infiltrated the haze in her brain, telling her that there was no place she'd rather be, she hoped Scott felt the same way.

When the song ended, Scott took a half step back. He looked tense. "I like that song."

That was his explanation, and Lauren finally saw clearly again. It was a cop-out if she'd ever heard one. But his face held more than what the words implied, so she held on to that to keep herself from beating some sense into him. "Me too."

Scott led her off the dance floor and back to the table. The girls had returned with their drinks and were making small talk with Scott's friends.

"Here, we got you another drink," Simone said as she handed Lauren a glass.

"Thanks." Lauren drained half the glass before setting it down. She felt scattered, and she didn't like it. She was so deep inside of her own head that she barely paid attention to Scott and his friends joking around with one another until she forced herself to join into the conversation.

"In college, Scott had a thing for a TA in one of his classes. A *big* thing. He worked on her for months," Xavier joked.

"Looks like I'm not the only one who was hot for teacher," Lauren muttered for only Scott to hear.

Scott glared at his friend, clearly making an effort to ignore Lo's comment. "It wasn't months. I talked to her one time."

"You may have only tried once, but you thought about it for much longer," Alex added.

"Dude, you're supposed to be the nice one," Scott chastised playfully.

"Aww, poor Scott. I didn't peg you as the pining type," Lauren teased. She was glad she'd started engaging with the group. She was sure the steady flow of alcohol was helping occupy her mind. Which she was thankful for because this story was going to be good. She could feel it.

"That's because I'm not. This whole story is assbackward." Scott set his beer down on the table so that he could wildly wave his hands to better get his point across. "This girl had been fucking me with her eyes since the first day of class. But I really wasn't interested in getting involved with someone who could impact my grade." Scott paused and looked down at Lauren. "No offense," he smirked at her.

Her eyes widened as she looked around at the group. The guys hadn't even registered his comment, but the girls had, and their faces were somewhere between shocked and thoroughly amused. "Dick," she whispered. But even she couldn't fight the smile overtaking her lips.

Scott continued like he hadn't just put her on blast in front of the entire table. "But a guy can only take so much. So about midway through the semester, I got tired of her drooling every time I walked into the room, so I went up to talk to her." Scott picked his beer back up and held it as though the story was over.

Xavier wasn't having it. "No way, Casanova. Tell them the rest."

"Rest of what?"

"Fuck you. You know the rest of what. That is *not* how that story ends."

"Spill it, Doctor. I'm not above beating it out of you," Cass threatened.

"She didn't think it was a good idea to get involved. She needed the TA job to help pay her tuition."

"Bullshit!" Xavier bellowed. "The truth is that she hadn't been looking at Scott at all. She'd been eye-fucking the guy who sat *behind* him. He was some big-deal lacrosse player. I think they eloped soon after that."

The table burst into hysterics. Lauren looked up at Scott, whose eyes were boring a hole into Xavier.

"It was an honest mistake. And he wasn't *that* big of a deal. It was lacrosse, for Christ's sake, not football or basketball."

"It's okay to admit that he was better looking than you," Xavier teased.

"You're always wrapped up in how good-looking guys are. You're such a fucking queer," Scott retorted with a laugh.

The floor seemed to fall away beneath Lauren, and

her ears began to buzz. She sobered instantly as she was catapulted back to almost seven years ago: the last time she'd heard almost those exact same words. Except it had been Cooper who'd said them—no, *yelled* them—at Sam when he didn't realize she was there to hear. She remembered the disgust and anger in his voice. The loathing he felt about who he was. And the contempt he felt then worked its way through her body like bile. She had to get out of there.

"Sorry. I—I need to leave."

"Wait, Lauren. What's wrong?" Scott asked.

Lauren didn't respond.

"Let it go, Scott." The words came from Quinn—the only one who knew the effect Scott's comment would have.

Lauren sprinted from the bar, the cool night air hitting her, sobering her a little. Darting her eyes up and down the road, she noticed how desolate it looked. *God, can I relate to that right now.* Lauren needed to move. Walking briskly up the street toward the corner where she would hopefully find a cab, Lauren tried to calm her rapidly beating heart. Taking off from the bar had been dramatic, but Lauren had needed to get the hell out of there. Just as she was getting her wits back, she heard heavy footsteps behind her. But she didn't slow down. She knew whose they were, and while she wasn't going to give the asshole the satisfaction of seeing her run away like a little girl, she sure as fuck wasn't going to stop for him either. Finally a hand on her biceps stopped her, and she flew around, filled with rage at what both Scott *and* Cooper had said.

"Don't fucking touch me, Scott." Her voice was level,

but it held a venom she hadn't even known she was capable of.

Scott quickly jerked his hand off of her and dropped it to his side. "What's going on, Lo?" His face and voice were full of concern, and she knew it was sincere. But she just couldn't bring herself to care.

"Don't you dare call me that." Hearing Scott use the nickname, the one her brother had given her, only to have them both act like assholes made her angry. Totally and unwaveringly angry.

"But you told me I could. Lauren, *please*. Talk to me."

She wanted to. Logically, she knew that she was being irrational. But she couldn't. She didn't want to explain her reaction to Scott then. One, because she didn't believe he deserved to hear it, and two, because she didn't trust herself in that moment to tell it the way it needed to be told. She took a deep breath, mustering any remaining willpower she had. "I can't talk to you right now. Just . . . just leave it alone, Scott."

"I can't just let you walk off. How will you get home?"

Lauren motioned to a pack of cabs waiting in front of a restaurant down the street. "I can handle myself."

He looked at her for a minute, probably trying to figure out what the best thing to do was. He finally must have realized what she already knew: there was no best thing. So he simply took a step back, pushed his hands into his pockets, and murmured, "I know you can."

Lauren felt an instant of remorse at the dejected look on his face before she forced her legs to carry her to the waiting cabs. But she couldn't leave it like that. Because a part of her, the hurt, furious part of her, wanted Scott to know what he'd done. Wanted him to experience perhaps just a fraction of the wound that she still carried all these years later. So once she had gotten a few steps away from him, she stopped, turned her head slightly, and said, "My brother was gay." She wanted to say more. Call him an asshole. Berate him. But she didn't. Because as those words left her, so did the fight, and all that was left was emotional exhaustion. So before he could reply, she resumed walking toward the cabs. And as she climbed inside one and gave directions to her apartment, she wondered if people were ever who they said they were.

The next day sucked almost as much as the previous night had. Lauren spent most of the day dodging calls and texts from the girls. Quinn was the only one she responded to, mostly because she needed someone to call off Cass and Simone. If she stayed MIA, they'd show up at her apartment, and she sure as shit wasn't up for that. Quinn understood, had mourned Cooper, knowing all of the circumstances surrounding his death. So when Lauren texted her saying she needed a day to think, Quinn took care of the rest.

She'd also received a text from Scott, asking her if she had gotten home safely and if she was okay. Lauren reread it a few times, trying to figure out whether or not she should reply. She didn't want to open herself up to a conversation with him, but she didn't want him worried about her either. Not that she should've cared. Being worried is the least he could feel after what he'd said. But Lauren also knew that she'd stress over the stupid text all day if she didn't say *something*. Eventually she decided that a simple *I'm fine* would suffice as a reply. And since she didn't hear from him again, she guessed it had.

By the time Monday morning rolled around, Lauren was glad that she had class instead of having to go into the office. Part of her was glad Scott hadn't texted her again, but the other part of her was irked that he didn't have the decency to try harder to get her to talk to him. Not that she would have, but still. Sometimes it was the fucking thought that counted.

Lauren plopped down into her seat and pulled her laptop from her bag. Even if her mind wasn't into the psychology behind intimate relationships today, she at least wanted to put on a good show. And as class began, Lauren tried her best to be attentive. Though ultimately, her attempt was unsuccessful.

"Ms. Hastings?"

Pulled from her daydream by Dr. Peterson's voice, Lauren pushed off of the hand she'd been resting her face on for the last half hour.

"Do you have any thoughts on today's topic of discussion?"

Lauren glanced from side to side at the classmates nearby, hoping to get some indication of what Dr. Peterson had been discussing. Normally, *she* was the one who had notes filling her laptop screen. But her head was so clouded she hadn't even been paying attention. "Uh ... not right now. Sorry."

Dr. Peterson dropped his head. "Fair enough," he said. "We won't *make* you talk." Dr. Peterson shrugged off his jacket and tossed it over the chair a few feet away from him. "You just usually have something insightful, that's all." Then he paused, slipping one hand into the pocket of his gray slacks. "If you have something to share, you'll let us know?"

Lauren nodded. "Of course," she replied, making every effort to focus her attention on the lecture so she knew what the hell was going on.

"How about you, Mr. Thornton? Thoughts on how important openness is to intimacy?"

Damon Thornton tapped his pencil for a moment before speaking. But Lauren knew he probably already had his response composed in his head. The two of them had been Peterson's go-to's since the beginning of the semester, always trying to add another element to his lectures. "I think it depends on the stage of the relationship."

Peterson gestured toward Damon with an open hand. "Elaborate, please."

Damon's lips turned up into a sort of a clever smile. "People share different things about themselves at different times, depending on the level of trust they have for the other person. Like . . ." Damon raised his eyes to the ceiling as he seemed to be trying to think of an example, "telling your partner that your parents are divorced could be seen as being fairly open when you don't know a whole lot about each other and you're trying to share a little about yourself." He cleared his throat quietly before continuing. "But if you waited six months to tell your partner that same piece of information, he or she may think you've been hiding that from them for some reason."

"Very good, Damon. You see, true intimacy involves sharing things about yourself or topics related to you that you wouldn't necessarily share with just anyone. And Mr. Thornton's point is an interesting one." Dr. Peterson stepped toward the front row and looked out, gesturing with one hand toward the rest of the students to participate. "But openness is more difficult for some people than others, don't you agree? There are some people who feel completely at ease sharing the most private details of their lives with you in an elevator while it—"

"That always happens to me!" someone yelled out. "Strangers tell me all sorts of things about themselves like I want to hear it."

Peterson chuckled. "That probably means you're in the right graduate program then. And believe me, hearing about strangers' lives will become more tolerable when you're getting paid for it."

The room grew louder with the students' laughter and verbal confirmations of Peterson's statement.

Once it seemed that the lecture hall had quieted down, Dr. Peterson continued. "As I was saying, some people are able to share easily while it takes others a while longer. Why is that, do you think?"

The room was quiet for a moment before Lauren heard a soft voice speak up from the back of the room. "Because some people just don't like to talk about themselves."

"That is one reason, definitely. But let's examine it a bit more deeply, shall we?"

"Because being closed is easier than being open."

"Right," Peterson said, pointing proudly at the person who had answered. "People have been lazy since the beginning of time. We take the easy way out, do things out of pure convenience, and prefer the quick and painless route to the slow and uncomfortable one. That, ladies and gentlemen, is simple human nature." Peterson smiled. "It's the reason someone thousands of years ago invented the wheel."

A few students laughed at Dr. Peterson's analogy. But Lauren stayed silent, used to his creative references.

"Still, there's more to it than that," Peterson added. "It might seem obvious—why some people share more about themselves—but really examine it, analyze why that is."

Finally Lauren was unable to stay quiet. She'd match Dr. Peterson's wheel parallel with one of her own. "Because openness is like taking off your clothes in front of someone for the first time," she suddenly spoke up. "You peel it off one layer at a time. And usually there is an understood reciprocity to it. I take off my shirt, you take off yours." Dr. Peterson raised his eyebrows humorously while Lauren continued. "Rarely does one person remove all of their clothing without the other person removing *any*. It's too uncomfortable to open yourself up to judgment that way. Revealing personal information about yourself when the other person's revealed nothing is akin to standing in front of someone completely naked while the other person's fully clothed."

A slow smile spread across Dr. Peterson's face. "Very astute comparison."

Lauren simply nodded, proud that she'd been able to draw a parallel that impressed her professor.

"Let me ask you one thing though," Peterson said.

Lauren waited quietly.

"Why take off anything at all then, if you're in fear that you're the only one who will? Why risk this emotional nakedness you speak of if you don't know the other person will reciprocate it?"

Lauren bit her bottom lip as she realized the implication of what she had said. She'd expected Scott to accept everything about her—all her baggage, her history—but she hadn't even shared much of it with him. She'd left him clues about Cooper but had never spelled it out for Scott in black and white, never told him the link between his comment and Cooper's death. "Because," Lauren sighed, "someone has to be the brave one and put themselves out there. Someone has to make the first move."

"Or what?"

"The relationship will be stagnant, devoid of any true closeness, any true intimacy."

Lauren watched a slight smile lift Dr. Peterson's lips. "Welcome to class, Ms. Hastings."

Lauren left class slightly shell-shocked. Like Oscar Wilde said: "Life imitates art far more than Art imitates life." It was as though Lauren was living so that her psychology classes could make more sense to her, be more relevant. Totally creepy, but effective.

As Lauren walked toward the library to do some work between classes, she dug into her bag and pulled out her phone. She figured she might as well send a text to the girls letting them know she was okay. But when she looked down at the screen, she saw that she had a voice mail from Scott. *Of course there is. Because my life is clearly one huge cosmic experiment.* Clicking on the voice mail, she held it up to her ear with an agitation she didn't really feel, but still felt entitled to.

"Uh, yeah, um, hi, Lo. I mean Lauren. It's me. Scott.

I . . . Christ, I'm so fucking awkward. I just wanted to call and apologize. I know you probably don't want to talk to me, but I just needed you to know that I'm so incredibly sorry. What I said was completely out of line and inappropriate. Even if your brother hadn't been gay, it was still insensitive for me to say. And I hope that you can forgive me."

There was silence then, and Lauren looked down at the screen, wondering if her voice mail had cut him off. But the screen showed that there was still more to the message. She put it back to her ear and waited.

"You're a good friend to me, Lauren. Please tell me I haven't fucked that up. Talk to you soon."

The hand that was holding her phone dropped to her side. She knew it had probably taken a lot for Scott to say that last part. He'd put himself out there a little. For her. And maybe, just maybe, he deserved the same courtesy.

Sighing, Lauren decided that it was time to be brave. Lifting her phone, she clicked on Scott's name. It only rang twice.

"Hello?"

"Hey. I got your message. I . . . I want to explain a few things. You going to be home tonight? Around seven?"

"Absolutely. I'll be there."

"Okay, guess I'll see you then."

"Yeah. And, Lauren?"

"Yeah?"

"Thanks for calling."

Lauren didn't know how to reply to that so she didn't. Disconnecting the call, she continued on her way to the library, hoping she didn't chicken out by seven.

Chapter 13

Post-Traumatic Stress Disorder

Scott didn't know what to expect. He knew he'd epically fucked up, and wanted nothing more than to fix it. But he wasn't sure if that was what *Lauren* wanted. So when her knock came a few minutes before seven, he was so anxious he nearly sprinted to the door.

But as he pulled it open to see Lauren holding a cup of coffee out to him, he felt relieved. Maybe it wouldn't be as difficult to fix as he thought.

"Here." She thrust the cup toward him. "Peace offering."

Scott took it from her warily, confused as to why *she* was the one bringing peace offerings.

"Don't worry. I didn't lace it with insecticide or anything."

She gave him a slight smirk that made some of the heaviness in his chest lift. "Thanks."

"Can I come in?"

Scott shook himself into action. "Of course," he said

as he stepped back from the door and allowed her to enter.

Lauren walked into the living room and sat down on the couch. "So, you're probably wondering what caused my temper tantrum Saturday night. I mean, I told you part of it, but I want to tell you the whole thing."

"You don't have to explain. It isn't my business." Scott desperately wanted to know where her anger had come from the other night, but he didn't want to push her into telling him. If she wanted to let it drop, then he'd force himself to do the same.

"No, you deserve to know. I just . . . What you said, the gay slur. I have a hard time with words like that, and not just because he was gay. It's . . . deeper than that." Lauren took a sip of her coffee and then wrapped her hands around the cup.

Scott waited, knowing Lauren was taking the time she needed to prepare herself to open up to him. Finally, she made her way further into his apartment and took a seat on the couch. He followed, settling in next to her, but consciously leaving a bit of distance between them.

Scott's eyes met hers, and he could see the pain in them. But this pain was different from the pain he saw Saturday night.

Scott watched Lauren fill her lungs with air before exhaling deeply. "He . . . he killed himself because of comments like the one you made Saturday. Because of people throwing words like 'queer' and 'fag' around like it's nothing. Like those words don't hurt, don't rip people apart, don't have the power to make people so ashamed that they can't bring themselves to share who they are with the people close to them. The people who wouldn't even care about their sexual orientation."

"I'm so sorry," Scott said as he moved to place a hand on Lauren's thigh tentatively. He expected Lauren to tense, maybe even pull away. But instead, she moved a little closer toward him. "I had no idea."

"No one did." Lauren sighed and let her gaze fall to the floor before bringing it back up. "Cooper was the best big brother. He was six years older and always looked out for me. I think he threatened every boyfriend I had growing up," she said with a sad chuckle. "When he was twenty-two, he graduated from college with a business degree that he didn't want to use. And since he didn't know what he actually did want to do, he just bounced around. When nothing stuck, he decided to join the Marines. I remember when he told us. We were shocked. He'd left to go on a job interview and then came home and announced that he'd joined the military."

She shook her head like she still couldn't believe Cooper's decision.

"But that was Cooper. He was so damn impulsive. He left for basic training a few months after that. I was almost through my sophomore year of high school when he shipped out to Afghanistan. I'd never been so terrified in my entire life."

Lauren took a moment to collect herself, and Scott remained quiet.

"He was gone for a little over a year. I expected that when he came home, Cooper would walk back into our lives just as he'd left it: happy, carefree, a little wild, funny. But he was different—more serious, regimented, distant.

He never talked about his time over there, and I was too self-absorbed to ask."

"You were a teenager," Scott interjected. "We were all like that." Scott shifted to a slightly more comfortable position and fell quiet.

"I guess. He was scheduled to be home for a few months before he'd have to report back to base and serve out the rest of his term. We all thought that was the plan. So when he announced that he'd be leaving for another tour in Afghanistan, we were devastated. Everyone tried to talk him out of it: my parents, me, Sam."

Lauren hesitated as if she'd said something she wasn't supposed to. And Scott picked up on it immediately. Though he already had a feeling he knew the answer, Scott couldn't help but ask. "Who's Sam?"

Lauren was quiet for a few seconds and leaned against Scott's shoulder so he could put his arm around her and stroke her biceps with his fingers.

"He was Cooper's best friend."

Scott wanted to let her go at her own pace, get out what she needed to, what she wanted to and not an ounce more. But something about it felt important, so he decided to pursue it and hope he wasn't making a mistake. "It sounds like there was more to it than that."

Lauren pulled away slightly so she could look up at him, a seriousness in her eyes he'd never seen there before. "The only other person who knows about this is Quinn, Scott."

She wasn't saying that she wouldn't tell him, but rather seemed as though she desperately wanted to. But he was pretty sure he understood her message: he was to take this to his grave or she'd put him there early. "You can trust me, Lauren."

She looked at him a beat longer before settling back down into the crook of his arm. "As far as I knew, no one had any idea as to the extent of Cooper and Sam's *friendship*. They seemed like typical best friends. Sam spent almost every spare minute at our house, but I never questioned it as being more. Until I saw them kiss in our pool one day when I was thirteen. I never told Coop that I'd seen them. I figured that if he'd wanted me to know, he'd have told me. I did kind of bring it up before his second tour though. I was home to see him off and I overheard him and Sam getting into it in his room, and then Sam stormed out. I remember standing in his doorway, afraid to walk in because of the anger that was radiating off of him. He finally whipped around, looked at me, and said, 'Spit it out, Lo.'" She laughed quietly at the memory. "He could read me like a freakin' book. I asked him why he was leaving, and he said it was just something he felt he had to do. Then I asked if it had to do with Sam, and he stopped dead in his tracks. He turned toward me, looking at me like he was trying to figure me out."

"So that's where you get that look from," Scott joked.

Lauren giggled. "Guess so. Anyway, he asked why Sam would have anything to do with his decisions." Lauren sighed heavily. "But I chickened out. I didn't tell him that I knew about them. It's one of my biggest regrets because I feel like if he'd known that I was okay with it, he maybe would have confided in me more—" Her breath hitched. "Like maybe if he had known that I knew and still loved him that he would still be here. But I just shrugged my shoulders and let the conversation drop. I didn't want to press it—and I regret that I didn't to this day."

"Do you really think he didn't know why you were asking?"

Lauren seemed to be thinking about Scott's question, as though she'd never considered it before. "I think he knew," she said quietly. She cleared her throat and continued. "He was gone almost nine months the second time. And whatever fragments of Cooper that had remained intact after the first tour seemed to be completely obliterated after the second. He was a shell of who he'd been. It makes me feel like an awful person, but at that time I was happy to be away at Dartmouth. I didn't want to have to watch him disintegrate. My parents tried to get him into therapy, but he refused. Said he was fine. We hoped that with some time, he'd come back to us. I'm pretty sure that he was suffering from undiagnosed PTSD, but I had no idea what that even was at the time."

Scott felt her quickly swipe at tears on her face. His heart broke for her, and part of him wanted to pull her closer and tell her she didn't have to say any more. But he knew that she needed this. Needed to get all of this off of her shoulders. Even if that meant putting some of it on his.

"I was home from school one weekend and I overheard him on the phone. My parents were out somewhere and he obviously didn't realize I was there. I don't know who he was talking to, but I always assumed it was Sam. He was yelling about how he couldn't do it anymore. That he felt like so many things were beyond his control, and that he wouldn't let that be one of them anymore. I figured that he meant being gay because he went on about how he almost killed some guy who'd called him a fucking queer." Lauren looked up at Scott briefly.

That's why it set her off so badly. It was the exact phrase he'd used the previous night. Scott hadn't even thought twice about saying it, and that made him ashamed.

"He asked the person on the phone how they could be so calm about it. Then Cooper yelled that he was done with it. That he'd endured more than any person should have to, and that when he came home, he wasn't even accepted by the people he'd risked his life for. My brother put his life on the line for over two years so that other people wouldn't have to. He did the dirty work so people could go on with their lives as if soldiers weren't losing theirs. And what did he get for it? He was called a queer for doing what made him happy. What felt natural. He hadn't been himself since he was deployed, and the *one* time he tried to, he gets harassed for it." Lauren's voice had steadily risen as she spoke. She took a calming breath before continuing. "Anyway, he ended the call, threw his phone against a wall, and took off. I can't explain why, Scott, but I was angry. I was mad because that man wasn't my brother anymore. I didn't know him at all and in that moment I didn't want to. I went upstairs, packed my stuff, and drove back to school."

Lauren shuddered as her tears started to come harder. "I turned my phone off because I didn't want to explain why I'd left early. I just wanted to use the drive to think. But when I walked into my room my roommate was frantic. She said my parents had been calling, that something had happened to my brother and I needed to call them back right away."

Scott shifted toward her and Lauren buried her face in his chest.

"When he left, it was to go out and buy enough pills to kill a fucking army. He had a few unfilled prescriptions for sleeping meds to help him readjust. He got them all filled at once from different pharmacies. Then he came home to an empty house, a house I should have been in, and took all of them. No note, no explanations, nothing. The war took a huge piece of my brother, and then assholes in his own hometown took the rest. And I wasn't there to stop him. I wasn't there to make it better, the way he'd made so many things better for me over the years. Instead I ignored him, I ignored his problems, and I let him suffer when I could have helped. He was only twenty-six. The same age I am now. What sense does that make?"

Lauren wiped away a tear that slid down her cheek, and Scott didn't know what else to do but to hold her. So that's what he did.

"I'm sorry," she laughed humorlessly.

"You have nothing to apologize for."

"Well, you know the rest of this story. I returned to school after taking a couple weeks off, went looking for a distraction, and found one in the form of a certain philosophy professor."

Scott wasn't sure why, but his stomach turned at the thought of a vulnerable, hurting Lauren getting involved with that scumbag because she needed an outlet. The bastard probably saw a weak, damaged girl and took immediate advantage. Scott was nearly overcome with the urge to hunt him down and follow through on the threat her father had no doubt issued. But instead, he tried to remind himself that comforting Lauren was more important than his own anger issues. But he couldn't resist saying what had been plaguing his mind since he'd first thought of it. "Cooper was the one who called you Lo?" He'd said it as a question, though it really wasn't one. He already knew the answer.

Lauren let out a noisy breath. "Yeah."

Scott held her tightly, and Lauren let him. Even though he was the one who had caused all of these emotions to surface, he was also the only one who could quiet them down again. She felt safe and comfortable in his arms, so much so that she found herself striving to get closer, wanting to melt as far into him as she could. Lauren felt the moment the air changed between them. She'd poured out her heart, and now she needed to forget about it, just for a little while.

Scott lifted his hand to her face, allowing his thumb to smooth over the worry lines that marred her forehead. "It's just you and me right now, Lo. No one and nothing else is allowed in here."

She understood what he was saying. Right then was all about feeling good. He was going to help her escape from regrets and hurt feelings. And she wanted nothing more.

He slid his hand down to cup her cheek, looked into her eyes for the briefest of moments, and then brought his lips to hers.

He took her mouth like he owned it. His hands groping at her waist, pushing her shirt out of the way so he could touch her bare skin.

Lauren wrapped her arms around Scott's neck and dug her fingers in his hair. The kiss was carnal, their tongues waltzing to a rhythm they could feel but not hear.

Scott began to walk them toward his bedroom. The movement should've been fumbling and clumsy, considering their size difference and the fact that they were too wrapped up in each other to be coordinated. But it wasn't. Everything about them in the moment was fluid and graceful.

When they arrived in the bedroom, Lauren decided she was going to take advantage of the opportunity to touch Scott as she'd so often fantasized. Their first time had been so rushed, so frantic and needy. Deftly, she began to undo the buttons on his shirt before sliding it down his arms, and letting it drift to the floor.

Scott pulled her tank top over her head in one motion, and then immediately crashed his mouth back to hers. His hands ghosted along the waistband of her jeans before he popped the button, slid down the zipper, and dropped to his knees. Thankfully Lauren had already kicked off her shoes, allowing Scott to easily pull her jeans from her legs. He kissed, licked, and nipped his way up her flat stomach, over her heaving chest, and along the ridge of her jawline.

Once he was standing again, Lauren went to work on his jeans, pushing them off his hips and moving backward slightly so he could undress.

He used his index fingers to pull her bra straps off of her shoulders before he reached around to unclasp it, letting it fall to their feet. He then pulled her flush to him.

Lauren had never felt anything as incredible as Scott's hard body. The taut muscles of his chest leading into the long, hard plane of his abdomen. She wanted to touch every part of him, so she did. She shifted back just enough to slide her hands over the ridge of his abdomen, the cut of his hips, the dusting of hair that led down to the last piece of the sexual puzzle in front of her. Deciding that she couldn't wait, she hooked her thumbs into the band of his boxers and dragged them down his thighs. She then took a step back to admire him. *All* of him. She hadn't done that before. And fuck, was Scott Jacobs impressive. His perfect cock demanded attention as it jutted from his body. She wanted her mouth on it yesterday.

She wrapped her fingers around the sides of her thong and drew it down her legs, leaving herself as bare as he was. Her gaze lifted to his, and she watched his eyes roam her body, taking her in as she stood before him. She took a step toward him and slowly dropped to her knees.

He briefly seemed like he was going to stop her, but didn't. She wanted this, and he let her have it.

Gingerly, she touched his cock, running her fingertips over it, feeling the hard steel covered in soft skin. Then she took him into her mouth, letting her tongue swirl over the tip before taking him deep. She felt him glide over her tongue as she forced herself to swallow so she could take more of him.

"Fuck," Scott said, his voice deep and rough. "That is so fucking good."

His words spurred her on, made her work him quickly and deeply.

Scott's hand rested on her jaw as he released one of the sexiest moans she'd ever heard. He allowed her to continue for a minute longer before stepping back, forcing her to release him. "Lie on the bed."

His command was simple and Lauren followed it without hesitation. She sat down on his bed and used her arms to pull herself to the middle of it, all the while keeping her eyes on his. She lay back, letting her hands rest by her sides.

Scott walked over to the bedside table and opened a drawer, removing a foil wrapper. "I had plans to do mind-blowing things to that magnificent body of yours, but you sucking my cock made me ache to be inside of you." He used his teeth to rip the wrapper open and then sheathed himself with the condom.

"I'm pretty sure mind-blowing is still in the cards," Lauren rasped.

Scott loomed over her as he placed his hands on either side of her head to support himself. "I'm pretty sure you're right," he uttered before he launched an assault on her mouth, his tongue pushing inside and wrestling seductively with hers. He moved one hand down to where she ached for him the most. "Let's see how wet you are for me." He plunged a finger inside, then two. "Goddamn, you're soaked. I'm dying to fuck you."

"Then fuck me," Lauren countered.

Scott leaned down again, his lips touching hers only briefly before he bit down on her lower lip. It wasn't enough to draw blood, but she got the message. Dr. Scott didn't take orders. He withdrew his fingers quickly before thrusting inside.

The movement was so fast, Lauren hadn't fully expected it, which made her gasp in both surprise and pleasure. He was seated deeply inside of her, giving her body time to stretch around him. The adjustment was a delicious mix of pleasure and pain. And then the pain subsided, and only pure, unadulterated pleasure remained. She craved friction, needed him to fucking move, but she knew better than to ask for it.

Finally Scott began to thrust, his cock rubbing against her walls, hitting every nerve ending on the way in and out. He growled as he lowered his head to her breast and he sucked her nipple into his mouth, teasing and nipping it in the best ways possible. His hands slid up and laced with hers, pulling them above her head on the bed and holding them there as he rocked into her. After a few minutes, he picked up the pace, pushing into her with a groan and hard, measured movements.

From the moment Scott had entered her, Lauren had felt her orgasm building. Tingling spread throughout her entire body, and she knew she would tumble over the edge soon.

As though he could sense her impending climax, Scott trained his eyes on hers. "You want to come? I can feel you tightening around me. You want me to get you off now?"

Lauren highly doubted he'd be able to stop her, but decided against voicing it. Mostly because she adored this side of Scott. And more importantly, she needed it. She needed him to take control. To let her forget everything but the feeling of him moving inside of her.

"Please. I'm so close."

Scott dipped a hand between her thighs and stroked her clit with his thumb. "Let go, Lo."

Lauren wasn't sure what made her orgasm harder, his thumb or his words. Not that she pondered it long. She was too caught up in the convulsions of release, the feel of his cock twitching inside of her as he exploded.

His whole body tensed with his climax, and the sight of his flexed muscles was almost enough to catapult her over the edge again. He pumped into her a few more times as he came down from his own orgasm. Then, as if he knew exactly what she needed, he pulled out, got up to throw the condom away in the bathroom, and returned to bed, pulling Lauren to him so he could hug her close.

And as she felt herself begin to drift off, there was nowhere else she'd rather be.

Chapter 14

Binging and Purging

Tuesday morning brought with it a whole new issue for Scott. Even though Lauren had left the previous night having forgiven him, he still knew that what he had said on Saturday was affecting her. It had to be. She'd been through something traumatic, and he'd catapulted her back to that time in her life with one sentence. So when she'd shown up for work, Scott gave her some space. Despite his intense desire to touch Lauren in any and every way he could imagine, he didn't. Because even though she looked the same, he could see the pain still clouding her eyes. He wanted to be there for her, though when the fuck being a good person trumped getting his dick stroked, he wasn't sure. But it had. And if he were honest with himself, he wasn't all that broken up about it. Someone else's feelings were more important than his cock. It was a relatively novel thought for him.

But when Lauren didn't go down to the cafeteria for lunch, he didn't let his disappointment show. And when she didn't initiate in any witty e-mail banter, he refused to send one just to bait her. But by the end of the day, he was exhausted from all the things he'd *refrained* from doing.

As he was staring at his computer screen, trying to waste time so that he didn't go into the office and pester Lo like an attention-starved puppy, she appeared. And she was smiling.

"You hiding out in here?" she teased.

"If I were, I should probably find a better spot." His lip quirked up in one corner.

She leaned against the doorframe and crossed her arms over her chest. It was one of the sexiest positions he'd ever seen a woman in.

"So, how ya been?" He didn't want to ask, but he had to. Because what else was there really to say? He couldn't ignore what they'd talked about Monday, and he also couldn't pretend that it wasn't causing a certain level of awkwardness between them.

"Working through it. Feeling better now than I was yesterday, or even this morning, for that matter." She dropped her hands and stood up straight, pinning him with that look that he'd started growing accustomed to—the deeply assessing one that made him feel like she could see through to his soul. "Thanks," she added.

"For what?"

She took a deep breath and let it out slowly. "For everything. For listening. For letting me freak out, for letting me fall apart, and then for helping put me back together again. And for giving me some space today. You obviously know how distracting you are." She said the last part with a grin that was both playful and seductive.

Scott didn't return the smile though. "First of all, you

didn't fall apart or freak out. I was a prick and you called me on it. As for the rest of it, I should be thanking you for trusting me with all of that. I know it took a lot for you to share it, and I'm ... just ... it was my pleasure." And then, because he was uncomfortable with his own seriousness, he added, "And you know how I love pleasure."

Lo rolled her eyes, but smiled wildly. "I do know. I also know you're pretty damn good at giving it."

"Very true," he agreed.

They just looked at each other for a bit, letting all of the weirdness that had settled between them evaporate.

"Well, my indentured servitude is over for the day. I'll see you Thursday."

"Wait. All that talk of pleasuring and now you're just going to leave?" Scott joked.

"Good things come to those who wait, Doctor."

And then she was gone. The tease.

As Lauren hefted her book bag onto her shoulder, she quickly rolled her neck from side to side before beginning to climb the steps toward the exit of the large lecture hall. She was so friggin' exhausted. Since classes had started back, she had been exceptionally busy with schoolwork, staying up later than usual to knock out a few papers and case studies. She'd also somehow allowed Scott to talk her into going to a Thursday night Redskins game the previous night. She didn't even really like football, but she had to admit that she'd had a good time. Not because of the game, but because Scott was simply a ton of fun to be around. He was funny, and flirty, and even downright goofy at times. It was a sharp contrast to his ever-serious demeanor at work. It was why she ultimately agreed to go with him even though she knew she had an early class the next morning. Watching Scott act his age was truly something to behold, and Lauren took advantage of every opportunity she got to witness it.

It also helped that Scott had two extra tickets and allowed her to invite someone. She chose Quinn since she could have fun doing just about anything. Scott was bringing Xavier for pretty much the same reason. She was a little worried about seeing him out again after her freak-out, but quickly decided that worrying about it wouldn't do any good, so she just let it go.

They'd decided to meet at Scott's apartment and leave from there. Scott was leaving work early, and told Lauren to do the same so she could get ready and be at his place by five. The building's security let her and Quinn right up when they arrived. She was surprised they'd even asked her who she was there to see this time. When she'd shown up the Monday after the club, she'd walked right up behind an old man and no one had questioned her.

"Does he have a butler too?" Quinn jibed.

"Only on weekends," Lauren replied as she hit the elevator button for Scott's floor. Once the elevator arrived at their destination, Lauren led Quinn toward his apartment. But just as she was about to knock, the door flew open and a man nearly barreled into her.

His hands shot out to keep her from falling over. "Shit, sorry."

Lauren's eyes looked down at the tattooed arms that held her upright. She began skimming her eyes up his biceps, over his broad shoulders, before finally landing on his face. She noticed a familiar pair of green eyes, but the man in front of her wasn't Scott. He was lean like Scott, but had a reddish copper tone to his hair and a light scruff over his jaw. He was taller too. Lauren wouldn't have called him attractive in the traditional sense, but he definitely held a girl's attention with a sort of bad-boy appeal.

"Trying to mow down my guests?" Scott's voice snapped Lauren out of her shock at almost being trampled by a stranger.

"You know how I like to make an impression." The man let go of Lauren and stepped back. "Are you okay?"

Lauren smoothed down her sweatshirt with her hands. "Yeah, I'm fine. You just startled me," she said with a smile.

"Lauren, Quinn, this is my brother, Tim. Tim, meet Lauren and Quinn."

Tim extended his hand toward Lauren first and she shook it. "Nice to meet you, Lauren."

"You too." She hoped her tone hid her surprise over not knowing Scott even had a brother.

Then he put his hand toward Quinn. "Pleasure, Quinn."

Lauren noticed the slight blush at Quinn's neck, probably at the double meaning of his words. She watched them shake hands, holding on to each other for a beat longer than what would have been considered normal.

Finally, Tim shook his head slightly as if to clear it. "Let me get out of your way. I just had to drop something off to my brother. Enjoy the game, kids." And with that, Tim took off down the hallway and disappeared onto the elevator.

Lauren looked at Scott, who smiled at her. "Come on in."

*   *   *

Lauren wasn't surprised that the tickets were practically on the field, though she was surprised by how caught up in the game she got. But sitting with two nut-job fans like Scott and Xavier would drum up excitement in anyone. She was almost sad when the night ended.

It had been weird—to be out with Scott when they both knew sex wasn't really an option—but a good kind of weird. It was actually crazy how their friendship had blossomed since Lauren had revealed how mortifyingly damaged she was. Things had been a little awkward at first, but she ultimately felt closer to Scott. They were even becoming good friends. *Friends.* Lauren tossed the word around in her mind as her class was about to start. *Who the hell saw* this *coming?*

But Lauren liked it—maybe a little more than she should. She was well aware that her sexual relationship with Scott had an expiration date, but maybe their friendship didn't. She was spending more time with Scott than her girlfriends lately, but she couldn't help it. And she knew she'd better damn well take advantage of it before he decided to move on. She tried to ignore the fact that she was now certain that it would be *him* that did the moving on. Lauren was at a point in her whatever-the-hell-it-was with Scott where ignorance was bliss. And she'd been spending *a lot* of time blissed out.

Scott leaned his hip against Lauren's desk. The past week or two he'd taken to pestering her as often as humanly possible. It was starting to matter less who saw him do it too. He explained it away by reasoning that he was entitled to bother whomever he wanted in his own practice. Lauren was typing on some spreadsheet, ignoring him completely. But he saw the curve of her lips, telling him it was intentional.

"I thought we'd moved past your weird staring tendencies," she said.

"I'm not staring at you. I'm looking at this disgrace you call a desk."

"Well, maybe if my boss didn't make sweatshop owners look lax, I'd have more time to tidy up."

Scott could barely hold back his laughter. The thrill that always shot through him when she referred to him as her boss never ceased to excite him. His dick twitched in his pants, but the invitation on her desk snagged his attention before he could reply and he picked it up. "Are you *really* going to this?"

Lauren slid her hands away from her keyboard and relaxed back into her chair. "Probably. My dad wants no part of it, and since I got an invite too, I figured my mom and I could go as each other's date."

Scott tried to keep his face neutral. On one hand, he didn't really want Lauren there for various reasons that he didn't want to explain to her. But on the other, he suddenly wondered what it would be like to take Lauren as *his* date. Not that he wanted a date. He didn't even want to go. But the curiosity was there all the same. "You heading down to the cafeteria?" he asked, feeling the need to change the subject.

Lauren locked her computer and stood. "Yup. Just let me grab my lunch."

Scott wasn't sure when exactly they'd started leaving

the office together—not caring who saw, but they had been doing it for a while. He was suddenly a little overwhelmed by how much their relationship had changed since they'd first decided to give into their mutual lust. They were no longer concealing their friendship, so it would be easy for people to get the wrong idea. He wasn't sure why he cared so much, but it seemed important in that moment. He was just beginning to slide his hand into his pocket when Lauren reappeared and handed him a brown paper bag.

"Don't act like you don't want it. It's better for you than whatever crap you'd buy downstairs."

Once her mom had grown tired of packing Lauren's lunch and started forcing her to pack her own, Lauren had brought Scott lunch a few times. Mostly whenever she was having something she knew he'd like. It had never felt like a big deal before. But right then, it did. Everything did.

"Thanks, Mom," he said dryly as he grabbed it from her.

She cocked her head slightly and observed him, probably noticing the change in his demeanor. She always fucking noticed. It was starting to piss him off how he couldn't get anything past her. "You're welcome, Son. You want to hold Mommy's hand as we walk downstairs? Or are you too big for that now?" Then she turned and led the way out of the office.

And even though he doubted whether he should or not, he followed her. Who cared if people talked? The two of them knew where they stood, and that was all that mattered.

As Lauren stepped into the hallway, Scott walked

closer to her. "I don't need you to hold my hand, but I have something else you could hold if you wanted to."

"Such a sweet-talker," Lauren teased. "It's nice today. Wanna eat outside in the courtyard instead?"

"Sure." He began to rummage through the bag lunch as they walked toward the elevator. "What's in here anyway?"

"Arsenic and rat poison."

"Very funny," he retorted, nearly laughing at how much he sounded like a ten-year-old.

"I'm not laughing." She boarded the elevator, which already held a few other people.

Scott followed her inside, and then reached over and snatched her lunch out of her hand. "I'll just take yours then." He started pulling things out of her bag and adding it to his.

"Don't you dare. That's mine!"

She tried to make a grab for it, but Scott lifted both bags above his head. "Not anymore."

She gripped his biceps and tried to pull his arm down, but he was too strong for her. "Scott, I'm about to start fighting dirty," she warned.

"Bring it, princess," he challenged with a smirk.

He watched as Lauren's hands flew toward him like wild birds, digging into his armpits, tickling him mercilessly. When the hell was the last time he'd been tickled? He had no idea. But he'd missed it. He tried to lower his arms enough to cover the area under attack, but she wedged her hands in. "Don't start a war you can't win." His breath caught at his words. He wasn't sure how Lauren would react to his mention of war, but she didn't seem to notice as she continued her ten-fingered assault.

She only ceased when the doors slid open and three more people boarded. But she continued to scowl at him until they arrived in the lobby.

As soon as the elevator doors opened, Scott squeezed out before the other riders, leaving Lauren to wait until the others got off. He made it outside to the courtyard, dropped the bags on the grass, and turned just in time to catch Lauren as she launched herself at him. He immediately took her down to the ground—not caring that he wouldn't normally act that way—pinned her hands above her head with one hand, and set about tickling her to death with the other.

She began to squirm uncontrollably, laughing so hard she could barely catch her breath. "No fair. You're cheating," she forced out between deep breaths.

"Cheating? You're crazy. I warned you not to start with me, but you didn't want to listen."

"But I didn't pin you down. You have an unfair advantage." She tried to wiggle out of his grip.

"You didn't pin me down because you *can't* pin me down. Don't blame your weakness on me."

"Whatever." She continued to try to fight him off, but when it became clear that he wasn't going to stop out of the goodness of his heart, she relented. "Okay fine, you win."

Scott stopped moving his fingers. "What was that? I didn't hear you."

"You're such a sore winner."

He wiggled his fingers against the soft flesh of her stomach.

"Okay, okay!" she yelled. "I said you win."

He reached his free hand up so he could use both to hold her hands above her head. "And why do I win, Lo?"

"Because you're freakishly strong," she quipped.

He leaned closer to her, their faces mere inches apart. "That's strike one."

"Because you're a stubborn ass."

"Strike two."

She studied him, looking into his eyes with her brilliant blue ones. Her voice was lower when she replied. "Because you'd never let yourself lose."

He looked down at her for a few seconds longer, letting whatever it was between them sink in until he had to pull back for fear of drowning in the feelings swirling there. "Can we eat now?"

"You're the one holding us up," she replied as she fixed her clothes and sat up.

He pulled the food out of both bags and set it before them. "Tuna salad?" he asked.

"Yeah. I kept it light on the mayo so I didn't have to hear you complain about it like I do when you order it from the cafeteria."

They ate in silence for a while, enjoying the sunny day and refreshing breeze. Scott watched an older woman walk up the sidewalk toward the building that housed his office.

She smiled as she approached them. "You two make a beautiful couple."

Scott froze, not sure what to say.

Lauren didn't hesitate though. "Thank you," she replied with that sweet, genuine voice of hers.

The woman nodded to them before she passed and went into the building.

Lauren nudged his arm with hers. "Don't overthink it. She was probably really only referring to me anyway."

He felt the tension leave his body. It was exactly what he'd needed her to say. The little wiseass.

Chapter 15

Heatstroke

Scott's eyes wandered around the large ballroom. Easily over two hundred people filled the space, making their way around the perimeter to bid on jewelry, tickets to sporting events, vacations, paintings, and other donated items. The philanthropic nature of many of the guests always surprised him because it was in such sharp contrast to their exterior, which—for many of them—was cold and unsympathetic. But as he watched them bid thousands of dollars for items that weren't worth anywhere close to that, he felt himself warm to the attendees a little more. Scott brought his attention back to the group of people in front of him at the sound of Hal Overton's chuckle.

"Scott, did you hear what Brian said? Isn't that funny?"

I have no idea, but it probably wasn't. The only thing that kept Scott from actually voicing his sentiment was the fact that he didn't want to be intentionally rude. These people hadn't done anything specific to make him not like them. In fact, he should have gravitated *toward* people like Brian and Hal—people who were used to fancy cars, fine dining, and ass-kissing. They were the type of people Scott had grown up around. But instead, he found himself annoyed by them. He preferred a loose pair of jeans, a cheeseburger from Charlie's, and people who were genuine. Maybe that's why he'd gotten along so well with Lauren over the past few months. He could sense her authenticity.

In an attempt to prevent Brian and Hal from picking up on his momentary absence from the conversation, he quickly flashed them a smile and exhaled a slight laugh before taking a bite of the crab cake on the plate in his hand. "Food's great," he said as a poor attempt to change the subject. Hal nodded his confirmation, and then continued talking to Brian. Scott was glad that his company seemed content to occupy each other, because what little attention Scott had been paying to the conversion disappeared completely when his eyes locked on Lauren, who had just entered the ballroom. Even over the distance that separated them, she was stunning. "Gentlemen, if you'll excuse me for a moment."

"Of course," came an equally distracted reply.

Scott wasn't sure who had said it because he was already moving toward the entrance to the ballroom. He tried to concentrate on making his stride seem casual and effortless. But the truth was, he couldn't cover the distance between them fast enough. As he said his "pardon me's" and "excuse me's" to pass through the crowd that had formed on the dance floor, he felt his heart thundering in his chest. He put his plate on a server's tray as he approached Lauren, finally catching her eyes as they struggled to peer above the mass of heads in front of her. She looked timid, unsure. It was the first time he'd ever seen her appear out of her element; and it didn't suit her.

Scott forced himself to slow down as he reached her, not wanting to seem too eager as he took his last few steps. He wasn't sure why he felt so happy to see her. He'd seen her at work a few days a week for the past two months, and spent time with her privately too. He chalked up his enthusiasm to how much more comfortable in his own skin she made him feel. With her there, he may actually enjoy the evening. But despite his internal self jumping up and down, wanting to yell *You're here!* his cool, collected exterior settled for a teasing *You look a little confused,* instead.

A subtle laugh escaped her. "And you look," she let her eyes roam his body from top to bottom and back up again, "pretty hot actually."

Part of Scott wished he could take back his greeting—say instead what he'd really been thinking. Maybe something about how Lauren's navy dress made her eyes bluer than ever. That he wanted to run his hands along the soft satin that hugged her chest until he couldn't bear to have her clothed anymore. Maybe he should have told her how beautiful she was with her hair up in loose curls, a few falling on her exposed back above her strapless dress.

But the larger part of him would never say any of those things to her, no matter how much he wanted to. Because even though those words would have been the absolute truth, they implied a level of intimacy that just wasn't there between them. So instead, he flashed her a charming grin, adjusted the jacket of his tux, and slid a hand in his pocket. "I do, don't I?"

"You're such a doofus," she said on a laugh.

"Doofus? What is this, the nineties?"

"Oh, please. Don't act like you remember anything about the nineties. You were too busy studying your way to excellence," she teased.

Scott took a step closer and spun around so he was standing beside her. "That's where you're wrong, Lo. I was *born* excellent."

"Do those cocky lines usually work for you?"

"*You* tell *me*. They've worked on you thus far," he said with a smile.

Lauren shook her head slowly. "Bastard," she whispered.

"Come on. Since you insisted on coming to this thing even though I tried to warn you about how boring it would be, I may as well show you around a little."

"How bad could it be with the great Scott Jacobs in attendance?"

"Still pretty fucking bad. Where's your mom? Why didn't you drive with her?"

"She doesn't understand the importance of being fashionably late, so I came by myself."

Scott's mind focused on the "came by myself" part, but again he filtered his thoughts. "Let's start by finding your table. It should be near mine. Since I own the practice, I get stuck sitting with the higher-ups, but I always insist that they keep me close to my team so I can escape when I need to and sit with familiar faces." With Lauren here this year, he wished even more that he could change his seat.

Lauren inched her head up again in an attempt to see where Scott was leading them.

Scott chuckled, and Lauren tilted her head in confusion. "What? What's so funny?"

"It's cute the way you think you can see over everyone if you stretch. You should have worn higher heels."

"I don't think they get much higher than this." Lauren slid her leg out from the slit in her long dress, allowing Scott a view that caused his cock to twitch.

Fuck the satin. I want to run my hands along her skin. "Those *are* pretty high. I don't even know how women walk in them."

She stepped closer to him. Not close enough to draw attention, but close enough to make Scott wish they were somewhere more private. "I'll let you in on a little secret," she whispered. "We don't either."

Scott laughed softly before resuming the walk toward Lauren's table. As he ushered her toward the other side of the ballroom, he consciously restrained himself from putting a hand on the small of her back, or tucking a stray strand of hair behind her ear. Instead, his hand gripped the coin in his pocket so tightly, he thought he might bend the metal.

Scott found Lauren's name at the table beside his. Some of their coworkers were already sitting down. Having already said his hellos, he waited beside the table while Lauren greeted everyone. "They should be serving dinner soon," Scott informed them, wanting to provide a reason for why he was still standing there.

"Okay, sounds good," Lauren said with a smile, but she remained standing. "I think I'll just take a look around at the auction while I wait. Do any of you want to go with me?

They all declined.

"I'll go," Scott offered. "I haven't checked it out yet. Before you got here, I'd been talking to Hal Overton for the past half hour."

Tammy rolled her eyes—a gesture Scott wanted to do himself.

"Should I know who that is?" Lauren asked.

"Consider yourself lucky that you don't," Tammy said, taking the words right out of Scott's mouth. "He's one of the hospital's upper admin, and possibly one of the most narcissistic people on the planet."

Lauren smiled. "Okay, so stay away from Hal Overton. Check. We'll be back. Lead the way, Doctor."

Lauren and Scott spent the next fifteen minutes perusing the silent auction. A few hospital employees stopped to talk to Scott as they made their way around the tables along the perimeter of the room, and Scott was surprised at how easily Lauren engaged in conversation with them about current events, their families, and even a few medical theories. "You're an anomaly—you know that?" Scott said, as Lauren admired a platinum heart necklace. He thought about how great it would look on her. Especially if it were the only thing she had on.

"Of course I am," Lauren answered playfully. "Why though?"

"I've never seen anyone who can engage every person they meet in meaningful conversation."

Lauren shrugged as if it were no big deal. "I like to talk."

"No, seriously. You can find something in common with *every*one within seconds. I've known some of these people for years, and know less about them than you found out in the first minute and a half."

"Thanks, I guess. It's really not that hard. I just ask them questions. People love to talk about themselves. I just let them talk. You can easily find a common interest, or maybe someone you know lived in the area where they grew up or something. You just have to try to look for it."

"Well, you're about to have to look pretty hard," Scott whispered.

Lauren seemed to take Scott's hint as she plastered a wide smile on her face and extended her hand toward the woman approaching them.

"Lauren, this is my mother, Susan. Mom, this is Lauren Hastings. She just started working in the office." Every year since his father had passed, Scott tried to figure out a way to dissuade his mother from attending the benefit, but could never come up with a viable excuse. So he settled for trying to limit his interaction with her as much as possible.

Lauren extended her hand. "It's a pleasure to meet you, Ms. Jacobs."

"Likewise," Susan replied, giving Scott a peck on the cheek after shaking Lauren's hand.

"Did you get a chance to take a look at the items for auction?" Lauren asked. "We just took a walk around."

"I did. I bid on the trip to St. Lucia. I've never been, and I've heard such great things about it."

Lauren stole a glance at Scott and gave him a smile that let him know she was about to work her magic once again. "St. Lucia's beautiful. It's different from most islands because it has so many trees. And they're all just so green. I took the most amazing pictures when I was traveling there."

Scott wasn't sure how he felt about his mother and Lo interacting. It felt like introducing an angel to original sin.

"I've been trying to take more pictures myself actually. Scott bought me one of those fancy digital cameras where you don't have to change the lenses, but I still need to learn to use it."

"Yeah, I know what you mean. They seem like a good idea in theory, but they're so hard to use. I just used my phone to take pictures when I was there."

Scott listened to the conversation, jumping in when he thought he should, but was mostly content to stay out of it.

After a few minutes, his mother excused herself to find her seat. "Lauren, it was lovely meeting you. Scott, I'll see you at the table, honey."

"Your mom's sweet," Lauren said once Susan was at a safe distance from them. "You don't get along well?"

"Like I said, you're an anomaly."

Fifteen minutes later, most of the guests were seated at their tables, eating the first course. Though Scott preferred his salad without grass and leaves, he did his best to eat it. He made small talk with some of the people at his table, but his attention was focused elsewhere. From his vantage point, he could see Lauren out of the corner of his right eye, and she seemed to be enjoying herself as she chatted with the others.

"So how are you enjoying working for us?"

Scott stopped chewing midbite at the sound of Jim

Prescott's voice. Clearly, his question had been directed at Lauren since she was the only new employee in the office, and Scott's muscles instantly tensed. Lauren had spent the last hour effortlessly engaged in conversations she'd probably rather not be. So he wasn't sure why he felt the need to protect her from *this* one. But he did. He wanted her out of Prescott's line of fire.

The bastard had been bitter since before Scott's father passed away. But truth be told, Scott couldn't say he blamed him. Jim had worked with Scott's father for over twenty years. He was a good doctor who had dedicated his life to the practice. He'd never married, had no children. His job was his entire life. And Jim assumed that those qualities would make him a sure partner in the practice.

Unfortunately for Jim, Edward Jacobs had different intentions. Once he learned of his son's plans to go to medical school, Ed had his heart set on Scott taking over his practice one day. It was the ideal situation. Ed had spent his life building his practice, devoting every free minute that he wasn't with his family to ensuring that his life's work would be successful long-term.

But despite Ed's honesty about his hope that Scott would one day be a partner and eventually take over the practice, Jim held on to a different hope—one that involved Scott deciding that medical school wasn't for him. For years, Jim waited, holding on to a slim chance that all of the time he'd put in to the practice would eventually earn him partner status.

But it never happened. Instead, Scott had graduated from medical school, and his father had passed away unexpectedly, making Scott the sole owner of the Jacobs'

Family Practice. Had Jim been less resentful of Scott's success, he might have made Jim the partner that Ed never had. But Jim let his bitterness get the better of him, and there was no way Scott would make someone like him a partner in what his father spent his life building.

But Scott couldn't bring himself to get rid of Jim either. He was a friend of Scott's father, and Scott wouldn't dishonor his dad by firing a man Ed had worked with for so many years. No matter how much he wanted to.

"Working there's fine most of the time," Lauren answered. Out of the corner of his eye, Scott could see her smile politely from across the table.

"Not exactly a ringing endorsement," Dr. Atler chimed in. While she was also bitter about Scott's inheritance of the practice, her anger was more rooted in having to call a much younger man her boss.

Not wanting Lauren to feel attacked, Scott almost spoke up, but instead cleared his throat loudly, hoping Florence and Jim would get the message.

But if the message was inferred, Jim didn't bother listening to it. "I agree—interesting that you should feel lukewarm about a job that was basically handed to you on a silver platter. What do you mean *most* of the time?"

Scott had had enough. It was one thing for them to be rude to *him*. They had a history. But Lauren hadn't even been around the other two doctors very often. Just the one Friday she had worked, and the few times they'd needed to fit patients in at that office. They had no reason to go after her. She wasn't involved in any of the intraoffice drama. Scott knew they were only targeting her because he had hired her without consulting them. But he didn't owe them that courtesy. He didn't owe them *anything*. And Scott would be damned if they were going to insult her and not expect him to stop it.

Just as Scott was about to stand and speak up, Lauren beat him to it. Evidently she wasn't going to tolerate their rudeness either. "I didn't think it needed much explanation," she said calmly as she put her fork down on her plate.

Assertive Lauren was making an appearance, and Scott instantly felt like a kid staying up to watch a movie he shouldn't be seeing. He settled back in his chair with his imaginary popcorn and waited for the show.

"With the exception of a few days here and there, I've loved my job at Jacobs' Family Practice. Dr. Scott and the nurses are wonderful to work with.

Scott watched her sit back and fold her hands in front of her out of his periphery. She was gearing up for battle. He almost felt bad for Jim and Florence.

"Lauren," Pam scolded.

"That's okay, Pam," Prescott stated. "So I'm assuming you neglected to mention me in your list of people you love working with intentionally."

Scott felt bad for Pam. After all, she had to continue to work with the two doctors Lauren was probably going to verbally eviscerate in a matter of seconds. But ultimately Scott was the boss, and he had no intention of stopping Lauren from defending herself.

"If we're speaking candidly, then yes, it was intentional."

Scott felt his chest vibrate with the chuckle that he tried to suppress. *That's my girl.*

Prescott huffed out a bewildered laugh. "And you think the what—maybe four times we've crossed paths—were enough to form a lasting opinion of me?"

"I think four times is *more* than enough. Especially since our current interaction isn't exactly proving my opinion inaccurate."

"If I may ask, what *is* your opinion, Miss Hastings?"

Lauren hesitated for a moment. "My opinion is that you're probably a very knowledgeable doctor who somewhere along the way let resentment cause him to lose sight of himself."

How Lauren's observation had been so dead-on, Scott didn't know. Not that he should've been surprised. Lo had always been able to read him like a book, and he knew better than to think this was something unique to *him*. Scott wasn't sure how Prescott would respond to that, so Scott prepared himself to intervene if necessary.

After a tense minute, Prescott cleared his throat. "I stand corrected. Maybe you did have enough time to form an opinion of me. If you'll all excuse me." Jim stood and made his way across the ballroom, eventually leaving Scott's line of sight.

"Lauren, not every battle needs fighting," Pam scolded.

"Hey, you raised me," Lauren retorted, clearly trying to lighten the mood.

"Yeah, well, I blame your father."

"Whatever helps you sleep at night." Lauren smiled as she leaned over and gave her mom a quick hug.

Thankfully, the rest of the dinner passed without incident, and when there was an announcement made that there would be a fifteen-minute break before dessert so people could place the last of their bids, Scott excused himself from the table because he wanted to take a last-minute look at a few of the items for auction. He couldn't go to this event and not bid on something. So he placed a bid on some tickets for a Redskins game and a few other small things before turning to head back toward his table.

Weaving through the chairs and people as others found their seats too, he heard his mother chatting up a small group of people. Knowing he'd regret stopping, he willed himself to keep moving and not even bother trying to hear what she was going on about, but he couldn't help himself from listening in as he passed.

"It's so good of Scott to participate in work like this for the less fortunate. So many of them turn to drugs. It's the lack of a strong family that drives them to it. I'm just so glad I was able to instill better values in my boys."

Scott felt his entire body tense. *Is she fucking kidding?* Scott wanted to interrupt. He wanted to march up to his mother and tell her in front of those people whose asses she was kissing that she destroyed their strong family. That she hadn't instilled anything but bad examples. It was why he believed so strongly in this charity, because it was the kind of thing that may have helped Tim, since his mother clearly wasn't up to that task. But she was up to glad-handing around a party where her presence forced his brother's absence.

But he couldn't. Making a scene wasn't the answer, though he wasn't sure what was. *Fuck it.* He stalked back to his table and willed himself not to let her ruin his night.

*   *   *

Scott returned to his table just after dessert had been served. Lauren took note of his rigid shoulders and the firm line of his mouth as he approached. He ran a hand across the worry lines in his forehead and then down his smooth face before he sat down, scooting his chair in roughly and turning it toward the stage.

Clearly, something had happened when he'd gotten up from the table. She just wasn't sure what. For a brief moment, she considered getting up and going over to him, but she logically knew that that wouldn't be well-received. Not with a room full of important people watching. It would definitely go past the invisible boundaries of their relationship—of that she was sure.

Lauren took slow bites of her chocolate ice cream and every so often stole a glance at Scott, whose expression hadn't softened since returning to the table. She wasn't sure exactly how much time had passed as she watched him. Several people got up to speak but Lauren hadn't been listening.

Until she heard a name she recognized: Dr. Scott Jacobs. *What the fuck?* He hadn't told her he'd be speaking. Not that he really should have. But he'd said he hated these events, and now he was a part of it.

As Scott stood, buttoned his jacket, and made his way to the stage, she saw it—the cool facade she knew so well. On the outside, he appeared calm, at ease. But she knew the inside held something entirely different. Especially as she watched his hand drift into his pocket once he settled himself at the podium on the small wooden stage. She wondered if anyone else had noticed it. She assumed his mother would have. He glanced from side to side with a practiced confidence, silently waiting for the applause to die down before speaking. If he didn't have it already, his deep voice commanded the audience's attention. "I promise to keep this short," he began. "I know you all have families to get home to. I'd just like to thank everyone for coming tonight. As many of you know, when this foundation first began five years ago, we only had a handful of people and some small donations to speak of. But gradually, as more people learned of the First Chances organization, donations grew." And that's when Lauren saw Scott's face become more genuine. Whatever had burdened him earlier no longer seemed to hold any weight. His eyes revealed the emotion he seemed to be trying to convey. "And now, because of all of your generosity, we've been able to keep hundreds of children from making decisions that ruin not only their own lives, but also the lives of their families." Scott paused to allow the audience to applaud, and Lauren found herself clapping along with them. "Your money has helped to build rec centers, fund after-school programs and activities, and teach kids about the dangers of drugs and alcohol."

Lauren leaned in toward her mom to finally ask the question she'd been wondering about since Scott began speaking. "Why is *Scott* the one discussing the charity?"

Lauren's mother turned toward her, obviously surprised at Lauren's question. "Because," she answered quietly, "he's the one who founded it."

Lauren had been too distracted to listen to the rest of Scott's speech. She'd spent the remainder of it contemplating her latest discovery. Scott hadn't told her the charity was his. In fact, he hadn't said much about it at all.

Except not to go because he hated events like it. But she wasn't sure why he'd tried to dissuade her from attending. It didn't seem like Scott to shirk credit he'd worked hard to earn. But before she could think too deeply about it, she was interrupted by people standing to applaud again. She noticed a number of people go up to him to shake his hand and talk to him after he left the stage.

Finally Scott made his way back toward their tables as some of the guests moved to the middle of the floor to dance. When he reached Lauren's table, he slid into an open chair beside her. "Thought that would never end," he confessed.

Lauren's eyebrows furrowed in confusion, and Scott seemed to get the message.

"I know you'd probably assume someone with looks like mine would love a room full of people staring at him, but I actually hate public speaking."

Scott laughed, but Lauren remained serious.

"Are you kidding me right now? This charity is *yours* and you didn't tell me? I feel like such a jackass."

"Hey, if the shoe fits."

Lauren slapped him on the arm, but couldn't resist smiling. As much as she enjoyed serious, demanding Scott, she liked playful Scott just as much. "I'm being serious."

"Okay, I guess I may be slightly to blame for you feeling like a jackass." Scott gestured with his finger and thumb to show just how small of a role he believed he played. "Although, in my defense, I figured your mom would have told you."

"She thought I already knew. Which I *should* have." Lauren widened her eyes at him, putting on a show of pouty disapproval. "And why'd you tell me not to come?

You made up all of that bullshit about how it would be boring and you'd have to kiss people's asses."

Scott leaned back in his chair, which put him closer to Lauren, who at some point had shifted in her seat to face him. "First of all, I have never and will never tell you not to come. That's blasphemous." He smirked, clearly pleased with his play on her words. "And second, I have kissed my fair share of asses tonight."

Lauren looked at him skeptically.

"Fine, I may have been a little vague." He flashed a boyish grin that Lauren wanted to slap and kiss off of his face simultaneously. "I stand by my warning about it being boring though." Scott glanced at the dance floor, which was becoming increasingly crowded.

He seemed to be contemplating something, his bottom lip pulling under his teeth ever so slightly. When he looked back at her, he looked younger—more open— almost carefree. "Dance with me."

It wasn't a question. And everything inside of Lauren told her that she wouldn't have refused him even if it had been. But she also didn't want to cause issues for him. So she hesitated.

And as if he could read her mind, Scott stood and extended his hand to her. "I don't care what they think, Lo."

Scott's reply had been simple, but it sent a rush of heat through Lauren's core. And the way he led her to the dance floor without any concern for the pairs of eyes that fixated on them made her want to skip the dance and leave with him right then. Visions of Scott's mouth on hers dominated her thoughts, probably because she knew they wouldn't be able to touch each other the way they'd want to there.

They danced easily—two people moving to the rhythm of the soft music. Somehow, both of them knew where the other was headed. Lauren got lost in Scott's cool green eyes, which looked darker than they'd seemed to her before. She asked about the charity, and Scott told her how he'd started it with his father's help. Drawing in closer to him, she rested her head against his chest. "Why this charity?"

Lauren felt Scott's grip tighten around her waist, and he dropped his chin to her shoulder. "I guess the charity's my way of fixing something for others that I wasn't able to fix for someone close to me. It probably sounds stupid, but I'm hoping I can do some good to make up for a time when I didn't do enough."

Lauren drew back so she could look up at him. She could see the unease in his face, hear the self-consciousness in his voice. It didn't suit him. "Oh come on. Like you've ever sounded stupid."

And Scott did what she'd hoped he would: he smiled. "Let's talk about something else," Scott said softly as he dropped the formal hold he'd had on her and slid both hands around her waist. "Like what I plan to do to you once I get you back to my apartment."

Lauren's face tilted innocently to the side as she prepared to play his game. "And what might that be, Dr. Scott?"

"I think I'll start by taking down this hair. I want to be able to pull on it later."

Lauren's whole body nearly shook with the need to push her hips hard against him. She wondered if Scott was as turned on as she was. She seriously doubted it. "What else?"

Scott thought for a moment before answering. Though

something told her he already knew exactly what he planned to say. "What would you say if I asked you to strip for me? Seeing you in this dress," he slid his fingers delicately up her spine, "makes me want to see you out of it."

Lauren bit her lip, reminding her how much she missed Scott's teeth on her skin. "I'd say that sounds like a plan."

They held each other for a while longer, moving at their own pace before Scott spoke again. "This is nice. Having your here. Dancing with you like this. Though it's a lot different from our previous experience."

Lauren laughed softly, remembering the last time they'd danced together at the club. It had been hot—full of sweat and sensuality. But this ... this was something different entirely. It was more real. The man who guided her across the dance floor effortlessly was the man who'd gradually emerged over the past two months. And dancing with *that* Scott felt different. She loved that he'd finally let her in a little—let her see the man behind the rigid, cocky curtain.

"Yeah," she finally said. "I've actually never done anything like this before."

"Well, I'm glad I got to be here for it."

And so was she.

Lauren and Scott made it back to his apartment a little after midnight. The moment the elevator doors had closed, locking them away from the outside world, Scott couldn't keep his hands off her. He'd spent the majority of the benefit waiting to move his lips across her neck, down her collarbone, and he'd be damned if he'd have to wait a second longer.

He pulled off his tuxedo jacket, throwing it somewhere before brushing Lo's soft curls to the side so he could plant a trail of kisses along her jawline. She inhaled a sharp breath as Scott stroked the side of her throat with his thumb and gripped the back of her neck so he could pull her closer. "You like that?" He already knew the answer, but there was something about hearing Lauren's breathy "yes" that he couldn't get enough of.

"I love *everything* you do."

Well, fuck if that didn't turn him on even more. "You haven't even begun to see everything I can do." He guided her toward his bedroom, sucking on her neck and letting his hands roam over her body the entire way. "This slit pisses me off," Scott said against her neck as his hands rubbed the exposed skin on her thigh.

"Why?" Lauren panted.

"Because ripping clothes off of your body is a fantasy of mine. But on this dress, the job's already been done."

"I'll choose more carefully next time."

"Good idea." Once in his room, Scott left Lo standing while he reclined back on the bed, using his elbows to prop himself up, raising an eyebrow to see if she was as good at reading him as she seemed to be.

He watched a slow, sexy smile overtake her lips. As she reached behind her back and slowly dragged the zipper down, she didn't try to stop the satin from dropping to the floor. With Lo standing before him in a dark purple, strapless bra with black lace overlaid on the cups with a matching thong, he somehow got harder. And the stilettos she still wore made every muscle in her legs flex in the sexiest ways.

She's trying to kill me. As with every time Scott was

with Lo, he felt as though his cock had never been so hard. He felt the precum bead at his tip and soak into his boxers.

Lauren's hands stayed at her back as she unhooked her bra. But this time, she didn't let it drop. Instead, she crossed her arms over her breasts as her eyes remained locked on his. Her seductive smirk made his whole body tingle with anticipation. Then she dropped her hands, letting her bra join her dress at her feet.

He watched as her fingers ghosted down her flawless skin until her thumbs hooked into her thong. She lifted her eyebrows at him.

"Do it, baby."

She immediately pulled the material down her thighs until gravity took it the rest of the way.

"The heels stay on," he warned.

"I had no intention of taking them off." She moved toward him, bending over him when she reached the bed. "You have too many clothes on."

"You'd better do something about that then."

He watched her tongue dart out and wet her bottom lip as she pulled off his shoes and socks. Then her hands trailed up his legs, over the inside of his thighs, narrowly and purposefully missing his cock. She undid his belt, popped the button on his pants, and unzipped them before freeing his body of them. She then went to work on his shirt, starting with the buttons at the bottom, smoothing her hands up his torso as she worked.

After she'd gotten all of the buttons undone, he sat up to remove his cuff links so she could push the shirt off his shoulders. Lauren gripped his undershirt and lifted it over his head. Only his boxers remained.

Lauren pushed him back onto the bed, rested her weight on one hand beside him, and grazed the fingers of her other hand over his chest, down his muscled abdomen, before caressing the skin just above his waistband.

As much as Scott was enjoying the seductive temptress side of Lo, if he wasn't inside of her soon, he was going to lose his fucking mind. "Take them off."

Her eyes lifted to his, her fingers still fluttering across his skin. "Whatever you say, Doctor." She straightened slightly so that her legs could support her weight as she grabbed the band of his boxers and pulled them down, allowing his cock to finally spring free. Her eyes immediately went to his hard length.

Scott let her ogle him for a moment before he pointed at his bedside table. "Get a condom out of that drawer and then get your sexy ass over here."

Lo felt the smack of Scott's palm on her ass as she leaned across the bed to retrieve the condom. Then she settled back over him, straddling his thighs. She ripped the condom open, tossing the wrapper to the floor before slowly dragging the latex down his length as it stretched to accommodate him. He let out a low growl in response. And as she remembered what it was like to sheath Scott's cock with her own body, she felt her internal muscles clench.

Scott's hands skated over Lauren's breasts, feeling their fullness until one hand settled on her nipple and his fingers gave it a sharp pinch. His other hand landed solidly around his erection as he pumped himself slowly. Lo let out a soft moan as she watched him grip himself tightly, pull on his cock, and drag his palm over his tip in quick circles.

Before long, her own hand slid down her stomach to massage her clit while she ground against the base of Scott's dick. After a few minutes, Lauren leaned down, her chest almost flush with Scott's as she pressed her lips to his. Scott reached both hands around to Lauren's back, his fingertips pressing roughly against her skin to massage her. She felt relaxed, comforted, and more fucking turned on than she'd ever remembered feeling. "This feels so good, Scott."

Scott let out a soft chuckle against her throat before speaking. "I've been aching to be inside you since I saw you walk into that ballroom." Scott slid his hand between them, pushing Lo's out of the way so he could be the one to stroke her. "And by how fucking wet you are, I bet you can't wait much longer either."

Lauren let out a heavy breath at Scott's expert touch. "That's a bet you'd win." When she felt the tip of Scott's cock graze her entrance, she wiggled to help him inside her.

Scott seemed to understand her silent plea, and in one movement, he grabbed the base of his cock to direct himself right where Lo wanted him. When she felt his tip push inside her ever so slightly, she couldn't stop herself from coming down hard on top of him. She took all of Scott at once, and the fullness she felt as his cock rubbed her walls in all the right ways let her know she wouldn't last long. At least not if she kept grinding on top of him like she was.

Scott's hands guided her hips back and forth, causing

her orgasm to build rapidly as her clit brushed just above his cock. Then his hands moved to her ass, his fingertips digging into her flesh in the most delicious way.

"Faster, Lo," he said, moving her so that she had no choice but to comply with his request. His hands moved up to fist in her hair, pulling on it just hard enough to tilt her head back so he could kiss the front of her throat.

She relished the feeling of being on top of him, riding him while his lips and tongue brushed over her skin like they were searching for a spot they hadn't discovered yet. But Scott already knew every inch of her—knew every touch and movement that would make her come undone.

And she was dangerously close to it. She rocked against him, swiveled her hips in circles, and leaned up until only his tip remained inside her. Then she'd push onto him again, enjoying the feel of him filling her completely.

He plunged in and out of her, letting their rhythm guide his every thrust. Intentionally, she clenched herself tightly around him, feeling how hard he was inside her. She could feel her climax nearing whether she wanted it to or not.

Scott groaned as he sped up, the sound vibrating against Lo's neck. "You with me?"

And she was. In every way. "Yeah," she breathed. "I'm with you."

Scott's eyes found hers, his gaze settling on her face as she dangled on the verge of release. "Good," he said as he pumped into her harder, faster until she felt she'd let go at any moment. "Come with me." His breathing was heavy, and she could tell he was trying to hold off as long as possible. "Right now, Lo. I want to feel it."

If his movements hadn't already gotten her so close that there was no turning back, his words would have been her undoing. Waves of pleasure spread through her, and she knew he could feel them too. Then Scott jerked sharply into her a few more times, groaning as she felt his cock twitch with release.

She collapsed on top of him, not wanting to separate her body from his. But realizing she had to, she climbed off of him—holding the ring of the condom so it stayed on—and lay down beside him.

"God, that was so fucking good," Scott said to her before placing a kiss on her forehead and getting up to remove the condom.

"It always is," Lauren said so quietly that she wasn't sure he heard her.

Chapter 16

Addiction

The weeks following the benefit were much like the weeks leading up to it: class, work, Scott. Lauren had spent a little time with her friends, but still not as much as usual. They didn't call her on it, giving Lauren the space to do her own thing. Though she had to admit that she missed them. So when Quinn called to see if Lauren wanted to get together and just putter around town the Sunday after Thanksgiving, she jumped at the chance.

She had just finished pulling her hair into a ponytail and applying a little makeup when her phone rang.

"Hey, I was just about to leave to meet you. What's up?"

"Don't kill me, but I need to cancel," Quinn said, sounding frazzled. "My boss just called and I need to cover some stupid community festival. My job sucks. I swear, as soon as I get home I'm sending my résumé out to every newspaper and magazine I can find. I'm so sorry, Laur."

Lauren laughed as she plopped down on her bed. "No problem. Maybe one night this week we can all get together."

"Yes, totally. I'm in. Let's talk to the girls and see if we can set something up."

"Okay, sounds good."

"All righty. Thanks, hooker. I'll talk to you soon."

"Later, tramp." Lauren hung up but kept looking down at her phone. She was all dressed with nowhere to go. Scrolling through her contacts, she decided to stop pretending she wanted to hang out with anyone else. She found the number she was looking for and pushed Call.

"Dr. Scott's Sex Hotline."

"Aww, you got a second job?" Lauren asked with a laugh.

"It's more of a hobby. What's up?"

"I'm bored and am officially appointing *you* in charge of rectifying that."

"Oh really? I bet I could come up with a few things. I'm actually on my way to my brother's for dinner if you want to come."

"I don't want to intrude," Lauren drew out.

"Yes, you do. It's not a big deal. Just a meal and some football watching. I'll pick you up in twenty minutes."

As Lauren approached the door to Tim's apartment building, she found herself getting surprisingly nervous. Though it was just a casual dinner and she had met Tim briefly before, Lauren was starting to realize that she really didn't know much about him at all. Scott had only mentioned him a handful of times in passing.

"Is this weird? That I'm here, I mean?" She could hear the panic in her voice.

Scott stared at her for a moment, the lines in his forehead revealing his confusion. "No, why would it be weird? You're just eating dinner with us."

"I don't know . . . I just . . . This all feels very domestic."

Scott slid his hand around the back of Lauren's neck, letting his fingers tangle in her hair a moment before using his other hand to tilt her chin up to him so their eyes locked. "It's dinner. It's supposed to be. Wait 'til I tell Tim you said he's domestic." Scott chuckled as he knocked on the door.

"Come on in," a deep voice called from inside.

Scott opened the door, gesturing for Lauren to go in first. From the front door, she could see the majority of the apartment. It was small and sparsely furnished, but neat. To their left was a living and dining room combination, which had only a cream sofa and small glass table with four chairs. Several open boxes were scattered around the floor. She could see Tim in the kitchen straight ahead, but he was busy chopping something on a cutting board.

"Smells great," Scott said. "How can we help?"

"We?" Tim asked, clearly confused as he spun around and grabbed a dishtowel to dry his hands. His eyes seemed to light up at the sight of Lauren, and he took a few quick strides toward her with his hand extended. "Sorry. Scott didn't tell me he was bringing someone." He shook Lauren's hand and gave her a welcoming smile.

Scott shrugged. "What's one more? Let's eat. I'm starving."

"I apologize for my brother's lack of common courtesy, Lauren," Tim joked as he headed to the cabinet and set three glasses on the counter.

Lauren laughed, impressed that Tim remembered her

name. "It's nice to actually get to talk to you this time. Scott's told me a lot about you." Lauren had meant for her comment to be standard: a polite greeting. The problem was, it wasn't the least bit true.

"Oh, he has, has he?" Tim turned toward them again, casually leaning against the dark granite counter.

Lauren felt her stomach drop. "Um—"

"Let me guess," Tim said as he slid a hand over the strawberry blond scruff on his face. "He told you how ruggedly handsome I am?" And that *was* the truth. Tim looked a little more rough around the edges than Scott, but she had no doubt that he attracted his fair share of women.

Lauren shifted her focus to Scott as Tim opened the fridge. "Guess the cocky gene runs in the family," she said with a laugh, and the men joined in.

"Now what can I get you to drink?" Tim opened the fridge before waiting for her to reply. "I have iced tea, Coke, water. Sorry. I don't keep alcohol in the house."

Lauren's brain stuttered at his words, trying to figure out if there was a deeper meaning behind them. But she recovered quickly. "Oh, iced tea's great. Thanks."

Tim poured the tea and handed her the glass. Then he handed Scott a glass of milk.

Lauren looked at him, disgusted. "Why are you drinking milk?"

Scott shrugged. "Old habits die hard, I guess. My mom used to make me drink it every night for dinner. I still do. Unless we're at a restaurant. That would just be too embarrassing."

"For *you* or the people you're with?" Lauren teased.

Scott smiled. "I guess both."

"That's my baby brother for you." Tim continued to chop up some vegetables. "Make yourselves at home. I'm just finishing up with the salad. Turkey and stuffing should be ready in a few minutes. Do you eat homemade cranberry sauce, Lauren? Or are you one of those weirdos who prefers the canned stuff?" Tim's expression let her know he was only partially kidding.

"Either really. It all smells delicious," Lauren replied as she wandered through the living room and plopped down on the couch with Scott, who grabbed the remote to turn on the TV to Sunday football. They relaxed on the couch, Lauren snuggling into Scott's chest and Scott pulling her in close to him as they watched the Redskins game.

Twenty minutes later the three of them were seated around the table with their plates piled high. "It's all amazing. Where'd you learn to cook like this, Tim?" Lauren asked after she swallowed a bite of mashed potatoes. "Actually, the better question is if *that* trait's hereditary like the cockiness gene." She looked to her left at Scott. "Does your talent extend beyond breakfast foods?"

Scott ignored Tim's widened eyes and gave Lauren a seductive smirk and laughed. "Oh, I have many talents you've yet to enjoy." He put a hand on Lauren's thigh under the table. "But unfortunately for you, cooking's not one of them."

Tim shot Scott a look of feigned disgust. "Could you at least wait until you leave before you start seducing my guest?"

Scott threw a napkin across the table at Tim.

"My mom taught me to cook," Tim said, finally answering Lauren's question. "I used to help her in the kitchen when this one was still running around in diapers." He gestured across the table at Scott, who had just started buttering his corn bread. "But I also went to culinary school and work as a chef." Tim picked up his water and took a sip. "I'm starting to think Scott didn't tell you as much about me as you insinuated," he added with a wink.

Lauren felt herself blush and quickly changed the subject. "I can't believe you made an entire second turkey for just the two of you. I figured you would still have leftovers from Thanksgiving," Lauren said.

Tim looked across the table at Scott questioningly and then back at Lauren. "Scott, didn't you tell her?"

"Tell me what?" Lauren asked slowly, and Scott reached his arm around her shoulder to rub the side of her biceps with soft strokes.

"This *is* Tim's Thanksgiving," Scott said simply.

Lauren shook her head, confused. "I don't get it. What about your mom?" she asked Tim.

Again Scott spoke for Tim, who didn't seem to know how to respond. "She eats with me on Thanksgiving. This is just like a brother thing, I guess. It's a tradition we do with just the two of us each year. Tim cooks a feast, and I eat it."

Scott tried to laugh the tension away, but Lauren wasn't put more at ease. She wanted to ask why their mom wasn't there, why they had Thanksgiving dinner on Sunday with just the two of them—or in this case three. But thankfully her brain caught up to her mouth for once and kept it from opening.

Tim shifted uncomfortably in his chair and cleared his throat. "So who's winning the Skins game?"

Lauren could sense Scott's relief at the subject change.

"They are. About time too. I don't want to be a band-wagon fan, but they've played like shit most of the season. Makes it hard to watch."

"Yeah, well, you always liked rooting for the under-dog anyway," Tim said.

Once the residual awkwardness from Lauren's question had diminished, they spent the rest of dinner discussing more benign topics, like Lauren's upcoming internship and her current job in Scott's office. She also learned about Tim's plans to move. He'd recently landed a job as an executive chef at a new restaurant in D.C. He'd gotten a new apartment about thirty minutes from his current place so he would be in between his job and Scott's house. "Gotta keep an eye on my little brother," he joked.

When Scott discovered that there was nothing for dessert, he shouted something about Thanksgiving without dessert being unacceptable and stormed off to the store. Lauren stayed behind to help Tim clear the table and wash the dishes. "It's the least I can do," she said. "I mean, I pretty much crashed your Thanksgiving," she joked. But she couldn't help but feel that there was some truth to it.

"Are you kidding? Scott's never brought anyone over. Especially to Thanksgiving. He usually keeps his personal life and his . . . personal life separate." Tim shook his head. "Sorry. That doesn't really make any sense."

Lauren stopped drying the plate she had in her hand when she understood the implication of what Tim had said. Everything in Scott's life was compartmentalized. He kept work separate from his personal life, and he kept the women he slept with separate from the rest of his life too. Although, he hadn't this time. Not with her.

"It's great to finally see Scott *with* someone. You know? He's been alone for so long. I actually never thought he'd find—"

"Oh," Lauren stopped Tim midsentence, "we're not together. Scott and I are just ..." Lauren let her voice trail off. For some reason, hearing herself say the words aloud had an effect on her she hadn't expected. They felt wrong.

"I'm sorry. I just thought ..." Tim left his sentence unfinished as well, and he avoided Lauren's eyes by putting some dishes in the cabinet. "For Scott to bring someone here ... I just think you should know how huge that is for him."

Lauren wasn't sure why, but she felt close to Tim already. She leaned against the corner of the counter, preparing herself to hear what Tim was telling her. "I'm not sure I understand."

"I'm not sure Scott told you my history. For him to bring you here, I'd think he would have."

Lauren let her silence answer Tim's question.

Tim exhaled. "I've been clean for seven years."

Lauren didn't know how to respond, so she remained silent, certain that Tim would explain.

"Today is the anniversary of my first day sober. I haven't spoken to my mom since I was twenty-two. Or more accurately, *she* hasn't spoken to *me*. And I can't say I blame her. When you steal your mother's wedding ring and pawn it to pay for drugs, it puts a little bit of a strain on the relationship. And that was the last straw really. I'd been fucking up for a lot of years before that."

Instantly, things became clear: why Scott hadn't told her much of anything about his brother, why Tim's relationship with his mom seemed so strained, the charity that Scott and his father started. All the pieces began to fit together, and Lauren was finally able to see the puzzle for what it was: complicated. "I didn't know. I'm sorry."

"Don't be. I deserve whatever I get." Lauren guessed Tim was trying to portray a level of comfort about the situation that he probably didn't feel. "They were my decisions. I've been in and out of rehab five times since the age of sixteen. They should have reserved a parking spot for me there." He spit out a humorless laugh before continuing. "I made dumb decision after dumb decision. I lost every decent friend I ever had and most of my family. Scott was the one person who always stuck by me unconditionally."

Lauren could tell that there was more Tim wanted to say, but just as he opened his mouth to continue, a booming voice came from the hallway. "Pumpkin pie," Scott announced. "No Thanksgiving's complete without it." Scott walked into the kitchen, grabbed a few forks, and returned to the table, cracking open the pie tin and sinking a fork into their dessert.

"What are you, a caveman? I have plates," Tim offered, though he contradicted his own words as he sat beside his brother and picked up a fork.

"You already cleaned up. Why do more dishes?"

Tim shrugged and dug in, as if that explanation made all the sense in the world.

Lauren watched the brothers for a moment, observing the similar mannerisms, the easy conversation that flowed between them. She felt a sudden pang of jealousy, realizing that she'd never have a moment like that with her own brother again.

Finally, after Lauren wasn't even sure how long, Scott's voice interrupted her thoughts. "I'm not saving you any of this. So if you want some, you'd better get over here."

With a roll of her eyes, Lauren moved to sit with them, grateful that, even if she couldn't be with her *own* brother, Scott had cared enough about her to share his.

After they'd demolished the pie and talked for a bit longer, it was time for Scott and Lauren to head home.

The brothers gave each other a manly hug good-bye, and then Tim leaned down to embrace Lauren. "Thanks for coming. I hope I didn't make you feel uncomfortable," Tim said, his voice low so only Lauren could hear. "But I needed you to know what his bringing you here means to him. And to me."

In the car, Lauren was quiet but it wasn't an uncomfortable quiet. She looked satisfied. Content. He realized he liked seeing that look on her face. Liked knowing he had something to do with putting it there.

The night had gone even better than he could have imagined. Thanksgiving was an important tradition between him and Tim, and having Lauren fall into it so seamlessly did something to Scott. It made him want to share more with her. Made him want to be as open with her as she'd been with him.

"Tim's been a drug addict from about the age of fifteen. Or at least that's when it became noticeable." Scott hadn't meant to blurt it out like that, but there was no easy way to share what he had to say.

He could feel Lauren's stare fixed on him, prompting him to go on.

"One night," he continued, "my dad told me to go up

and get Tim for dinner. I was ten, which would have made Tim sixteen. Anyway, I went up and knocked on his door, but he didn't answer. So I knocked again. I remember feeling like something was off. I can't explain it, but I knew that I did *not* want to open Tim's door. I kept knocking until my dad yelled up to see what was taking so long. I finally sucked it up and pushed his door open."

Scott tightened his grip on the wheel. "And that's when I saw him. He was sitting on the floor, slumped against his bed. He wasn't moving. I must have screamed because I remember my dad running past me, and my mom grabbing me and taking me out of the room. It was a blur after that. There were ambulances and police. He almost died. That was the first time they sent Tim away to rehab."

Scott chanced a quick glance at Lauren to find her watching intently. No pity, just genuine interest.

"I had a lot of anxiety after that. I was always afraid of new situations, unsure of what to expect, of what could happen around every corner. It drove my mom nuts. She just wanted us all to forget about what had happened and move on. But how does a ten-year-old move on from watching his brother OD on his bedroom floor? So one day my dad gave me a silver dollar and told me to grab onto it and rub my fingers over it when I felt like I couldn't handle a situation. He said to focus my brain on trying to feel every ridge, dip, and detail of the coin. And it actually worked. It kept me grounded and focused on something familiar, rather than on all of the unknowns out there. I still carry it with me." Scott looked down at her with a smirk. "As you already know.

"Tim was in and out of rehab for over eleven years.

Finally, one day, November twenty-fourth to be exact," he added with a slight smirk in Lauren's direction, "something clicked for him and he's been clean for seven years. I think what bothers me the most about it all is how my parents reacted to the whole thing. At first they acted like the problem didn't exist, and then when Tim didn't respond to their help immediately, they completely abandoned him. Kicked him out on his ass the second he hit eighteen, and then cut off all contact with him a few years later."

Now that Scott was talking, he couldn't stop. It was like a massive purge that he hadn't even known he'd needed. Granted, he'd told Gwen all of this stuff a million times, but telling Lo was different. He wasn't paying Lauren to be interested; she was interested because she gave a shit about him. "The real kicker is that they're the ones who drove him to the drugs in the first place, especially my mom. She was so hard on him. He couldn't do anything right: he made his bed the wrong way, his grades weren't good enough, he had bad manners, he didn't keep his clothes clean enough. It was exhausting just watching her go at him." Scott stopped speaking abruptly. He needed a second to get his shit back under control.

"She was that way with him but not you?"

Scott nodded.

"Why?"

He found himself at the part of the story he didn't want to share. "Because she blamed him."

"For what?"

Scott took a deep breath, and his words came out harsher than he intended. "Because she accused him of trying to fuck up her marriage with my dad. Because she's a completely insane individual who thought it was okay to take her small boys to her lover's house so she could have an affair while she let her children play in the next room."

Anger was rising up in his words, but Scott couldn't help it. "Because she blamed an eleven-year-old for answering honestly when his dad asked what he'd done that day. And even though she conned my dad into sticking around, and she didn't stop having affairs, she still decided that Tim was to blame for all the trouble that existed between my parents. So she spent the next however many years convincing him he was worthless until he finally believed her and turned to drugs to numb the pain *she'd* caused. And then to top all of it off, she cut him squarely out of her life when he got to be too much of a hassle to deal with."

"God, Scott, I don't even know what to say."

Scott ignored her words, needing to get the rest of it out. "Do you want to know what the worst part of it is? Tim doesn't blame her for any of it. He still thinks he deserved all the shit she put him through. And it scares the hell out of me because how can a guy ever truly get better when he believes all the nasty things she said are true?"

"Because he has you."

"What?"

"He has you. Maybe his love for you is all he needs to stay clean."

Scott shook his head. "Even if that were true, it's not a good enough reason. He needs to be better for *himself*, not for me."

"Getting to be a good brother and having you in his life *are* for himself. And don't sell yourself short, Doctor." She tugged gently on his hand, causing him to look over at her. "You're worth being better for."

Scott didn't know what to say to that, so he pulled her hand to his lips for a quick kiss and let himself enjoy her words. As he got closer to home, Scott realized that, as sour as the night had turned, he wasn't ready for it to be over yet. His hand slid over to Lauren's inner thigh, and he felt her let out a heavy breath. They didn't exchange words. Scott's touch was all that was necessary to know that both of them wanted the other's skin against their own.

By the time they made it inside Scott's bedroom, he'd already begun slipping a hand up Lauren's shirt to scratch the soft skin of her back until she raised her arms enough to let him pull her shirt over her head. No matter how much Scott pressed his lips against hers, it never felt like enough. Her mouth was much too sweet and the feel of her tongue against his—gentle strokes against hard licks—made him that much more aggressive.

She moaned into him as his hand gripped the back of her neck, and the vibration made his cock ache with the unbearable need to be inside her. "If you weren't so fucking beautiful, I'd throw you against this wall and take you from behind. But I need to see you," he groaned, "because nothing is sexier than seeing your face when I'm inside you."

Lauren quivered against him as Scott toyed with her bra before unhooking it and letting it slide slowly down her arms to the floor.

Scott's erection pressed against the inside of his jeans,

and Lauren ran her palm lightly over it just enough to tease him. He couldn't remember the last time he'd been this hard just from a woman's hands on top of his pants. "I'm not going to let you make me come in my pants." *Again.*

"Is that a challenge?" Lauren countered, a playful laugh escaping into his mouth.

Scott ground his cock against her, wanting nothing more than to feel her lips around him as she took him deep. "More of an order," he replied, popping the button of her jeans and helping her shimmy them down her hips.

"Mmm."

"First," he said seductively, drawing out the word as he nipped along her neck, "I'm going to get you so ... fucking ... dirty." His fingers skated down Lauren's stomach and under the fabric of her thong. *Fucking soaked.* "Then," he said, thrusting his fingers deep inside her and letting his thumb rest on her clit, "you're getting in the shower to clean up." He smiled against her throat. "But this time I'm getting in *with* you."

Lauren moaned softly as Scott's fingers moved inside her, hitting the spots he knew drove her wild. The way he pinched her nipple between his fingers—sucked and nipped at the spot just below her collarbone—had her arching off the bed. He could anticipate Lauren's every response with complete accuracy. And it comforted him to have a sexual partner he knew inside and out. Literally.

Lauren's hands fisted in his T-shirt as he helped her pull it over his head. And when her fingertips traced the lines of his abs on their way down toward the waistband of his jeans, he nearly exploded with the need to have her hand wrapped tightly around his cock while her tongue stroked him toward orgasm. "You know how much I want your mouth on me right now?"

He let out a low hiss when he felt Lauren's fingers clamp hard around him. "Well, if past experience is any indicator, I have some idea."

He smiled when he felt her tongue trail slippery lines down his stomach. With her mouth just above the base of his shaft, he guided his cock to her lips. "Suck me, Lo."

Lauren complied, her tongue working tantalizingly up and down the throbbing vein of his dick. He heard the suction created by her lips gripping tightly around him. And the sound made him ache at the base of his spine as he struggled to hold off his orgasm. With small tugs of her hair, he moved her head back and forth as he thrust sharply inside her. Scott couldn't remember getting so close to coming so quickly before. Lauren's mouth couldn't have been on him for more than two minutes, and he felt like he could lose it any second. But as much as he wanted to let go—feel himself jet into her mouth as she swallowed every drop he gave her—he wanted to come *with* her more. "Stop before I have to make you."

Scott felt Lauren swirl her tongue around him once more before sucking hard on his tip and then pulling away. "What do you want?" Lauren whispered against his stomach as she stood.

"You." He realized too late the unintended significance of his response and immediately tried to recover. "But first I need to return the favor." Scott pulled Lo's thong down her legs and tossed it on the floor before lying on the bed and spinning Lauren around so her ass hovered above him. She lowered herself down onto his mouth before taking his cock in hers once again.

This time neither one of them was gentle. They sucked, licked and stroked each other until the sound of moans and wet mouths on each other's skin filled Scott's room. He growled against her and he knew that Lauren could feel the vibrations in her clit because of the way she then moaned while taking him deeper. When he felt he couldn't hold off any longer, he pressed a wet finger against her perineum just enough to get her attention. He knew Lauren wouldn't expect it, but it elicited the desired response — her bucking against him as she pulsed around Scott's tongue.

Scott knew the feeling of Lauren's pussy clenching over and over would be his undoing. He could never hold back after she came, her pleasure being a direct trigger for his own. Hard bursts shot to the back of Lauren's throat, and the feeling of her swallowing against his tip prolonged his orgasm. Lauren didn't let up until he'd finished completely, milking every drop with her clenched fist.

When both of them had come down from their orgasms, Lauren rolled off of Scott and positioned her head near his as she lay beside him. Thoughts of running slippery hands down Lauren's wet body in the shower caused Scott to remain semierect. But he didn't want to move yet. Just lying there with Lauren's arm draped across his chest gave him a satisfaction he wasn't used to feeling. But after a few minutes, the temptation of the awaiting shower was too much for him. He rolled off the bed and held out his hand to her to help her stand. Then he spun her around so she faced his bathroom, and Scott got a thorough look at her from behind. "So how about that shower?" he asked with a playful slap to her ass.

The feel of the cold tile against Lauren's nipples made them harden further. Scott pushed his erection against her ass as he rubbed body wash over her shoulder blades and around to her stomach. Lauren leaned back into him, allowing his solid chest to press against her and his hands to work their way up to her heavy breasts.

"So you've wanted me in this shower since the first time I stayed at your apartment?"

"Mm-hm," Scott groaned against her neck. "I've wanted you in here since the day I met you."

Lauren let out a small laugh that was barely audible over the sound of the hot water spraying them.

"If I'm being completely honest, I've jerked off to the thought of you in here too."

Scott's confession sent a rush of pleasure through her body. "Well, you know how I like honesty."

Scott pulled her wet hair back and began to lather it in shampoo, his fingers working aggressively into her scalp. She relaxed at his touch, but her body was still worked up. She craved the man with every molecule of her being. And she could tell by how hard he felt against her ass, that he craved her too. He leaned her head back toward the water, pulling the soapy strands through his fingers until it was clean.

"So, Dr. Scott," Lauren said with a flirtatious grin he could see as her head leaned back and he kissed her neck. "Are you gonna stand behind me and tease me all night, or are you gonna fuck me?"

Scott's hands slid down to give her nipples a sharp pinch. The subtle pain turned her on even more. "Don't ask questions you already know the answer to," Scott said before sliding open the shower door and leaning out. The crinkling of foil told her he was retrieving a condom he had stashed somewhere.

Before Lauren knew what had happened, Scott had spun her around to face him. Tearing the packet open and tossing the wrapper aside, he sheathed himself with the latex. As his hands moved over his hard length, Lauren pictured him masturbate—pictured him making himself come for her—and the image made her beg to have him inside her. "Please, Scott."

Roughly, Scott pinned both her hands above her head with one hand applying the perfect amount of pressure. His lips seemed to attack her mouth and her neck. With every kiss, their tongues tangled with the water that streamed down them.

Scott ground against her clit, hitting her in a place that made her think she might lose it right then. Finally, just when Lauren didn't think she could wait any longer to have Scott inside her, he grabbed the backs of Lauren's thighs and lifted her up until she felt his tip at her entrance. Then he thrust hard and deep inside her, stretching her with every stroke.

Her back slipped against the cool tile as Scott's warm body pressed hard against her. Her orgasm had been building since they'd entered the shower, but she tried to hold off, wanting to enjoy the fleeting feeling of the two of them moving together as one.

"Fuck, Lo," Scott groaned. "This is better than any fantasy I had of you. You're so fucking soft."

He pumped into her faster and without reservation until she let go and allowed herself the release she'd been craving. Her nails clawed Scott's back as she yelled in relief. The spasms that coursed inside her were enough to make her legs loosen their grip around Scott's waist. But she wanted to give Scott the same pleasure he'd given her, so she focused on him—a look in his eyes like he wanted all of her and didn't want to let her go.

He slammed into her long and slow until he finally came—a look of complete satisfaction on his face. Scott stayed inside her for a few moments longer before pulling out of her and slowly lowering Lauren down. At his absence, she nearly shivered even while standing under the warm spray of the shower.

Scott grabbed two towels and put one around Lo, hugging her with his warmth before discarding the condom and putting his own towel around himself to dry off. When both of them were dry, Lauren raised her lids to look up at Scott, whose eyes held a possessive sweetness.

He pressed a knuckle softly under her chin and raised her head to kiss her gently. "Stay," he whispered.

Chapter 17

Delusional Disorder

Scott drove Lauren home the next morning on his way to work so she could get ready for class. Despite the fact that she'd only stayed the night two other times, it had felt surprisingly natural. They'd stayed up to watch *Wedding Crashers* on TV—a movie they quickly realized they both could quote on demand. And they'd spent the rest of the night in Scott's bed. But they hadn't had sex again. Instead, Lauren enjoyed the comfort of Scott holding her as she drifted off to sleep and thought about how perfectly she fit in his arms.

Scott parked his car in front of her apartment and gave her a gentle kiss. His lips lingered on hers for what seemed like a moment too long to be a just a quick kiss good-bye. "Call you later?" he said as he pulled away slowly.

Lauren felt her brows furrow in confusion. "Are you asking me or telling me?"

"Well, I mean I don't want you to think I'm a Stage Five Clinger or anything."

Lauren laughed at the reference from the movie they

had just watched, but she couldn't ignore its implications. It was Scott's way of asking if he was overstepping. She hoped her laughter made him feel more at ease. "I'll talk to you later," she said with a smile that she was sure would stay with her as she got ready for class.

After getting dressed, Lauren trotted toward the kitchen for a cup of coffee when her cell phone rang. "Hi, Mom," she said as she brought it to her ear.

"Hi, Laur. What are you up to?"

"Nothing. Just getting ready for school. What's up with you?"

"Not too much. We're having a little bit of a lull this morning, so I thought I'd check in since I haven't spoken to you since Thanksgiving."

Perfectly executed guilt trip, Mother. "Yeah, I was getting caught up on schoolwork and then I was bored so I went with Scott to his brother's house for dinner yesterday."

Pam was quiet for a long moment, taking a deep breath before she began speaking again. "What are you doing, Lauren?"

"What do you mean?"

"With Dr. Scott. What is going on between you two?"

"Nothing. We're friends. Can't I have friends?"

"Don't be smart, Lauren. Of course you can have friends. But don't try to convince me your relationship with Dr. Scott is that simple. I know it isn't."

She was right, and Lauren didn't have it in her to try to convince her any differently. "Why does it matter what we are?"

Pam sighed, her voice softening when she spoke. "It matters because he's your boss. And sleeping with your boss is not a stigma you want to carry, especially just as you're getting ready to pursue your own career in the health field. I don't want you getting mixed up with another authority figure who could derail your entire life again. It isn't responsible."

Lauren opened her mouth, but quickly closed it again, finding herself in too much shock to reply. Unsure of what exactly to say, she settled for the only truth she had. "This is different, Mom."

"How? Explain it to me, Lauren, because I desperately need to understand."

"That thing at Dartmouth was a bad patch. You know that. I'm not that immature, naive little girl anymore. I can't explain to you how it's not the same with Scott other than to tell you that the way I feel, the way he *makes* me feel, is totally different."

"I don't like it, Lauren."

"I can't change it, Mom. And I don't want to."

She heard her mom's heavy sigh through the phone.

Lauren hated disappointing her mother, and she had the sinking feeling that that was exactly what she was doing.

"I'll talk to you later, okay?" her mom finally said. "I love you."

"Love you too." Lauren brought the phone down from her ear, but continued to stare at it for a few seconds after her mother had hung up. Finally Lauren got her coffee, gathered her stuff, and headed out the door to school, trying desperately to ignore the fact that what she'd just admitted to her mother, and herself, had changed everything.

*   *   *

Somehow Lauren managed the drive to school without giving much thought to what was happening between her and Scott. She'd assured her mom that the situation with him was different from the situation she'd gotten herself into with the professor at Dartmouth. And it hadn't been a lie. It *was* different.

It wasn't until she sat in her Advanced Psychology class listening to Dr. Bauer's lecture that she took the time to evaluate just how far the relationship with Scott had progressed.

Her *relationship*. She let the word bounce around in her head like a racquetball in an empty court. Though she tried, its echo rang much too loudly to ignore.

She and Scott were more than just friends with benefits, whether they wanted to admit it or not. For months they'd both believed that they were nothing more than two people who had an undeniable sexual chemistry, two people who laughed with each other and enjoyed spending time together. But she was crazy if she thought that all of those elements, when combined, did not equate to some sort of relationship beyond the casual sexual arrangement they'd claimed to maintain.

"Almost *everyone* exhibits some form of delusional behavior during their lifetime," Dr. Bauer insisted. "It's only natural for our brains to want to hold on to what they'd like to believe is true, rather than what *is*. It's easy to accept a false belief even with overwhelming evidence to the contrary."

Lauren's hand shot in the air before she'd even decided what she'd planned to say. She just knew she had to say *something*. Since her undergrad days, she'd made it a habit of trying to participate in all of her classes, but she usually found it tougher in Bauer's class. Though his lectures were always informative, he just didn't have the same charisma as Dr. Peterson. But today's topic begged her to engage.

"Yes, Miss Hastings?"

Lauren sat up straight and glanced from side to side as if someone nearby could help her make sense of her jumbled thoughts. "You said nearly everyone exhibits some sort of delusions, right?"

"That's correct."

"So then, almost everyone could be diagnosed with a delusional disorder?"

"They wouldn't be diagnosed with a delusional *disorder*, necessarily, if that's what you're asking." Dr. Bauer paced back and forth slowly at the front of the room as he ran a hand through his thick gray hair. "Nonbizarre delusions serve as our mind's defense mechanism—a way of protecting ourselves from how the truth will make us feel, so it isn't uncommon for even people without any psychological problems to exhibit that behavior from time to time."

Lauren's mind was a jumbled mess of information and emotions, and she couldn't even begin to make sense of any of it. *She* could admit that what she had with Scott was more than what they'd claimed it was. But she was almost certain that Scott couldn't.

Lauren sat back in her chair, feeling herself sink down a little lower as the implications of what Dr. Bauer was saying settled over her. "So," Lauren continued, "if someone exhibits that behavior, as you said, how would you get them to stop having those delusions? If we had a patient like that, I mean."

Dr. Bauer cocked his head to the side and looked at Lauren a moment too long, as if he knew the real reason for her question.

Damn psychologists.

"Well, since delusions are a symptom, and not the problem in and of itself, our best course of action," he continued slowly, giving Lauren time to process his words, "would probably be to figure out what was causing those delusions. Once we can assess the underlying issue, we can finally begin to make some progress. With the patient, of course."

Lauren probably would have been embarrassed by Dr. Bauer's callout, had her mind not been reeling. She knew the underlying issues Scott was dealing with. He'd told her not twenty-four hours ago. But his first instinct was to brush those issues aside, ignore how much they really affected him. Lauren sunk back in her chair, her teeth nibbling on her pen cap as she contemplated that even though *she* was ready to move forward with Scott, he was more than likely not in the same mental place. Her heart sunk at the realization that Scott may walk away from her before they ever really got a chance to take any steps together.

Most of Dr. Scott's morning had been hectic. Three back-to-back appointments—two of which were new patients—had kept him busy for the first few hours. By the time he got a chance to breathe, it was nearly time for lunch.

He was at the nurses' station, looking over the chart from his last patient of the morning, when Pam's voice interrupted his thoughts. "I don't know how else to say this, so I'm just going to say it."

Scott made his last note on the chart before putting it on the desk and turning his attention to Pam, who had appeared next to him. He heard the abruptness in her voice, but something about her expression held concern.

"I know about the two of you."

Scott opened his mouth to respond, though he wasn't exactly sure what he would have even said. No explanation would justify the fact that he'd been sleeping with her daughter.

Pam continued, her voice softening as she spoke. "She'd probably kill me if she knew I was even saying anything to you, but I'm her mother and my job will always be to protect her. I need you to know that she's been through a lot."

He felt a deep pang in his chest as he thought about everything Lo had revealed to him. Things she hadn't even told her own mother. "I know."

"She assures me that this is different, Scott. And I have to believe her. When I saw you dancing with her at the benefit . . . Well, I should have known what was going on then. Even before then really. So I'll just say this once and expect you to do the right thing." She sighed heavily as if the weight of what she was about to say had been physically pulling her down. "When Lauren loves someone, she loves them with everything she has." Then Pam touched Scott lightly on the arm as she spoke. "Just be careful with her heart. She's all I've got left." Without waiting for him to reply, she turned around and walked down the hall.

Chapter 18

Pathological Lying

Scott tried to ignore the unsettled feeling in his gut. Ever since his talk with Pam the day before, he'd been racked with nerves. How the hell had he and Lo gotten so off track? How had he *let* them get so off track? They had agreed to a certain set of rules before they'd begun their sexual relationship, and Lauren had broken the most important one: she'd gotten attached when she'd promised she wouldn't. And now they were in one hell of a predicament.

He felt his face get hot as he clenched his jaw. She'd screwed everything up, but *he* was the one who'd have to fix it. And it'd be a messy fix, one filled to the brim with hurt feelings. Scott fucking hated messy.

Scott hadn't called her the previous night like he said he would. He didn't want to be that guy who ended things over the phone. Not with Lo. Because no matter how pissed off he was, he still respected her more than that.

So he'd waited until she'd come in Tuesday. Waited until she'd gotten herself situated and started on her work for the day. He waited . . . for a reason not to do what he knew he had to. Finally, as lunch was approaching, he saw Lauren go into the filing room. *This is as good a chance as any.* So he gave a discreet look around before following her inside and softly shutting the door.

And because he just couldn't resist pressing her up against the wall once more, he leaned one hand above her head and rested the other on her hip. Then be lowered his face to hers, needing the proximity. One more time.

He noticed her physical response to him, and it only twisted his stomach more. "You promised," he whispered.

When she replied, her voice was thick with desire. "Promised what?" She licked her lips and he had to bite back a moan.

He didn't answer right away. He just looked at her, thinking about how much he'd miss being up against her. Scott wished he could go back and change the course they were on so they wouldn't end up where they were. But there was no going back. If he allowed it to continue, he'd only hurt her more. "You promised you wouldn't fall in love with me, Lo. You promised." He heard the regret, the disappointment, the hurt in his voice. And part of him hoped that she heard it too, so she'd understand that this wasn't what he wanted, but what needed to be done.

"I . . . I'm not." Her eyes were wide, the panic clear in them.

It was all the confirmation he needed. He lowered his forehead so that it was flush against hers. "You also said you weren't a liar." His head drifted into her hair and he inhaled her scent. Then, he pressed a soft kiss to her temple and pulled away. He allowed the finality of the moment to pass between them. He didn't need to say it. It was clear from her slackened posture and the moisture building in her eyes that she knew. It was over. Summoning a willpower he didn't know he had, he stepped back from her—knowing that he could ease the pain in her eyes, but refusing to allow himself to do so. He couldn't be weak now. It was better for her to think he was a prick than to give her hope that he could be what she needed. He gave her one last look before turning and walking away, closing the door behind him as he left.

Lauren went through the rest of the day on autopilot, too focused on the whiplash she'd received, compliments of Dr. Scott. *What the hell happened?* The previous morning they'd been fine. *More* than fine. She'd felt like they'd finally gotten over the defenses the other kept so firmly locked in place. But then Scott had swooped in and slammed his down again, effectively shutting her out.

The more she contemplated it—the more she watched him actively avoid her—the less upset she was about his rejection. Instead she was pissed. If Scott thought that he could cast her aside like she didn't matter, then he had another thing coming.

At six, she couldn't take it anymore. She waited a little while longer for everyone else to leave for the day before she barged into his office, taking in his shocked expression when she threw the door open. "We need to talk."

He released a heavy sigh, like he was annoyed by her.

She was going to fucking kill him.

"Okay. Talk."

She shut the door behind her in case anyone was still left in the office, before rounding on him. "You have a lot of fucking nerve."

"You're just figuring that out?" He shuffled some papers around on his desk like he was too busy for her nonsense.

"Stop being a dick and look at me, Scott."

He did. And she saw it. The hurt, the unhappiness, the longing. All of it. He didn't want things to be over. He couldn't.

But that only made her rage grow stronger. What was he punishing them for? Lauren felt a peace with Scott she hadn't felt in seven years. How dare he take that away without giving her a chance to convince him otherwise? "Why are you doing this?"

He stood. "We had a deal, Lauren. I'm not the one who broke it. You are."

She felt as if he'd slapped her. "You can't be serious. We've grown so much since that stupid deal. You *know* me, Scott. Like no one else does. Are you really going to sit there and tell me that I'm not worth more than a good fuck from time to time?" Her eyes watered as she said the words.

Scott didn't speak for a moment. He continued to look at her blankly, as if he were looking at a stranger.

"Answer me." Her voice was strangled, so full of emotion she could scarcely breathe over it all.

"I never lied about who I was or what I wanted," he stated plainly. His tone was so detached and distant, her heart broke even more.

"So why are you lying now?"

He flattened his hands on his desk and leaned on

them. Scott was finally bringing some emotion to the table, but it wasn't the emotion that Lauren had hoped to see. "You have a lot of nerve. You barge into *my* office, demand that we talk about something that never should've happened in the first place, and then call *me* a liar? *You* lied. You said you could handle this. But then I get a lecture from *Mommy* that I need to be careful with your heart. Well, I didn't sign up for that, Lauren. I didn't ask for your heart, and I don't want it."

Lauren felt herself wince from the impact of his words. The venom in his voice, the disdain that he used when he mocked her with the word "Mommy" had her reeling. *Who the fuck is this guy?* And worst of all was that she couldn't deny that she did love the bastard. Even though he was quickly proving that he didn't deserve it. Nor did he want it. "Really? You want to bring 'Mommy' into this, Scott? How about we talk about yours then. How about we talk about the fact that the reason you won't admit that you have real feelings for me is because you can't let go of what your own mother did to your father. Well, I got news for you, Scott. We're. Not. Them." She looked at him for a moment, scanning his face for any hint of remorse. When she didn't see any, she said the only thing she could think to say. "I'm sorry."

He pulled back slightly, his brow furrowing.

But Lauren wasn't apologizing for what he probably thought. "I'm sorry I let my guard down. I'm sorry that I allowed myself to believe the bullshit you fed me. All that crap about how the last thing you wanted to do was hurt me." She saw the firm line of lips, the rigidity of his posture. In that moment, she wished she'd never met him.

"But I'm mostly sorry that I ever told you a Goddamn thing about me. How do you think that feels, Scott? You know things about me my closest friends don't know. Things about my brother ..." Her voice faltered as the rising emotion made her fight for control.

"I trusted you with more than myself. I trusted you with Cooper." Her voice was small, weak. But she couldn't have that right then. Taking a deep breath, she refocused her glare on him. "But you couldn't handle it, could you? You wanna know why? Because you're a fucking coward. You're so afraid of letting someone in, of opening yourself up to the possibility of getting hurt, that you run like the chickenshit you are."

"You finished?" Scott's face hadn't changed. She'd put all her emotions out there, and he was still standing before her, radiating nothing but anger.

"You bet your ass I am."

"Good. Because I have some things to say. I'm the same man I've always been. It's you who thought I was different. I never claimed that."

Lauren swallowed around the thickness in her throat. So this was it? All the past three months had boiled down to. "You're right. Guess the joke's on me." She gave a defeated shrug. She watched him for another second, allowing herself the briefest bit of hope that he'd take it all back. That he'd try to fix what he'd broken before it was irreparable.

But he didn't.

So Lauren turned and headed for the door. As her hand gripped the knob, she hesitated. Taking a deep breath, she spoke the last personal words she ever planned to say to Dr. Scott.

"I told you a while back that you always win because you never let yourself lose. But living this way ... This isn't winning." Lauren waited for a moment, letting her words sink in before she started again.

"And just so you know, since you never waited for me to say it, I do love you. You're the first person I've ever said that to outside of my family. That's a regret I'll have to carry with me. And the fact that I didn't give that gift to someone who actually deserves it sucks." Then she wrenched the door open and walked through it before slamming it shut behind her.

Chapter 19

Rebound Pain

Lauren spent Wednesday trying to get herself together. She felt emotional and depleted. Her classes trudged by, and she found that she could scarcely concentrate.

Thursday brought the added bonus of a severely unsettled stomach. She didn't feel sick per se, but she definitely didn't feel well. She chalked it up to having to spend the day around Scott. By midmorning, she was sitting at her desk with her head in her hands, trying to calm the aching throb in her stomach and keep her nausea under control.

"Lauren?"

Just what I don't *need.* "What?" She sounded completely wrung out, but didn't have the energy to sound normal to try to mask it.

"I just— Are you okay?"

"Sure," she replied dryly. "Do you need something?"

"No."

She heard Scott move and figured he'd left. Until she heard him speak again.

"If you're not well, you shouldn't be here."

Despite her pain, she whirled around in her chair. "Don't worry. I promise not to get close enough to infect any of your patients." *Why did I waste my time on such an asshole?*

His face softened slightly, which caused tears to threaten her eyes. *How dare he look at me like he gives a shit.*

"That's not what I meant. If you're sick, then you should be home resting."

Lauren turned back toward her desk. "I can't lose the hours. I don't want to spend a single extra minute here if I don't have to."

"I'll still pay you for the hours."

"I don't need your charity."

"That's not—"

"If there's nothing you need, I have some things I have to get done."

Scott exhaled a long breath. "Okay, well, the offer stands."

He scuffled away from her, and Lauren couldn't help but think that the only pain worse than the one in her stomach was the one in her heart.

Scott was miserable. He'd been an incredible asshole but he didn't know what else to do. He'd thought it was best for them both if they severed all ties, left no questionable feelings between them. A clean break was the easiest to heal from. But then he'd seen Lauren. She'd obviously been sick as hell, and it killed him that he couldn't help her. She wanted nothing to do with him; that much was clear. And while he knew she wouldn't let him examine her, he wished he would have at least *asked* her to allow him to examine her. But he knew that idea would get shot down, so he hadn't even offered. It had gnawed at him all night—not knowing if she was okay, not even having the right to ask. *How did shit get so fucked up?*

Friday morning he walked into his satellite office and began looking over his calendar. He was thankful it looked like it'd be a busy day. "May as well get to it," he said under his breath as he left his office and made his way toward his first patient.

By eleven, he had a brief break in his schedule. So he went into his office and took a seat. Scott immediately saw that his phone was flashing, letting him know that he had a message. He lifted the receiver and punched in his voice mail code. He was surprised to hear Pam's voice.

"Hi, Scott. It's Pam Hastings. I wanted to let you know I had to leave work early. The ER just called and said Lauren was just admitted with acute appendicitis. I'm sorry to be leaving a voice mail, but—"

Scott didn't listen to the rest of Pam's message. He flew out of his office, stopping only to give some instructions to the nurses as he took off for Trinity.

The bustle in the ER only further aggravated Scott. He stopped at the nurses' station to ask what room Lauren was in, and then took off in that direction. He paused outside the curtain, trying to get his breathing under control. He ran his hand through his hair and took a few calming breaths before pushing the curtain aside and entering her room.

What he saw stopped him cold. Lauren was lying in bed, holding her mom's hand. She looked pale and barely awake. His heart seized at the sight.

"Dr. Scott," Pam said in a way that let him know she hadn't expected to see him.

Lauren's eyes drifted toward him, then darted away quickly.

Scott saw Mr. Hastings sitting on the other side of Lauren, looking at his daughter with concern. He hadn't even registered Scott's presence.

"They just started prepping her for surgery to remove her appendix," Pam informed him. "It hasn't burst yet, but it's not far from it."

But he barely heard her. His eyes were glued to Lauren. She looked slightly dazed, probably from the pain meds. But she was still able to give her mom's hand a slight tug.

Pam bent toward her so she could hear whatever Lauren was trying to tell her. Her mom contorted her face in confusion. "Are you sure?"

Lauren gave a weak nod and shut her eyes.

Scott knew what Pam was going to say before she even approached him. "I'm sorry, Scott. But Lauren asked me to, um . . ." Pam looked back at Lauren.

Scott knew how uncomfortable she had to be. How do you tactfully kick your boss out of your daughter's hospital room? Scott decided to let her off the hook. "She doesn't want me here, does she?"

Pam looked back at him, concern written all over her face. "No."

Scott nodded and started to leave. But when he reached the curtain, he stopped. "Just . . . when she's out of surgery, just let us know how it went."

"I will," Pam assured him.

And with that, Scott left.

*   *   *

Scott knew that if he didn't stop pacing, he'd likely wear a hole in the carpet of his office. *What the hell is taking so long?* He checked his cell phone again, making sure his ringer was turned on.

Pam had promised she'd call, but Scott wasn't sure which phone to wait by. Would she call his cell or the office? He'd said let *us* know, which maybe made it seem like she should call the office. But obviously he'd be the most concerned, so maybe she'd call his cell. All of his employees had his private number in case they needed to call in sick or anything. So, since Scott didn't know where Pam would call, he did the only logical thing he could think of: he holed up in his office and stared at both phones.

It had been almost four hours since he'd been politely told to get lost, and he still hadn't heard from her. Scott was trying to respect Lauren's wishes by staying the hell away from her, but she wasn't making it easy. He was even tempted to call down there to see what information he could get out of the nurses.

Twenty more minutes passed before his cell phone finally rang. "Pam! How is she?" he blurted out before he'd even gotten the phone to his ear.

"She's doing well. They removed her appendix laparoscopically, so she should heal pretty quickly. I was just waiting for her to wake up before I called. The doctors think she can resume school and work in about ten days, depending on how she's feeling."

"Good. I'm glad to hear it." Scott hesitated a second before adding, "Would it be okay if I talked to her for a minute? I won't keep her long."

Pam was quiet on the other end for a beat. "Sure, Scott. Let me see if she feels up to talking. Hang on a second."

He heard the phone being jostled and then a groggy voice croak, "Hello?"

"Hey, it's Scott."

Silence.

"I just wanted to tell you that I'm glad you're doing better. You really scared the shit out of me." He didn't care what that admission implied. It was the truth and he wanted her to know it. "Take care of yourself. Plenty of rest and fluids. And make sure you take the pain meds. They'll make you a little loopy, but that's better than being uncomfortable."

"Am I going to receive a bill for this conversation?"

Scott couldn't help how her comment made him feel—like absolute shit.

Before he could say anything else, Lauren spoke again. "I'd better go. I'm really tired. We can talk more about when I'm going to make up the hours I'll owe you after I get out of here."

"You don't owe me anything," he said.

And he meant it.

Chapter 20

Relapse

Scott had been nearly monosyllabic since he'd arrived. He had things he wanted to discuss, *needed* to in fact, but he wasn't sure how to bring them up. So he sat back and barely engaged as he waited for Gwen to figure out why he was there. Was it immature? Yes. But he felt like he needed as much time to organize his thoughts as possible.

"How have things with the practice been going?" Gwen asked.

"Good," he replied. Scott thought of Lo for the tenth time since he'd sat down. Or maybe he hadn't actually *stopped* thinking about her. He had to find a way to stop thinking about her constantly. If he didn't, he feared he'd eventually go crazy. And he was in therapy to *not* go crazy, though he didn't think it was working.

Gwen looked down at her tablet. "How was your Thanksgiving dinner with your brother?"

"Nice."

"How did he look?"

"Sober." *Damn it! That was two syllables.*

"He's been clean for a long time. That must make you feel proud—seeing his progress."

"Yup."

Gwen sat back in her chair and set her tablet on the table beside her. "Scott, why are you here?"

"What?"

"You heard me. If you're not going to participate in your therapy session, then why even come?"

Scott straightened slightly, adopting a more challenging tone. "Before you were encouraging me to come whether I had anything to talk about or not."

"But you do have something to talk about. You're just refusing to discuss it."

He almost argued, but then decided it was pointless. If he delayed any longer, he'd have wasted his whole session and not gotten his head on right. But what did he say? That it was driving him nuts to see Lauren at work, to know that everything there had been touched by her, *infected* by her. He couldn't look anywhere without thinking about her, and it was starting to piss him off. Why couldn't he just move past her? It didn't make any sense. "I stopped seeing Lauren," he blurted.

"The girl working in your office? You didn't tell me you were seeing her."

"Sure I did," Scott insisted.

"No, you said you were friends with her, but you never said you were *seeing* her." The distinction seemed important to Gwen, though Scott couldn't figure out why.

"In my life, there isn't a big difference between the two. I don't have friends who are women, so I expected that you understood what I meant when I said Lo and I were friends."

"You have a nickname for her?" Gwen looked surprised.

"Yeah. Why?"

"Just seems very personal."

"Do you want me to talk or not?"

"I want you to talk, but I want that talk to be the truth. What is Lauren to you exactly?"

Was, he thought. She wasn't anything to him anymore, and he hated it. "Let's talk about the truth for a second." Scott knew that he'd ignored her question, but he had bigger issues to discuss. "I don't ask for much. Really, the only thing I require is complete honesty. And she couldn't even give me that. She promised . . . She promised she wouldn't fall in love. Now everything is a wreck, all because she had to go and develop feelings for me. Things were perfect as they were. We had a good time together, we each satisfied the other's needs, and then she admits to loving me when I told her that wasn't even a remote possibility for me."

"Why isn't love a possibility for you?"

"Come on, Gwen. We've been down this road a hundred times. It's just . . . not for me. I don't want to be tied down to someone forever. I don't want to make a mistake that I have to spend the rest of my life paying for. Life's too short for that."

"Did you ever think that it may be an even bigger mistake to *not* commit to someone? That you may actually miss out on more by refusing to belong to someone else?"

Scott thought for a minute, turning her words over in her head. "No," he finally stated.

She was clearly unimpressed with his answer. "What kinds of things did you and Lauren do together?"

"Just . . . normal stuff."

Gwen hesitated before saying, "Like?"

"Like go to the movies, or dinner, or hang out at my apartment, or a bar, whatever we felt like."

"Has she met any of your friends?"

"Yeah, she met Alex and Xavier. And Tim."

Gwen had been reaching for her glass of water, but stopped abruptly. "You introduced her to your brother?"

"Yeah," Scott replied uneasily. "Well, yeah, I mean she met him once by accident, and then one day she called and was bored, so I invited her to dinner—our Thanksgiving thing."

She settled back into her chair. "Let me see if I have this right: she met all of the people closest to you, you hung out beyond the workday—frequently I presume?"

Scott nodded.

"You were engaged in a sexual relationship with her, you took her to one of the most special traditions you and your brother have together, and you're angry that your friendship is over. All of that sound about right?"

"Sure. I guess."

"Describe a girlfriend to me, Scott."

Scott was confused. "What?"

"Give me your definition of a girlfriend. What kinds of things do you do? How do you act around each other?"

He saw what Gwen was doing. What she was implying. But she was wrong. Dead wrong. "Lauren was not my girlfriend. I'll admit, we did a lot of relationship-y things together, but we weren't dating. Don't get me wrong, I cared about her. *Care* about her. But I care about a lot of people—my friends, my brother. But I'm not *in love* with them. I know the difference."

"But you're sad? And angry that you've lost her?"

"Of course. We spent a lot of time together. She'd become a good friend. But now we can't even be that because she's going to want more. And I'm never going to be able to give it to her."

"You're not able to or you just don't want to?"

Scott rubbed a hand over his face. "They're the same thing," he said impatiently.

"No, they aren't. One is a choice and one isn't. So which is it?"

"A little of both," he said.

Gwen folded her steepled hands and rested them on her lap. "Scott, do you love Lauren?"

"What?" Scott was taken aback by the question. "No."

"Why not?"

"What do you mean, 'why not'? I just don't." He was beginning to wonder if Gwen needed a shrink herself.

Gwen studied him in that way only therapists could. "Is not loving her a conscious choice or is it just something that is? Something that happened?"

Scott didn't know how to answer that. He had decided at the outset of all of this that he wouldn't develop deep feelings for Lo. He also didn't think he'd ever be able to love another person. Love them in the kind of way that made you think about them incessantly, want to spend all of your time with them, put their well-being before everything else. It was too risky. He'd seen the devastation relationships could cause, and he didn't want to be part of that collateral damage. So in that sense, it was a choice. But he also knew he just didn't love Lauren. "It's both."

He and Gwen looked at each other, both seemingly waiting for the other to determine the direction the conversation would take. Scott gave in first. "Just tell me how to get her out of my mind. I can't—" Scott took a deep breath. "I can't keep feeling like this. I can't be her friend. It isn't fair to her. So I need you to tell me how to let her go."

"I don't think that's a decision you can will yourself to make." Gwen lifted her tablet off of the table. "Close your eyes, take a deep breath, and answer me this: when you picture yourself in ten years, who do you see next to you?"

Scott was annoyed that she'd ignored his question, but he tried to answer hers anyway. He expected not to see anyone in particular beside him. But he did see someone. *Of course I see Lauren. We just spent twenty minutes talking about her.* He'd picture anyone who was on his mind as much as she was. He was sure of it. Not willing to delve into a deeper examination of his hibernating "love" for Lauren, he replied to Gwen's question with the only truth he had. "No one will be there."

Gwen sighed, a brief look he couldn't quite identify flashing across her face. Disappointment maybe? "That sounds awfully lonely, Scott."

"Maybe to you. But I think we have different definitions of lonely." He wouldn't be alone, because he'd still be having exactly the type of relationships that he had enjoyed for the past few years. Lauren wasn't *that* special. She was just like every other girl he'd been with.

And if Gwen didn't believe him, well, then he'd just have to prove it.

As Scott sat alone in the small booth at The Curveball after work Friday, he was thankful for the peace and quiet that the night out provided. He normally didn't go out alone, but after the previous night's therapy session, he needed time by himself to unwind. Needed time to just be Scott. He took a long drink of his beer and settled back comfortably into the leather booth.

Scanning his eyes back and forth among the patrons, he noticed some people he knew from the hospital. There were too many familiar faces to allow his mind to fully wander. *Why did I come* here *looking for a random lay?*

But three beers and one quarter of the Wizards game later, he'd successfully been able to relax and let go of some of the thoughts that had plagued his mind since he'd broken things off with Lauren. He leaned his head against his closed palm as his elbow rested on the table. His other hand toyed with the silver dollar he'd removed from his pocket as he watched it flip back and forth between his fingers.

"Anxious about something?"

Scott instantly recognized the voice and allowed it to pull him out of his mindless trance. He raised his face to a doctor he'd once known intimately, though he hadn't seen her since she'd left Trinity over a year ago. "Not anymore, actually. Just kind of spacing out. How ya been, Mel?" Scott was instantly soothed by the reminder that Lo wasn't the only woman he'd had an "arrangement" with. The few months he and Mel had spent together were easy.

No talk of love. No messy feelings. And though his current anxiety was none of Mel's business, the fact that she could read him—knew his expressions and idiosyncrasies—comforted him.

"May I?" Melanie motioned to the seat across from Scott and he gestured back, letting her know that she could sit.

Scott watched Mel as she slid into the booth and downed the last of the clear liquid in her glass. "Another Seven and Seven?" he asked, pointing to her nearly empty glass.

Mel smiled. "Please."

Scott got up to head to the bar and returned a few minutes later with another round. They sat quietly for a few minutes, neither knowing exactly what to say.

"So how's the practice going?" Mel asked, relieving Scott of any obligation to start a conversation.

"It's good. Nothing much has changed." He took a sip of his beer before continuing. "Tell me about yours. How's everything working out at Inova?"

Mel's face lit up. "It's great, really great. Different from Trinity, but I love the practice. Everyone there's great."

"So it's great?" Scott asked.

They both released awkward laughs, and Mel propped the side of her head on her palm. "Yeah, I guess I said that a few times, didn't I?"

Scott smiled. "Just a few."

They fell into easy conversation from there. She told him about her sister's new interior design business and that Mel had taken up baking as a hobby after agreeing to help her niece with a school fund-raiser. Scott talked about the only thing he knew: sports. It was all superficial and comfortable. Exactly what Scott was looking for.

"So are you seeing anyone?" he asked out of nowhere.

Mel looked surprised at first, but then smirked slowly. "No. You?"

"No." He tried to ignore how bitter the word tasted as it left his mouth. "I'm not looking to either. Just ... enjoying the single life." He gulped down the last of his beer and inwardly acknowledged the cheesiness of his last line.

Mel reached across and grabbed his hand. "Being single has definite advantages." Then she stood, slinging her purse over her shoulder. "Walk me home, Scott." The gleam in her eyes told Scott what she wanted from him. And it just happened to be exactly what he needed.

The walk toward Melanie's apartment was more awkward than Scott had anticipated. Despite the fact that their conversation in the bar had been natural, it seemed that they'd used up all of the topics worth discussing. But once they got to Melanie's apartment, there would be no need for talking. Especially not in bed. That was something Mel never liked. But he didn't need that. What he needed was some relief, relief that he'd been craving since he'd broken things off with Lo.

He turned to look at Mel, gauging her expression before he spoke. She appeared ... relaxed. And the way she bit back a smile told him she'd been thinking similar thoughts. Instead of speaking, Scott grabbed Mel around the waist, spinning her a bit until her back pressed against the brick wall of the apartment building they'd been passing. She inhaled a sharp breath before Scott pressed his mouth to hers, needing to feel a physical connection. His tongue explored the inside of her mouth as if it hadn't been there a thousand times before.

But the familiarity he'd felt earlier had dissipated as soon as he'd kissed her. Instead, it felt . . . empty. It felt wrong. What he was doing with Mel wasn't going to make his world right again. It would only make it worse. Hers wasn't the touch he wanted. It wasn't enough. And the look in her eyes as he pulled away told him his touch would never be enough for her either. "I can't do this," he said, an unmistakable hint of apology in his voice as he pulled away and started to leave.

Mel let her gaze drift to his face for a moment before it moved downward to follow the hand that he'd slid around the coin in his pocket. "I know," she said softly.

Chapter 21

Optical Pathway Delay

Scott concentrated on the cup in his hands as he waited for his brother. Tim had seemed surprised when Scott asked to meet up at a coffeehouse. It made Scott feel guilty. *Like I need to feel any worse than I already do.* The truth was, though he spoke to Tim weekly, they didn't see each other nearly as often. *I should make more of an effort.*

But before Scott could wallow in self-recrimination, he saw Tim yank open the door and stride in. His brother threw him a quick wave before getting in line to order himself a coffee.

After a few minutes, Tim slid into the chair across from him. "Hey, what's up?"

Scott offered a small smile and shrugged his shoulders. "Nothing. You?"

Tim cocked his head slightly. "Nothing here either." He waited a beat before adding. "Everything okay?"

"Yeah. Why?"

"No reason really. You just don't usually ask me to

hang out last minute like this. You had me a little worried."

Scott forced himself to appear nonchalant. "I was just sitting around the house and felt like getting out for a bit. You were the first one I thought of, so I called."

Tim stared at Scott as if he was searing the bullshit right off the surface of him. He knew that look. Lauren had the same one.

"Well, I'm glad. Wish we hung out more."

Scott returned his gaze. "Me too."

"Enough of this sappy shit. Let's talk about more interesting things. Like Lauren. What's up with her?"

Scott didn't miss Tim's intentional avoidance of eye contact as he lifted his cup to his lips. He hadn't brought Lauren up casually. *The bastard.* "I think I'd rather talk about you."

"Ah, so there it is. The real reason why you called. What'd you do now? You look like somebody kicked your puppy, by the way."

"Asshole," Scott muttered.

Tim barked out a laugh before turning serious. "Really, Scott. What happened?"

Scott leaned back against his chair and took another sip of his coffee as he readied himself to speak. He wasn't sure what Tim would say. For that matter, Scott wasn't sure what he would say himself. But he knew he'd speak candidly. This was his brother asking. Not to mention, he couldn't ignore the hypocrisy of lying. "I'm not seeing her anymore."

Tim's eyes widened, letting Scott know he expected him to continue. "I kind of figured that much."

"Right. I know. Sorry. I just don't know what went

wrong. I mean, one minute we were fine. The next . . . we weren't."

Tim scooted back in his chair. "I'm surprised, man. You guys seemed great together."

"That's the problem—we weren't *together*. But she wanted to be. Or at least I assumed she did, but I . . . I panicked. When her mom told me to take care of her heart, I just couldn't—"

"Wait. Did you say her mom?" Tim narrowed his eyes as if he'd misheard.

Scott huffed out a short laugh. "Yeah, her mom came up to me at the office and basically told me that Lauren was in love with me."

"Damn, that's bold."

"Pam is definitely that." Scott shook his head, but smiled with the motion. Despite that being awkward for him, he respected Pam for it. She gave a shit about her daughter—he couldn't fault her for that. "Anyway, I called Lauren on it, and she barged into my office like the Gestapo and called me a coward. And she confirmed that she did love me. Can you believe that?"

Tim looked at Scott like he'd never seen him before. "So let me get this straight. A beautiful, smart, fun, compassionate woman tells you she loves you, and that's a bad thing?"

Scott quickly pulled himself closer to the table. "You're damn right it's a bad thing. I can't . . . I don't . . . That's not where my head's at right now."

"Yeah, because it's too busy being buried up your ass."

Scott looked at him incredulously but didn't respond.

"Don't look at me like *I'm* the crazy one. *You're* the

one who's lost his mind. How many girls like Lauren do you think there are in the world?"

"God, you sound like Gwen. You met her twice, and one of those times shouldn't even count. That somehow makes you an expert on what kind of girl she is?" Scott couldn't believe his brother was coming at him like this. *Last time I call you to get my mind off of my problems.*

"I may barely know her, but I do know you. I saw how you were with her, how you looked at her. The feelings swirling around you guys were mutual. Even a fuck-up like me could see that."

"We're both fuck-ups. That's why I can't go down that road." Tim looked like he didn't understand, so Scott continued. "We both knew something wasn't right when Mom would take us to his house. At least you had the balls to tell Dad about it." Scott raked a hand through his hair. "Fuck, even now I don't stand up to her. I'm still staying quiet when everything in me is begging me to tell her exactly what I think about her choices and what she did to our family. But I don't. Because ultimately, I'm exactly like Dad. I can't let someone in, Tim. I can't let someone destroy me the way she destroyed him." Scott shook his head. "And for that reason, I can never be what Lauren wants."

"But you *are* what she wants."

Scott dropped his gaze to the table.

"Look at me, Scott." When Scott raised his eyes, Tim continued. "I know that I'm no one to take advice from. But I do know what it's like to make a mistake so big that you can barely breathe under its weight. My choices isolated me from people who gave a damn, from the people who loved me, and you're doing the exact same thing.

I pushed people away through drugs, and you're doing it through some bullshit set of rules. I made my choices, and now I have to live with their consequences. But being alone sucks, Scott. Don't do that to yourself. Because it only gets heavier as the regret builds." Tim leaned back in his chair. "Besides, does Lauren really seem like the kind of girl who doesn't know what she wants?"

Scott took a deep breath and digested Tim's words. He tried to transport himself back to their Thanksgiving dinner. Tried to remember how he'd *felt*. Right now he was bogged down with denial, hurt, and a ton of other emotions he wasn't used to feeling. But then, his feelings had been pure, raw, honest. *So how did you feel, jackass?* He met Tim's eyes again. "I messed up."

"Yeah, you did."

Scott felt his face fall.

"But it isn't too late to make it right," Tim added. "Now go buy me another coffee and we'll make a plan for you to get your girl back."

Scott stood slowly. "Like I need your help getting girls," he joked. He started to walk around the table to approach the counter, but stopped beside Tim.

Registering the cessation of movement, Tim looked up at his brother with raised eyebrows. "What?"

"Thanks. For being the big brother I needed."

Scott watched Tim's face warm, his jaw tic with the emotion he held back. "It's my pleasure."

Scott nodded, and they left it at that.

Chapter 22

Remission

Walking to class, Lauren pulled her coat tighter as the sharp December breeze chilled her. She drew in on herself and quickened her pace. She had managed to only miss a week of classes after her surgery, and she was thankful that her professors understood her circumstances since it was nearing the end of the semester. She had been excused from a lot of the smaller assignments, and was able to make up the rest while she was recuperating. She was heading to her last Advanced Psychology of Intimate Relationships class before finals started, and she was actually a little sad that she wouldn't get to enjoy Dr. Peterson's lectures anymore. Though she knew that wasn't the only reason she was feeling a little sad.

The girls had gathered at Cass' apartment the previous night, and Lauren had come clean about everything involving Scott. Telling them they were right about him meaning something to her had been tough. But it was tougher telling them that he didn't feel the same way. She tried to push thoughts of him aside when she walked into the lecture hall. There was no way she was going to let Scott distract her from doing her absolute best in her classes even if this particular one reminded her of their slightly fucked up nonrelationship.

She took her normal seat toward the front of the room, pulled out her laptop, and waited for class to begin. She busied herself with making sure her phone was on silent and perusing her notes. When she heard Dr. Peterson's voice asking for their attention, she lifted her head to look at him. At *them*.

What. The. Fuck? Lauren felt her jaw drop and was sure the color drained out of her face. Standing at the front of the room beside her professor, looking smug as ever, was Dr. Fucking Scott. Lauren tried to regain her composure, but stopped when it became clear that he'd already registered her shocked expression. She knew because the bastard smirked at her. *The nerve of this asshole.*

Lauren wanted to leave. Whatever game he was playing, she wanted no part of it. But she wasn't going to give him the satisfaction of running her out of the room. Not to mention, she couldn't help the urge to sit there and take him in. He looked gorgeous, as usual. Black slacks showed the athleticism in his thighs, while his vibrant green button-down pulled across his chest in all the right ways while also causing his eyes to damn near glow. He was the sexiest man Lauren had ever seen and she hated him for it. Well, she would have hated him if she still didn't love him so much.

Her ravenous visual devouring of Scott was interrupted by Dr. Peterson. "I have a surprise for you today. This is Dr. Scott Jacobs. He runs a general practitioner practice at Trinity Hospital. Yesterday he contacted me, asking for a favor. Seems he'd like to improve his public speaking skills, and offered to be used as a review subject for your final exam if I would allow him to come in and get used to talking to a crowd. Since I knew his father quite well, I agreed. Especially since I felt like it would be a good way to review the material. Dr. Scott has promised to be candid with his responses, so don't hold back. Let's begin with a simple definition of intimacy. Anyone?"

Lauren's ears were buzzing. *Public speaking? That's the lamest thing I've ever heard. And what are the odds that he knows my friggin' professor? The universe really does hate me.* She forced herself to calm down. Whatever his angle was, Scott wouldn't get out unscathed. Lauren would make sure of it.

Scott noticed the second Lauren decided to give him a run for his money. Her posture straightened, her lips pulled tight, and her hand shot into the air. *That's my girl.*

He had to admit, he'd briefly enjoyed watching her shocked stare when she'd first seen him. He'd so rarely been able to surprise her that it was a jolt to his system. But after Dr. Peterson's question, he'd seen her become herself again—the strong, witty, confident woman he'd come to know. A fire had lit behind her eyes, and there she was. Ready to flay him alive.

He was sure she saw right through his bullshit excuse for being there. He and Tim had stayed at the coffee-house for three hours trying to come up with a plan, and embarrassingly, this was their best one. Scott wanted to make a grand gesture. He didn't want to just *tell* Lauren how he felt, he wanted to proclaim it. A lecture hall seemed like a great place for that.

"Yes, Lauren," Dr. Peterson said.

"Intimacy is a physical or emotional attachment to another person. It typically implies the inclusion of a sexual relationship, though it can also refer to relationships that are *strictly* sexual."

"Very good," Peterson said as he scanned the room for other volunteers. "So if Dr. Jacobs were your patient, and he came to you with intimacy issues, how would you delve in to the topic with him?"

Lauren spoke before he could call on anyone else. "I'd just ask him."

"Well, yes, obviously. But what, exactly, would you ask him? How would you phrase it? You can take the first stab by taking him through a series of therapeutic questions."

Peterson was speaking to Lauren that time, which was good because she looked like she had every intention of answering whether he asked her to or not. She cleared her throat and began. "Dr. Jacobs—"

"Scott. Please, call me Scott." He didn't even bother trying to hide the imploring tone in his voice. "For our purposes today, it's probably more appropriate."

Lauren seemed to falter for a split second before regaining her composure. "I think it's best if we keep things professional."

Her eyes never left his, so he knew she didn't miss him wince at her words. He started to slide his hand toward his pocket, but stopped himself.

"Dr. Jacobs, what types of relationships do you typically have with people you find yourself attracted to?"

"Typically they're purely sexual."

He saw Lauren's eyes widen. She looked surprised by his honesty. "So your level of intimacy is restricted to physical manifestations then?"

"Usually, yes."

"Usually, but not always?"

"No, not always." He could hear the challenge in his voice.

"So you have had intimate relationships that fulfilled a more emotional need?"

"Yes." His voice was soft but firm. He hoped she could see where he was going, but nothing in her posture intimated that she did.

"So you're capable of that level of attachment, though you don't frequently engage in relationships on that level. Why?"

Scott took a deep breath. *Here goes nothing.* "Because I'm a coward and because I like to win," he admitted, intentionally using the words she had hurled at him.

Dr. Peterson cleared his throat—a subtle cue for Scott to pause so that the professor could step in. "Thank you for your candid response, Dr. Jacobs. That's exactly what we need."

Scott wanted to speak up, to say that exactly what *he* needed was Lauren. But he remained silent.

"You see," Dr. Peterson continued, "humans have an innate desire to belong and to love. It goes against our nature to remain alone."

Finally Scott couldn't hold back any longer. "But when all some people see is others rejecting those they should love the most, it can cause them to rail against others for self-preservation. Because they know that type of rejection isn't just possible, but it's common."

Lauren took a deep breath. "I thought I was the psychologist in this scenario."

"You are. I'm just trying to answer your questions as fully as I can."

Scott heard a few murmurs from the other students who were clearly trying to figure out the reason for Lauren's brusqueness.

"Thanks," she replied dryly. "Does that mean you've never experienced love?"

"No, that's not what it means." *This was it.* She'd started down the path Scott hoped she'd go down. He just hoped they could both see it through to the end.

"Throughout this course we've learned that there are three types of love, Dr. Jacobs. Passionate, companionate, and sacrificial. Which type are you the most familiar with?" Lauren asked.

Scott looked around the room where students sat in rapt attention. Even Dr. Peterson seemed enthralled. "To be honest, I'm not sure. The type of love I feel is new to me. I'm still trying to figure out exactly how far it stretches. But if I had to answer, I'd say what I feel right now encompasses them all."

Lauren's mouth went dry and her heart began beating rapidly. *What the hell is he saying?* She finally forced herself to speak. "So you're familiar with the types of love I mentioned?" Her voice wasn't as strong as it had previously been. She felt weightless, as though she weren't even within the boundaries of her own body anymore.

"They seem pretty self-explanatory. But maybe I could get a little clarification . . . just so I can be sure."

He'd taken a small step toward her, and she was unnerved by the movement.

She took a moment to calm her nerves, knowing her voice would probably shake as she spoke. But thankfully, a deep voice from a few rows back beat her to it. "Passionate love is marked by a feeling of exhilaration when you're with your partner."

"Then that's a yes." Scott's voice cut in before anyone else could speak, his emerald eyes fixed on Lauren as he spoke. "When the woman I love is around, I don't want to be anywhere else."

Lauren tried to ignore his response and hold herself together. Though that was increasingly difficult since she'd forgotten how to breathe.

"What about the second type?" Peterson asked.

Lauren saw a hand shoot up out of the corner of her left eye.

"Yes, Ms. Neal."

"Companionate love is an enduring bond. It's a mutual commitment and based upon a deep level of caring for your partner."

"I want the commitment. I want the bond. I want all of it." Scott was slowly inching toward her, but stopped. "What's the last type?"

Lauren couldn't help it—her voice wavered as she tried to hold the emotion back. "Sacrificial love is the subsumption of an individual within a union. It's commonly compared to God's sacrifice for humanity."

Scott closed the remaining distance. And as he stood facing her, only the single empty row between them serving as a barrier, she allowed herself to hope.

Lauren could hear the soft whispers around her as she guessed students were beginning to realize that this was not just a typical review. But as Scott opened his mouth to speak, the faint noise in the audience died down.

When he spoke, his voice was low and raspy. "I'd give anything, *give up* anything, for her. She's all I need."

A single tear slid down Lauren's cheek, but she wiped it away quickly. She wasn't finished with him yet. He wasn't getting off that easily. "At the beginning of the semester, Dr. Peterson posed a question to us. He asked if there can be sex without intimacy. What are your thoughts on that?"

Scott smiled, and the sight thrilled her, but terrified her too. She wanted nothing more than for that smile to be hers. Only hers.

"I think it's possible."

The answer caused the air to rush out of her, and disappointment to creep back in.

"But when I'm with her, it's completely impossible. Because for the first time, I found someone who I want to share *every* aspect of my life with. Not just the physical side of things, but *all* things. If she'll let me."

"Is this going to be on the final?" someone yelled from the back of the room.

"Shut up, you idiot," another voice said in reply.

Scott continued as if they were the only two people in the room. "I'll never love anyone the way I love you, Lo. And I'm sorry that I was too dumb to see it before, but it's the truth. And I'm sorry I was such a selfish asshole. But if you give me the chance, I promise I'll never be selfish again because this"—he gestured between them—

"this was never about me, Lo. It was always about *us*. I just needed—"

Lauren stood and put a hand out to stop him. "Stop." She looked at him seriously, before letting a slow smile take over her lips. "Stop talking and just kiss me." And with that, she flew forward, leaning over the row that separated them and threw her arms around him.

He gripped her back tightly. "Did you just tell me to shut up during my heartfelt speech?"

Lauren laughed. "Basically."

"Damn, you're tough."

"You love it."

Scott pulled back slightly so he could look into her eyes. "I do."

Then he leaned in and captured her lips in the kiss she'd missed since she walked out of his office nearly a week ago. She had just started to lean into it when a sound interrupted them.

"Ahem."

"Oh shit," Lauren whispered against Scott's lips. "I totally forgot they were even here."

"I have that effect on women."

"Shut up," Lauren said on a laugh as she pulled back from Scott.

"I'm guessing you two know each other?" Dr. Peterson asked.

Scott smiled. "We may have met before."

"I've been used, haven't I?" Peterson charged. But his expression didn't match his tone. The twinkle in his eye and the ghost of a smile on his face let Lauren know that he wasn't angry.

"Yeah. Sorry about that. I just . . . needed her to know."

"And you felt that my class was the most appropriate place for that?"

Scott stayed silent, looking a bit like a chastised toddler.

"I'm honored," Dr. Peterson said genuinely. "Maybe you two can come back and reenact this every semester. It was a great review."

"We'll see what we can do," Scott replied.

"Okay, folks. I think that's enough. Study hard. I'll see you at your final." And with that, Dr. Peterson dismissed class and walked toward the exit.

The rest of the students began to follow, packing up their things and casting amused looks and smiles at Lauren and Scott.

"I can't believe you did that in front of the entire class," Lauren said.

Scott shrugged. "I love you, Lo. There's nothing I wouldn't do for you."

Lauren leaned in and rested her forehead against Scott's. "I love you too."

Chapter 23

Shock

Lauren shrugged out of her winter jacket and hung it on the back of her chair at one of the two wooden tables Scott and Alex had just pushed together. "Ahh," she said, looking around the bar and gesturing her arms wide for effect, "I never thought I'd miss the smell of grease and tequila as much as I have the last few months. It's good to be back," she added with a clap of her hands as she took a seat next to Scott.

Cass stared blankly at her and shook her head. "You're ridiculous. I can't believe you wanted to come to Mickey's for your birthday. You don't even like this place that much."

"It doesn't matter whether I like it or not. It's the principle of the thing."

"I'm surprised Mickey even let you back. Didn't he ban you for life?" Quinn asked.

"He can't dictate where I can or can't go. This is a free country. I paid my debt to society."

A laugh burst from Simone. "Calm down there, Dr.

King. You're allowed back in a local bar. You're not leading the Million Man March."

The table erupted in laughter, and Scott put an arm around Lo before pressing a kiss to her temple. "If my girlfriend wants a dive bar for her birthday, then a dive bar is what she'll get." He smiled but his tone grew more serious. "You're right though. This place makes me want to go home and scrub myself with Lysol."

Lauren's face twisted into amused confusion. "Lysol? Don't doctors have access to industrial strength body wash or something?"

"All right, all right," Xavier said, interrupting them. "Less talking, more drinking." He scooted back his wooden chair and made his way toward the bar, returning a few minutes later with three pitchers of beer. "I started us a tab. I figured we could just settle up later."

They spent the next half hour talking about Lauren's upcoming internship and Cass' latest promotion, which Alex seemed interested in hearing all about. *Very* interested.

Lauren pretty much zoned out on what they were talking about, but she did hear Alex tell Cass about his daughter, Nina, and describe his job at Quantico.

"So you're like a criminal profiler then?" Cass asked.

Alex chuckled. "Well, kind of. That's not actually the job title though. That's just what they call it on TV."

"So what *are* you then?"

"A special agent for the FBI."

Cass' mouth hung open for a few seconds and Lauren wondered if drool might start to drip from it. "Do you wear a uniform?"

"She really has no shame," Lauren said through a laugh.

Scott's eyebrow shot up in surprise. "And you do?"

Lauren let her small smile answer for her.

"So when do you want your birthday present?" Scott asked, looking like a kid on Christmas. "I'll give it to you now if you want."

Lauren grew serious. "Scott, I don't think the other patrons in this fine establishment have any interest in seeing you naked right now. Not to mention, I've already been banned from here once before."

Scott coughed out a laugh as he looked around. "I actually think there might be a few who would be up for it."

Lauren's chastising expression wiped the smile right off his face, but she was laughing inside. No doubt he was right.

"I'll give it to you after we leave. I've just had it for so long, I can't wait for you to finally have it."

Lauren wondered just how long he'd had it. It had only been a few weeks since he'd come to her class to win her back.

"Stop trying to guess what it is. Come on, let's dance." Scott took her hand and led her to the dance floor. The music was upbeat, but Scott pulled her close as they moved to a melody all their own. "I love dancing with you," Scott said in her ear before he gave it a nip.

Lauren tightened her arms around his neck. "I love doing just about everything with you."

And they stayed that way, swaying together without a single care about the world around them. Until Lauren felt a tap on her shoulder and turned to face its source. "Oh. Hi, Mickey."

The short, round man eyed her warily. "I just wanted to welcome you back. And to tell you not to start any trouble tonight."

Lauren put a hand on Mickey's shoulder. "No worries. I've got my babysitter with me tonight," she said as she jerked her head toward Scott.

Mickey cut his eyes to Scott, then back to Lauren. "Okay then," he replied gruffly before turning around and disappearing into the crowd.

"He's pleasant," Scott joked.

"Oh, yeah, Mr. Congeniality, that one. I'm thirsty. Want to head back to the table?"

Scott nodded as he slid his hand to the small of her back. Lauren wasn't sure why, but she always got a thrill when he did that.

They returned to find everyone at the table. Surprisingly even Tim had come.

"What are you doing here?" Lauren said excitedly as she hugged him.

"I'm here to see the birthday girl. I can't stay long, but I wanted to at least stop by."

Lauren wasn't sure if it was a good idea for Tim to be in a bar, but she appreciated the gesture.

As though sensing her concern, Tim leaned in and whispered, "It's okay. I have better self-control now." Then he pulled back and shot her a quick wink.

"Hey, stop trying to put the moves on my girlfriend," Scott said playfully as he wrapped an arm around her shoulders.

Tim laughed. "I'm not so desperate that I need to steal girls from my baby brother."

Lauren couldn't help but notice the way Tim's eyes cut to Quinn as he spoke.

"Anyway, like I said, I'm only stopping by to say hi to the birthday girl." Tim wrapped Lauren in a big hug.

"Happy birthday, Lauren." He released her and looked at both her and Scott. "See you guys soon?" he asked Scott and Lauren.

"Definitely," Lauren replied.

Tim smiled, said his good-byes, and left.

Lauren glanced around the table and noticed the empty pitchers. "I'll go get these refilled. I want to say hi to Sam anyway."

Scott nodded and took a seat next to Alex and joined in on his and Cass' conversation. Lauren had told Scott that Sam worked here, so she wasn't surprised that he understood her desire to talk to him. She leaned down to give Scott a quick kiss and then headed to the bar. She squeezed in between two women and waited until Sam came over.

Her eyes ran down the length of the bar in search of him, finally landing on him at the far end. He was talking to another man who was sitting alone.

Lauren knew she was staring but she didn't care. She took the stranger in: olive skin, navy blue graphic tee strained across an obviously muscled chest, defined biceps leading down to strong forearms, a Georgetown University cap covering wavy, dark hair. *God, Sam had better jump on that.*

Sam took a look around the bar. Despite the smile on the stranger's face, Sam looked uncomfortable. His eyes caught Lauren's, and he quickly excused himself, making his way toward her with a look of relief on his face.

"Hey, welcome back. How're you doing?"

"I'm doing well. The better question is how are *you* doing?" Lauren looked around Sam to the man at the end of the bar, making it clear what she was really asking.

"I'm fine," Sam replied quickly.

"Mm-hm." Lauren couldn't help the smile that slid across her face. "Things definitely look fine."

"Yup. So what can I get you?"

"We'll take three refills," she said as she pushed the pitchers across the bar toward him.

"Got it." Sam set about getting the beer, while Lauren looked back at the stranger.

He must have seen her staring because he waved at her. She looked at Sam, then back at the stranger and raised her eyebrows. The man smirked. That was all the confirmation she needed.

When Sam returned, Lauren wasted no more time. "So who's your friend?"

"What friend?"

"Oh, you know what friend. Don't play coy with me, young man."

"I'm older than you."

"Insignificant detail. Let's focus on important things, like who that hot guy at the end of the bar is. He's staring at you like he wants to eat you alive."

Sam sighed, putting his hands on the bar and dropping his head. When he looked back up, he seemed . . . sad. "I'll add these to your tab."

Lauren got the message. Got it, but didn't heed it. "Sam, just . . . he wouldn't want you to be alone."

"Yeah, well, if that were true he'd still be here." Sam's voice wasn't angry or harsh, just resigned.

Lauren nodded solemnly and watched Sam walk away. She grabbed hold of the pitchers carefully and turned to make her way back to the table. The bar wasn't overly crowded for a Friday night, but she found herself having to squeeze her way through some of the tables.

"Excuse me. Can I just sneak by you?" Lauren had stopped as she waited for the person in front of her to scoot his seat in so she could squeeze between him and the table. When she could tell the man either hadn't heard her or was just being deliberately rude, she shifted the pitchers carefully so she could get a better look at him. Had she been paying less attention to not spilling the beer and more attention to her surroundings, she probably would have known to take a different route before it was too late. A route that didn't involve running right into Josh and his group of *Animal House* rejects.

"Ha," Josh laughed in disgust as he looked up at her without making any effort to move. "You've got some nerve showing back up here after you pretty much destroyed the place. I'll have to talk to Mickey about the type of people he lets in."

A few of his friends laughed, though Lauren wasn't sure why because his comment wasn't the least bit funny. She kept her expression even. She wasn't going to let this douche bag ruin her night *again*. So as much as she wanted to fire back at him—maybe ask him if he was laughing at the size of his dick—she bit her tongue.

She'd been about to turn around and head back toward the way she'd come when he spoke again. "Although I can't say I mind the view." He made no effort to conceal his gaze as it ran the length of her. And she could almost feel the filth seeping from his body onto hers.

"You can't be serious." Lauren was almost laughing, although inside she felt a raging fire burning within her.

And Josh was only fueling it. "You must *like* it when women kick the shit out of you."

Josh's friends laughed again, and the one across from him pointed at Lauren with his eyes wide. "This one's feisty," he said with a twinkle of amusement in his eyes.

"Yes, she is," Josh answered before turning his attention back to Lauren and lifting his eyebrows into a silent invitation. "Bet you're a freak in bed."

"Too bad you'll never know," Lauren responded. But as she turned to leave and make her way back to the table, she felt a hand grip her wrist, causing beer to splash out of the pitcher and onto her.

His gaze flew to her newly soaked shirt. "Guess karma's a bitch," Josh said on a laugh.

Scott's chest tightened when he saw the asshole grab Lauren's wrist. He wanted to rip his arm off his body. In an instant, Scott was out of his seat, his legs moving with an urgency he hadn't ever felt before. Seeing another man put his hands on Lauren sparked a rage inside Scott that he didn't even know he had.

He knew what anger felt like. But this wasn't it. This was something that made him want to put this prick's head through a window and then wrap Lo up in a fucking cocoon and never let her go.

As he made his way through the maze of tables to get to her, Lauren spotted him. There was an unmistakable confidence in her eyes. It reminded Scott of what had drawn him to her in the first place. Lo was a self-assured, independent woman. One who could take care of herself.

Only she didn't have to anymore.

In the few seconds it had taken Scott to move through the bar, Lo had pulled her arm away and was staring at the prick, her eyes wide with fury. Clearly, she wasn't backing down. "That's the second time you've done that," she said, placing the pitchers on the table. "You're not a quick learner, are you, Josh?"

And that's when it clicked for Scott. Josh was the asshole who'd touched her before. And Scott would be damned if he'd get away with it twice.

Josh stood, obviously attempting to use his size to intimidate her. And as he closed the distance between them, invading Lauren's space, Scott's arm slid between her and Josh. Scott moved Lo backward gently, creating a wall between her and Josh with his own body. "I think you'd better sit back down," Scott warned, using every ounce of willpower to restrain himself. "And if I ever see you put your hands on a *woman* . . . on *my* woman again, I'll break every fucking bone in them."

By now, Scott and Josh were the center of attention, the rest of the people in the bar watching them intently.

Lauren put her hand around Scott, her palm resting on his solid chest as she moved to his side. "I got this. It's okay."

Josh crossed his arms and chuckled.

Scott turned to Lauren, hoping she saw the sincerity in his eyes as he spoke. "Lo, don't ever ask me not to fight for you."

"Lo," Josh said mockingly. "That's cute."

Hearing that douche bag use her nickname flipped a switch Scott couldn't turn off. Somehow he had been able to control himself until then, but that name held significance—had emotion tied to it. Josh didn't deserve to be a part of that. And he most certainly wasn't allowed to mock it. As soon as the words left Josh's mouth, Scott's arm drew back and his fist connected squarely with Josh's jaw. Caught off guard, the man fell back, holding Josh's mouth, from which his blood was already flowing freely.

Scott towered over him, silently challenging Josh to stand up, and it didn't take him long to respond. He rose clumsily, obviously still recovering from Scott's punch, and tried to return one of his own. But Scott was much too quick for him. He easily dodged Josh's fist, deflecting it before hitting him once more in the nose.

Though Scott had his eyes fixed on Josh, Krav Maga had taught him to rely on instinct rather than what he saw in front of him. So when Scott sensed Josh's friends moving in on him, he was easily able to fend them off without much trouble.

He actually had to consciously go easy on them. His martial arts training wouldn't advocate doing more damage than was necessary.

Finally Lauren's voice pulled his focus away from Josh and his friends, who had clearly given up. "Scott, that's enough," she said. "You have to stop. Mickey said the cops'll be here any second."

Scott surveyed his path of destruction: broken glasses and chairs. "I'm sorry, Lo. I . . . *shit* . . . I didn't mean for this to happen."

Despite the seriousness of the situation, a seductive smile swept across her face. "You really have no idea how hot that was, do you?" she whispered.

*   *   *

Scott attempted to clean up some of the mess inside the bar, but there wasn't much he could do other than put some of the broken items in a trash can. Josh and his friends had already made their way outside. And despite the fact that Scott had embarrassed them by beating them all senseless, he was sure Josh and his friends wouldn't hesitate to tell the police what had transpired. Finally, Scott exited the bar to find that a gray-haired officer was already talking to Josh about twenty yards away in the parking lot. Josh was leaning against the side of the police car, and Scott could see over the shoulder of the officer that he was holding a paper towel on his face to stop the bleeding. Scott turned back toward the exit to see that Lo and the rest of their friends had followed him outside. "Stay here," he said to Lauren. "I'm going to go talk to the cop. Josh is there, and I don't want you anywhere near that asshole."

"Okay," Lauren nodded.

As Scott approached him, Josh's eyes grew narrow but he didn't speak.

Scott introduced himself to the officer and told his version of the events—which seemed to match Josh's almost exactly.

"So you beat up *four* men?" the officer asked in disbelief.

Scott nodded.

"Well, Doctor, I'm not sure if you're familiar with how the law works. But here in Virginia, kicking the shit out of multiple people is considered simple assault."

Scott nodded. "Okay." He didn't know exactly what the charge would be, but the officer's explanation didn't surprise him.

The officer scrawled something in his notebook and then put it in his pocket. "Do you have any sharp objects on you that I need to know about before I search you, Dr. Jacobs?"

Is this guy serious? "No, sir," Scott responded politely, although it crossed his mind to say he always carried around a few hypodermic needles.

The officer directed Josh to move around to the front of the vehicle but to stay where he could see him until backup arrived. Scott put his arms on the top of the police car so he could be properly searched. Never in his life had he been in trouble like this, and as much as he didn't want an assault charge on his record, he didn't regret his actions for a second. Josh had deserved every bit of what he'd gotten and more.

The officer patted Scott down and removed his wallet, his silver dollar, and a long black box from the pocket of his jacket. He opened it, taking a look at its contents. "This looks expensive," he said. "Is there someone you want to hold this for you?"

"It's hers," Scott replied, turning around to gesture toward Lauren. "Happy birthday, Lo," he yelled across the small parking lot. Another police car pulled up, and a cop—who looked about Scott's age—exited the vehicle. When the officer who had searched Scott directed the other man to give the box to Lauren, Scott's eyes followed him as he neared her. There had been so many times he'd wanted to give her the gift—to see her eyes light up when she opened it. But he never did. Two months ago when he'd gotten it for her, he hadn't thought twice about it. Though he quickly realized that giving Lauren a gift like that would have blurred the lines between them even more. But for some reason he hadn't gotten rid of it. And now Scott knew why. Because somewhere, in the recesses of his mind, he must have known that one day he'd get to see her open it.

Lauren looked at Scott as she held the thin black box in her hand, and he smiled when she removed the platinum heart necklace she had admired at the benefit. "That's the one you wanted, right?" he called to her.

Lauren was moving toward Scott now, and the officer didn't stop her. Scott wanted to wrap his arms around her and never let her go.

"You gave me your heart before I was ready to give you mine," Scott continued, hoping she understood that he wasn't just talking about the necklace. "But I hope you'll take it now."

"I love it, Scott. I love *you.*" Her eyes stayed glued to his until she brought him into a warm embrace. "Thank you." When she finally pulled away and turned to glance at the cop standing beside Scott, she began laughing. "You've got to be kidding me."

Scott saw the man shake his head and let out a huff. But an amused smile spread across his face as recognition seemed to set in. "Not you again."

It didn't take long for Scott to put the pieces of the puzzle together. "Let me guess," he said. "You're the one who arrested her?"

"That would be me," the officer retorted dryly. "Looks like you two make quite a pair."

"I guess we do," Scott replied, a gleam in his eye as he looked at Lo.

"Will he have to stay in jail overnight?" Lauren asked, clearly concerned.

"Yes," the cop replied. "He'll have his arraignment with the judge in the morning."

"Okay, well, call me when you're allowed to leave, and I'll come get you. Oh, and tell the judge I said hello. We go way back."

"Will do," Scott answered. He couldn't avoid catching Josh's gaze when Scott spotted him standing with his friends by the car. Clearly Josh wasn't going to be detained. The bastard had gotten off without punishment again. Yet Scott's eyes found Lo's again and he thought, *I'm still the lucky one.* "Hey, Josh," Scott called, unable to resist, "your face looks pretty bad. You might want to get a doctor to take a look at that."

Scott could see Josh struggling to restrain himself. Finally, the cop put Scott in the back of his car and shut the door.

As the car started up, Scott heard Lauren say something about sirens and someone named Eleanor. Then just as the car started to pull slowly away, Lo began running beside it and tapping on the window.

Surprisingly, the cop stopped the car and rolled down Scott's window halfway.

"Just one more thing," Lo said softly. And as Lauren leaned into the car, Scott caught the reflection of the blue lights in her eyes before she kissed him.

Acknowledgements

We've got to start with Sarah Younger, whose belief in us has been steadfast and enduring. Never afraid to put us in our place, while still assuring us that we *have* a place in the literary world, you're the best agent a pair of wacky girls could hope for. Thank you to everyone at the Nancy Yost Literary Agency for supporting us. And to Mama Younger, thank you for coming up with the chapter title when we weren't able to.

To our editor, Laura Fazio, you've been fantastic throughout this entire process. Our first foray into the traditional publishing world has been quite the adventure, but you made the process painless and exciting. We can't thank you enough for believing in us and for trusting our judgment. You let us have our creative freedom while still leading us down a path we wouldn't have known existed without your guidance. And don't worry. One day we'll get better at Tweeting.

Thank you to all of the people at Penguin Random House who have helped us make *The Best Medicine* the best it could be. From the art department to the copy editors, you guys are incredible.

Alison Bliss, stumbling upon you and convincing you

to CP for us was one of our most fortunate moments. You're a terrific critique partner, author, and friend.

Amanda, you're the best personal assistant money doesn't buy. You've been our friend and our supporter from the beginning when all we had were ideas on a page. And nearly two years later, you're still here. Thank you for going on this journey with us. Hopefully the trip will be a long one.

Erik, I know I'm a total pain in the ass most of the time. Thank you for always loving me anyway. You and Mya are everything to me, even though I sometimes forget to show it properly. I love you guys. ~Elizabeth

To Hayley, you've helped me realize a dream and make it a reality. There's no amount of thanks that can satisfy the gratitude you deserve. Working with you . . . there's just nothing better. Love you. ~Elizabeth

Nick, thanks for being the Real Elizabeth Hayley when we don't know how to do something like set up a Web site, save a document, open a file; the list is really endless. You've been our biggest supporter when this was all just a crazy idea. Thank you for not only allowing me to pursue my dream, but for dreaming along with me. I couldn't ask for a better husband or for a better father for Nolan. Because simply put, there is no better. To both my boys: I love you. ~Hayley

Elizabeth, nothing I will say in a paragraph will accurately express how I feel about how far we've come together. I love you for being my friend, my partner in writing (and crime), and the sister I'll have forever. Thank you for always calling me out on my bullshit while somehow still letting me dream big enough for the both of us. Now, tell me about the rabbits. ~Hayley

Want to see how the girl next door finds love?
Read on for a sneak peek at Quinn's story
in Elizabeth Hayley's

JUST SAY YES

Available from Signet Eclipse in November 2015.

Tim shoved his hands in his pockets as he got out of his truck and walked toward the white house with blue shutters that his brother had told him to look for. He was happy to be there to celebrate the fact that Lauren had gotten her master's in psychology.

Withdrawing one of his hands as he approached the front door, he briefly wondered if he should just walk in, but decided against it before reaching out to ring the doorbell. Lauren's mom had worked for Tim's dad before he had died and Scott had taken over his medical practice. Therefore, he felt some level of formality was required.

A small, slightly round woman answered the door, smiling broadly.

"Hi, Mrs. Hastings."

"Tim, I'm so glad you made it. And call me Pam," she added with a wave of her hand.

Tim nodded and entered the house when she pulled the door open wider. "Your home is beautiful."

"You Jacobs boys are so polite. I'm not sure how either of you puts up with Lauren," she replied with a laugh. "But thank you. Make yourself comfortable. The gang is all out on the back deck."

"Thank you," Tim said as he started for the back of the house. It wasn't difficult to locate his brother; Tim heard his voice before he even reached the deck doors.

"Lo, if you don't stop spraying that damn bug repellent all over the place, I'm going to have to take it away from you."

Lauren huffed out a laugh. "I'd like to see you try."

Tim stepped out onto the deck in time to see Scott make a move toward Lauren, who quickly lifted the bottle as though she were going to spray him in the face with it.

"I'm not playing with you, Scott. This is my party, and I'll spray Off! if I want to."

"You're causing a haze to settle over the deck," Scott complained.

"That means it's working."

"Are you still getting bitten?" Scott challenged.

"Yes."

"Then it's not working. Give it to me." Scott rushed her, but Lauren threw the bottle into the backyard before he wrapped his hands around her. "Do you want to explain what the point of that was?"

Lauren laughed and turned into Scott's chest. "I panicked."

"Can you two stop canoodling? I'm trying to keep dinner down," Cass jibed.

Scott kissed Lauren on the cheek before he looked up and his eyes caught Tim's. "Hey, bro." He disengaged from Lauren and made his way toward Tim, pulling him into a one-armed hug.

Lauren hugged Tim after Scott moved away. "Thanks for coming, even though it's completely ridiculous to have a party for getting out of grad school."

"It's not ridiculous," Scott said, appalled. "You worked hard. You should get a party just like everyone else."

"*Who* is everyone else? No one else I graduated with is having some big shindig in their parents' backyard. You and my mother are insane for insisting we have this."

Scott raised a hand. "First of all, 'big shindig' and 'parents' backyard' are mutually exclusive terms. If you'd let me rent out Clay's like I'd wanted to, *then*—"

"Then it would be pretentious and obnoxious in addition to being unnecessary," Lauren interjected.

Scott glared at her for a second. "Forever with you is going to be a really long time, isn't it?"

Lauren smiled brightly, looking pleased with herself. "Yup."

Scott pulled her into an embrace. "Thank God." He chuckled right before kissing her chastely.

"Yuck. Get a room," Simone complained through a smile.

Tim shook his head at their antics. "How was your graduation?"

"Long-winded and dull," Lauren replied with a smile. "Have you eaten yet? There's a ton of food in the kitchen."

"I'm good for now."

"Okay. Well, make yourself at home." Lauren drifted back toward her friends.

"How's the restaurant been?" Scott asked.

"Going well. Business is starting to pick up."

"That's great. So being an executive chef is everything Wolfgang Puck made it out to be?"

Tim smiled at his brother in response before his eyes began to skim the crowd congregated on the deck. He tried to act uninterested, as though he were casually taking in the people before him.

But that wasn't the truth. And as he stretched his six-foot-two frame to get a better look around, he caught a glance of the familiar head of red hair that made his heart rate jack up every time he saw it. Quinn was sitting alone in the backyard by the pool.

"Who are you looking for?" Scott questioned, making Tim shrink back slightly.

"No one," Tim lied. "I'm going to grab a water. You want anything?"

Scott looked at him curiously for a second before shaking his head.

"Be right back," Tim said, though he hoped he wouldn't be. He walked over to the coolers lined up against the railing and dug around for a water before he descended the three steps that led to the yard and began walking toward Quinn.

Tim had seen her a dozen or so times since Scott had begun dating Lauren, and he had looked forward to it every time. Not that he'd ever let anyone know that. Tim was almost eight years older than Quinn, and he had a history that was seven shades of fucked-up. There was no way a girl like her needed to waste her time with a guy like him. But that didn't stop him from dreaming.

He couldn't help but feel a twinge of concern. Quinn's best friends were all at the party, yet she was sitting alone in the backyard. He took in her posture as he approached, immediately knowing that something was off with her.

He'd hardly spent any time with her since they'd met, but he could tell something was wrong.

"Hey, stranger," he said as he plopped down in the chair beside her.

"Hey," Quinn said quietly.

He noticed the way her eyes drifted over him, taking him in from head to toe. It made him feel like fucking Superman. "So what's up? Why are you sitting over here?"

Quinn took a long drink from the beer bottle she was holding. "That's an interesting question." The words were slow leaving her mouth.

Is she drunk? "That's why I asked it," Tim said with a grin.

"Cheeky."

Yup, she's wasted.

Quinn was sitting cross-legged in the chair, and she turned her entire body toward Tim when she spoke again. "Did you know that I'm safe and traditional and predictable and a whole lot of other boring things?"

Tim took a sip of his water. "I did not."

"Well, I'm glad that I was here to enlighten you," she said as she drained the rest of the beer.

"How many of those have you had?"

"I lost count at seven."

"Wow. Looking to dash that whole boring thing by getting your stomach pumped?"

"If that's what it takes," she murmured as she lifted the bottle back to her lips. Upon realizing that the bottle was empty, she muttered, "Figures," and set it clumsily on the ground under her chair.

"Who told you you were all of those things anyway?" Tim asked.

Her only response was a slight shrug as she looked out over the pool.

"Okay, I'll just ask all of them, then." Tim stood up and turned toward the deck. "Hey, everybody, I was just—" He was cut off by Quinn leaping onto his back.

"*Shh.* Don't be embarrassing."

Tim tried to ignore how good it felt to have Quinn pressed up against him, her long, thin frame molded against him, her full breasts pushing onto the corded muscles in his back. He quickly gave his dick a silent warning to behave as he reached up and unhooked Quinn's hands from his shoulders. He kept hold of one hand as he turned around to face her. "Then tell me who said you were boring."

"I just am."

"Bullshit."

Quinn's eyes widened slightly. "You said a bad word," she teased.

"I did. And I'm going to say a lot more of them if you don't tell me who was calling you names."

"Aww, you going to defend my honor?"

Tim didn't return her smile. "Absolutely."

Quinn tilted her head slightly, and he would've given anything to know what she was thinking. She blew out a breath, pulled away from him, and sank back into her chair, resting her arms on her thighs. "Do you ever wish you were someone different?"

Tim wasn't sure how to answer that question. He was sure she knew about his past, at least the highlights. He'd drunk enough water at bars while he was out with them to make it pretty obvious. Not to mention the fact that Lauren knew all about Tim's problems with addiction. The girls didn't seem the type of friends who kept secrets from one another. "I've been someone different," he finally answered as he sat back down beside her.

Quinn looked over at him. "Oh. Yeah. Sorry. That was a stupid question."

"No, it wasn't. Now, tell me why you asked it." Tim couldn't believe Quinn would want to be different. As far as he was concerned, she was perfect.

She sighed. "I don't know. I just . . . Sometimes I feel like this isn't how my life is supposed to shake out. That there's so much more out there waiting for me if I'd just grow a pair and go look for it."

Tim couldn't help but smile at Quinn's choice of words. She wasn't a saint by any means, but she didn't typically speak so candidly either. "What's stopping you?"

She looked confused.

"From looking for it," he clarified. "If you think life has more to offer, then why aren't you doing something about it?"

"I already told you. Because I'm safe and traditional and—"

"Don't give me that shit again," Tim interrupted. "Give me the truth."

"That is the truth. I'm cocooned so deeply into my own comfort zone, I can barely breathe, let alone get out."

"Just take it one step at a time."

"I kind of already did that actually," she explained. Tim gave her a look that told her to keep going, so she did. "I pitched an idea for an article. A kind of exposé of the life of a sheltered woman looking to spread her wings, if you will."

"That sounds great."

"Yeah, except now I have to actually go through with

it. I was only pitching the idea, but now my editor wants *me* to write the article. And I have no idea how I'm going to do that. I don't even know the kinds of things I should write about." Quinn sighed deeply. "How am I supposed to know what type of person I want to be? I can't even pick the right type of guy to date."

Tim felt his jaw tighten at the mention of Quinn and guys, but he ignored it because there wasn't anything that could be done about it. "What type *do* you date?"

"In a nutshell, mamas' boys," she said with a hollow laugh. "It's fine. I just couldn't understand why I always date these guys who still live at home and think playing video games is a stimulating activity. Then I started reflecting on it and realized that it's because I play it safe and look for guys who will be the least likely to hurt me. I don't take risks, and I don't like leaving things to chance. It's just how I'm wired."

He wanted to tell her that that was a good thing. There was a reason she was attracted to guys who were essentially the opposite of him: they were better. They hadn't spent years on the streets, doing whatever it took to get their next fix. They didn't hurt the people who loved them. They didn't fuck up everything they had to chase a high that was never as good as promised. "There's nothing wrong with that, Quinn. Trust me. I've taken enough risks in my lifetime to satisfy the quota for a football team. And it hasn't made me a better person or more fulfilled or happier. It made me stupid and thoughtless."

"You don't think you're those things now, happy and fulfilled?"

"I am them now, for the most part. But that's because I've stopped being a reckless jackass."

"Don't you think that those experiences enabled you to be them, though? That by making mistakes and seeing how bad things could get, you actually found out how you *did* want to live?"

She had him there. Tim was a hundred percent formed by the lessons he'd learned. He was a better person at thirty-five because he'd been such a bad person from ages fifteen to twenty-seven. Tim had hit rock bottom about four times, and each time that rock bottom had gotten deeper. It made him appreciate being firmly above ground. "I'm kind of an extreme case, though. I don't recommend my type of living to find out who you are."

Quinn offered him a slight smile. "I'm not saying I want to hang out in dark alleys and befriend gangbangers. I just want to push the envelope a little. I don't want to look back on my twenties and be bogged down by all of the things I *didn't* do."

Tim sat quietly for a minute. "Okay. You want to unleash your inner rebel, then we'll do it."

"We?"

"Oh yeah. There's no *way* I'm missing out on this."

About the Author

Elizabeth Hayley is the penname for "Elizabeth" and "Hayley," two friends who have been self-publishing romance novels since 2013. They are best known for their Pieces series, among other novels. **Elizabeth** lives with her husband, daughter, and dog in Pennsylvania. **Hayley** lives with her husband, son, and dog in Pennsylvania.